# THE RAVEN

SPIRITS OF THE NORSE BOOK 2

KATE ROBBINS

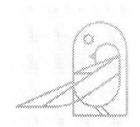

This is a work of fiction. Names, characters, places, and incidents are products of the author's imagination or are used fictitiously and are not to be construed as real. Any resemblance to actual events, locales, organizations, or persons, living or deceased, are entirely coincidental.

No part of this book may be reproduced, scanned or distributed in any printed or electronic form without permission from the author.

Copyright © 2022 Kate Robbins
Cover Art: https://www.wickedsmartdesigns.com/
Editor: Michelle O'Connell
All Rights Reserved
ISBN: 978-0-9940890-8-3

❀ Created with Vellum

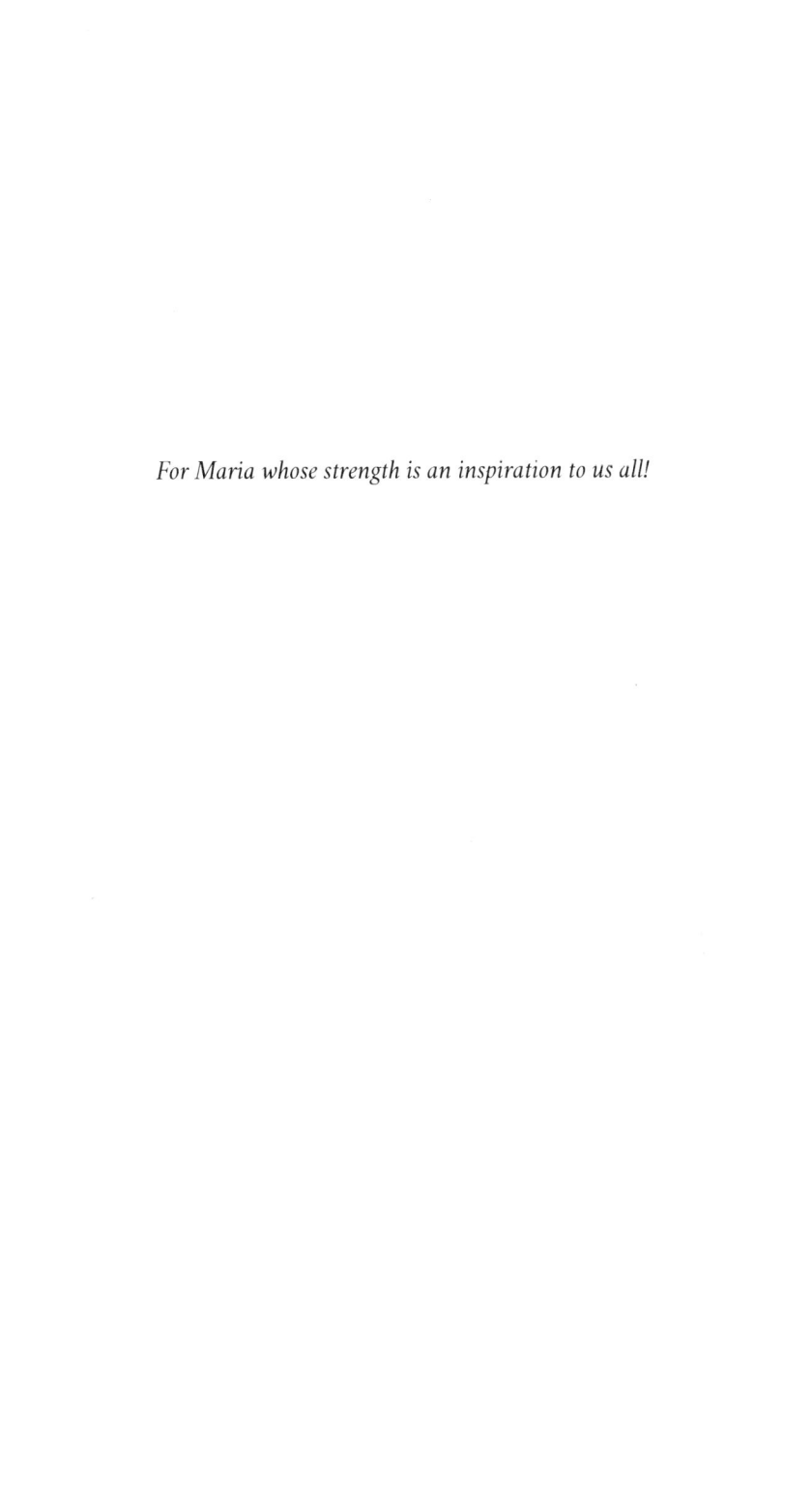

*For Maria whose strength is an inspiration to us all!*

## CHAPTER ONE

### DUBLIN, IRELAND, OCTOBER, 936 AD

The stench of rotting fish and burning peat was thick in the air as they docked. Magnus Haraldson followed his brother, Gunnar down the gangway and through the busy markets of Dublin. Magnus had been to many ports over the last few years, but none could match the trepidation and fear emanating from every corner of this one.

Pockmarked wenches pushed heavy carts with fly infested fish, toothless old men huddled together for warmth, and threadbare clothed children milled about by the dozens begging for scraps. The scene was not welcoming.

They'd been sailing for what seemed like an age from Ayr in Scotland and Magnus was hungry, tired, and in want of a woman. But all that would have to wait. As they meandered through the crowded streets and onward toward the gates, his fingers gripped his dagger. This might be a Norse settlement, but it was nothing like theirs on Islay. Nay, this was not a place one visited for pleasure. This was where one went to disappear, or in their case, forge a covert alliance.

They had recently aligned with Giric MacDomnail and through him, King Constantine of Scotland. Their goal was to band together to push back the English King Athelstan. King Olaf of Dublin was part of that plan.

They crossed the ramparts and stopped at the gates where they were questioned by the guards. Magnus wasn't worried about entry, but was not happy about leaving his weapons outside. Not here. The reeking air came from more than just the putrid provisions. Everything here felt soiled, like King Olaf had given up on the place. Well, by Odin, he would need to do better than this if they were to keep King Athelstan at bay. When the proposal from Magnus' Scottish brother-in-law to strengthen this alliance had been first suggested, Magnus scoffed. How could they possibly join together against such a foe? But somehow he'd been convinced, and so here they were on the doorstep of Olaf's kingdom, if one could call it that.

"You're very quiet, brother," Gunnar said as they passed through the gates.

"I do not like what I see," Magnus said.

"Nor do I, but we need Olaf's banner."

"That remains to be seen," Magnus said as he eyed the guard who took his weapons. The man wore a shiny chest plate of steel and a helmet that was far too polished for that of a seasoned guard.

"Through those gates and keep to the right," the guard said once their weapons had been confiscated.

Magnus looked left and right as they crossed over yet another bridge and toward two large wooden doors flanked by more guards with their spears crossed.

Once they reached the end of the bridge, the guards pulled open the doors and stepped back to permit entry.

The moment they stepped over the threshold, Magnus'

jaw dropped. The palisades were high enough to keep what lay beyond from view. Instead of amassed decay in the form of people or their wares, here were finely garbed men and women set about in what appeared to be a covered market. The aroma in the air could not have been in greater contrast; breads, roasting boar, and bubbling pots piqued Magnus's interest.

What lay beyond was even more surprising. Instead of a wooden longhouse, which was a common structure in his people's villages, it appeared Olaf had made one out of stone. The view from this angle suggested it was twice as long as his brother's on Islay and nearly twice as high. The only thing taller at the moment was the palisades.

"Gunnar, where in Odin's name have we landed?"

"I am not quite certain, brother, but I have envisioned such a place in my dreams when I think of Valhalla."

Magnus couldn't reconcile the contrast. Why the vast poverty outside and the appearance of decadence inside the gates? There was only one person who could answer that question at this point, and they were about to meet with him.

They approached the longhouse and waited until more guards opened the doors for them. Magnus turned around as a flash of green fabric caught his eye. Its owner was cloaked in black and walking away from him. A bright flaming lock of hair fell from the cloak and landed over a shapely shoulder. Magnus watched as it bounced and glinted in the sunlight. A large man walked beside her and held her elbow. He turned and glared at Magnus then urged her forward. A heady scent of cloves followed the pair and as he looked down, he could see leaves trickling from a pouch on her arm.

"Magnus, are you coming?"

Magnus blinked a couple times at Gunnar then shook his head. He nodded and followed Gunnar inside the longhouse.

It only took a moment for his eyes to adjust to the dark. The set up inside the stone structure was not entirely unlike any other longhouse. A grand fire pit was flanked by roasting, steaming, or boiling delights that made Magnus' stomach rumble in approval. He counted ten tables on each side of the pit leading up to the main table at the head behind which sat the largest chair Magnus had ever seen with great buck horns protruding from the back. Small groups of men and women took up most of the tables.

Before he could scrutinize any further he noticed the din in the hall had dwindled to the crackling fire and one spitting pot.

"State your name and business," a nearby scruffy Viking said from over his horn.

"Gunnar Haraldson of Islay. This is my brother Magnus. We are here to speak with King Olaf."

"What makes you think King Olaf wants to speak with you?" another voice could be heard amongst the crowd.

This was irritating. Magnus suspected Olaf was sitting among those gathered, and he himself may not be forthcoming among strangers either, but for Odin's sake, they had been permitted entry. Why the scrutiny here versus at any of the other guarded locations outside of here?

"King Olaf has created quite the kingdom for himself here. He will want to speak with us if he wants to keep it," Magnus said. Gunnar slowly placed his hand on Magnus' arm. He may have just overstepped, but he would rather face the man directly than play these games.

"What my brother means to say is that it is in Olaf's best interest to hear about meetings we have engaged in with King Constantine of Scotland. Should he not be interested, we will take our leave."

When no one spoke, Gunnar turned toward the door and

motioned for Magnus to follow. As they reached the door a voice spoke up.

"I am Olaf Guthfrithson, and I will hear you, Gunnar Haraldson of Islay."

As they turned, Magnus realized that Olaf had been sitting not farthest from, but closest to the door. He stood and approached. A man of great stature, but not nearly as tall as Gunnar or himself. He wore furs strapped around his chest and his blond hair hung shaggy around his shoulders. He did not look like a king.

"I welcome you to my hall. You have travelled far, and I will offer you food and drink. Then you will tell me your tale of this King Constantine."

Olaf walked on ahead with the presumption of a king that the two visitors would follow. Near the middle of the firepit, Olaf sat at a table and motioned for the brothers to sit opposite.

"Hilde! Bring food and ale!" His bellow was loud enough for the women at the far end of the hall to scurry to the pots and trenchers of food on display. Within short order, enough food and drink for their entire crew was placed before them. Magnus was hungry enough to simply stick his face into the mound of food and inhale, but he waited for the nod from Olaf to begin.

Gunnar heaped meat and bread onto his trencher and Magnus followed suit. He had to admit, though food in Gunnar's hall was always good, there was something extra special here. Be it the flavour or tenderness of the meat or the softness of the bread, Olaf's feast was superior.

When they'd filled their gullets to the brim, they sat back and waited. Olaf had merely picked at his food leaving Magnus to assume he'd already partaken.

"We are thankful for your hospitality, Olaf," Gunnar said after he'd finished the third horn of ale.

"Islay must not be as plentiful as I'd heard," he said with a grin. "I would swear you two haven't eaten in a month."

"You're not far off. We visited the MacDomnail before our visit here. 'Tis been nigh on a month since we ate in my hall."

"I can believe it. Please enjoy as much as you like. My table is your table."

Olaf sat back and watched Gunnar. Magnus could see the calculation in the man's eyes. He had many questions and had not yet decided if he would partner with them or not. Magnus was certain of it and Gunnar was too trusting. All of this could still result in them leaving empty handed. Magnus wasn't sure which outcome would be best, but he was certain, he didn't want to be on the opposite sides of Olaf. The man had a lot of resources at his feet—they would soon see how he used the power that came along with it.

"Tell me about your engagement with King Constantine," he said to Gunnar.

"The man is obsessed with Athelstan. He is convinced based on an attack on my sister that he has mobilized plans to invade the North lands and claim all for himself."

"And how is your sister involved?"

"My sister recently married a Scot. But I'm sure you already knew that."

"I did. The great shield maiden of Islay. I admit, I was disappointed to hear it."

"Is that so?" Gunnar asked. "I understand Constantine wants you to be part of his family."

Magnus was lost. "Are you saying that you already know the Scots king wants an alliance? If that is the case, what are we doing here?" His patience was wearing thin. Was he the only person who was in the dark at the moment?

"I pieced everything together from a long and enlightening conversation with your friend Snorri Short-Beard."

"I assure you, that man is not a friend," Magnus said.

"I also understand you have property of his that you plan to return once you leave Dublin."

Returning loot from a legitimate raid was unheard of. But he had agreed to just that for the sake of Gunnar's peace.

"I will return Short-Beard's loot. But I warn you that man is planning to invade. I merely delayed his ability for a while."

"Short-Beard will not step one foot farther east than the boundaries I have already set for him on Islay. I have given your brother my word on that."

"Now that business is resolved," Gunnar said, "what are your thoughts on the Scots and English?"

"I see our alliance tipping the balance in favour wherever we align. Mind you it will be a more challenging existence to be surrounded by English, which is why I will lean toward Constantine. Do you feel he is honourable? If I put my trust in him, will I make life easier or harder for the people entrusted to me?"

Magnus couldn't help but think about those outside of the gates.

"I sensed no dishonour," Gunnar said. "MacDomnail trusts him wholeheartedly and my sister trusts him. That is enough for me."

"Ahh, the shield maiden has a part to play in this after all. She is a fierce warrior, but do you tell me she has a strategist's mind as well?"

"She always has," Magnus said. He had to give her that much. He may never be perfectly happy with her having married a Scot, but he had to give her the credit she was due.

"Then that is enough for me as well. It appears I have underestimated women of late."

"What does that mean?" Magnus asked. Unbidden, a lock of flaming hair flashed across his memory and he swore he could smell cloves.

"It means, I plan to listen more," Olaf said and grinned.

"I am never given the chance," Gunnar said. "Between my sisters and our healer, I am usually in the wrong."

Magnus gave his brother a sidelong glance and noted the forlorn look about him. He suspected the man's connection to their healer Freydis and his missing her of late from her time spent with Saga in Ayr, but perhaps now was not the time to belabour that point.

"Where does this leave us?" Magnus asked. The conversation had taken an odd turn and he wanted to refocus and return to the ship. Something about this place unnerved him.

"You do not like my hall?" Olaf asked.

"I admire your hall, King Olaf."

"But?"

"Will you be offended if I speak freely?" Magnus usually did, but under circumstances where he understood the people in his company better. Right now, he wasn't even certain he knew Gunnar that well.

"Your hall and everything inside the palisade walls are bountiful and pleasant." Magnus glanced at Gunnar who shook his head slightly.

"Go on."

"Outside—"

"Outside people are starving and rotting like the food they are trying to peddle."

"That is what I viewed."

"And what is your question?"

Did this man have no conscience? "My question is how could you let that happen?"

Olaf smiled and leaned back. "You are the first man in two years to ask me this. I commend your bravery. The truth is the people inside of these walls have pledged their fealty to me and me alone. They are rewarded with food and drink and shelter as long as they continue to do so and rise to the occasion when they are asked. Those outside the walls have determined they do not need my protection as they do not want to serve a Viking king. Should they change their minds, they will be welcomed inside."

"And the children?"

"All orphaned children are immediately brought within these walls and paired with a family who will care for them until they come of age and can decide for themselves."

While it sounded like a reasonable arrangement, something still felt off about the place. The hair had been prickling at the base of his neck ever since he'd walked through the last gate, and he couldn't shake the feeling.

"And your men? Are they loyal?"

"No one truly knows if one's men are loyal, Magnus. Do you think your brother would bet on your loyalty with his life?"

"I would," Gunnar said quietly.

"I honour my family," Magnus said.

"Ja, but that has not always been the case. Did you not steal from a rival going against your chieftain's wishes?"

"I did, but that was to protect the clan."

"But you disobeyed him. That would be enough for me to question your loyalty to me."

Magnus sat back and considered what Olaf said. What he suggested was closer to tyranny and under those circumstances, neither Magnus nor Gunnar would be willing conformists.

"To be very clear," Gunnar said quietly, enough for Magnus' ears to perk up, "we are here to forge an alliance, not pledge fealty. That honour belongs to King Harald and him alone."

"I respect your current allegiances and assure you they will not interfere with the business we conduct this day."

A guard came toward them and whispered something in

Olaf's ear. He nodded and motioned someone forward from the door.

"Now please enjoy the rest of your meal. I have other business to attend."

With that, he stood and walked toward the large chair at the head of the hall. On the other side of the fire-pit, a black cloaked figure and a man walked toward Olaf and bowed low. The hair stood at the back of Magnus's neck again and he stared, willing a lock of hair to tumble loose.

"Magnus, did you hear me?"

He shook his head and turned to look at his brother. "We will return to the ship and make sail for Islay. We have come to do what we said we would and there's no further reason for us to stay."

"Ja, let's go," Magnus said and followed his brother outside where the sun shone brightly making him squint at the guard who directed them toward the gatehouse.

When they reached the last gate and had donned their weapons again Magnus placed his hand on Gunnar's shoulder. "Did you not find that place odd and unsettling?"

Gunnar shook his head. "That place has a great deal of history to atone for and Olaf is dabbling in dangerous methods to settle them."

"Do you mean, magic?"

"Of sorts. Olaf has been looking for a seer for a long time. Freydis has begged me not to let anyone outside the village know of her gifts for fear of being summoned."

"You would never let them take her, Gunnar. They have no jurisdiction over us."

"They do not, which is why I would be more comfortable if she returned to Islay."

Magnus grinned. "Then you will have to give her reason to return."

Gunnar said nothing as they meandered through the

stench and filth toward the ship. Magnus had to seriously question what he would do were it his family who was starving—align with a man who may not hold morals in high value, or let his family rot. There was no easy answer to that one.

# CHAPTER TWO

Magnus threw open the doors to the great hall and squinted into the sunlight. He grabbed an axe resting nearby and swung it wide above his head. Damned Gunnar. His sister Saga may have been conned into a marriage with a Scot, but he would not bend so easily. He should have known better than to trust the man's avoidance of the subject on their trip to Dublin.

Since their return, Gunnar had been hounding him constantly. He'd started by forcing Magnus to return the raided items to Snorri Short-Beard on the other side of the island. *Own up to the consequences of your actions*, he'd said. Each day Gunnar seemed more and more determined to find ways to irritate him and now he was bent of having discussions surrounding marriage. With everything else looming regarding King Olaf and the Scottish and English kings, Magnus didn't know where Gunnar still found the time to play matchmaker. Thor's breath, the man could be infuriating!

Magnus made his way to the wharf where various longships and shorter galleys were moored. He spied the one he wanted and hopped onboard. He needed to feel the sea spray on his face to help quell his irritation, nay, it was borderline rage.

"Well, isn't this a pleasant surprise," a sultry voice said from behind him.

Yrsa. Odin's teeth, he was not in the mood for her today. While she pursued him relentlessly, he'd been clear he was not interested.

"What do you want, Yrsa?"

"I heard you are getting married."

"I am not."

"That's not what I hear. Rumour is that you're going off to marry one of the fine ladies on the mainland and they will have you fitted into their fancy clothes before month's end."

"Yrsa, I am in no mood for your teasing or your mischief this day."

"Where are you going?"

"Nowhere, it would appear." The galley was moored close to one of the longships and the high seas from the previous night had jammed them just tight enough to prevent him from setting this one loose.

Magnus hopped back up onto the wharf and looked down at Yrsa. She was pretty enough, but her penchant for causing trouble was more than Magnus could bear. He'd been close to falling for her advances once and thanked the gods he'd resisted.

When he made to walk past her, she jumped in front of him. "Maybe you could take me out in your galley sometime."

"I don't think that's a good idea, Yrsa." He made to walk past her, but she got ahead of him again and placed her hands on his chest.

"Please, Magnus. You're all I think about."

"Is that so? And so you must think a lot, because I understand you've told Roland and Jagger the same thing."

Her cheeks flushed a crimson red. "How dare you make me into a loose woman!"

Magnus was about to lose the one shred of patience he had left. He leaned in close. "We both know you flirt, Yrsa. I respect you because of *your* brother, but if you approach me like this again, I will bring your activity to the attention of *my* brother."

Yrsa stepped back, her jaw dropping. "You would ruin me?"

"I have done nothing to ruin you that you have not done to yourself."

"Yrsa!" Bjorn's voice boomed loud enough to be heard across the inlet.

Magnus looked around at the high cliffs as her name echoed. "Nice to see you, Yrsa. Remember what I said."

As Magnus walked away from Yrsa, he met up with Bjorn. The man was more than a friend; he was a brother and strong ally. They'd learned to fight together and had been close until Bjorn developed an attachment to Magnus' sister, Saga. Now that she was married to a Scot and living on the mainland, Bjorn appeared a little lost.

"Is my sister bothering you again?"

"I'm telling you, Bjorn, find that girl a husband and do it soon."

"That's what I've been telling Fader, but he is adamant she will marry a nobleman from the mainland too."

"I suggest he speak to my brother. That is the flavour of all his conversations of late."

"He has, but Gunnar wants to speak to Yrsa himself first. He says he will not force her into a marriage she does not want."

Magnus shook his head. As chief, Gunnar could make arrangements for any of them, but instead he insisted on making sure all parties were in agreement. That was except for when it came to his own brother. Magnus was not opposed to marriage in the least, but he had not yet proved his worth to his clan, much less settle down with a wife. Since the Scots had landed in Islay several weeks ago, Gunnar was determined to play matchmaker whether his people were interested or not. And Magnus was decidedly not.

"Have fun meeting with Gunnar. I need to get out of here for a while, but the galley is jammed in too tight."

"Target practice?"

"Why not? I have nothing else to do at the moment but avoid Gunnar."

"I'll see ye later for a horn," Bjorn said and grinned as he walked past him and on toward his sister. "You've been summoned to see the chief," he said.

Magnus didn't stick around to listen to her response. No doubt she'd create a scene and he was in no mood for anyone's drama this day.

He made his way through the well beaten paths leading to the tannery and armoury. He'd been getting fitted for new trews and the tanner had them nearly ready. Their blacksmith was also working on a new broadsword for him, and he was anxious to see the progress on both.

"Have ye heard the news, Magnus?" the blacksmith asked as he pulled out the new sword for Magnus's inspection.

"What news?" he asked while taking the weapon into his hand and testing it for weight and balance. He twirled it in his right hand and then his left, then swung it over his head and spun around slashing at an imaginary foe. It felt good. More than good. It was like an extension of his hand, there being no separation between metal and man. This was a blade meant for battle. And mayhap that was at the heart of his issue. He wanted excitement in his life, not to settle down and marry. He'd been pestering Gunnar about sailing to

Iceland and Gunnar had refused, saying it was a dangerous time to leave the village with Earl Einar and Snorri Short-Beard still plotting against them from the other side of the island. Never mind the looming war with the English.

"Your brother has invited more Scots to join us before the snow falls."

"More Scots! Surely you jest. We are not long rid of the last lot. Who now?" And how did the blacksmith know this when Magnus did not?

"Word has spread about your sister's marriage and other nobles have an interest in making peace with your brother."

That made sense, but why had Gunnar not told him about it? Perhaps because of how each conversation ended lately between them. All of Gunnar's insistence over the past few days now made sense. He was setting Magnus up for a wife right now, not in the near future, but now.

"When will they arrive?"

"This day or the next, I'm told."

Magnus shook his head. Thor's breath, he needed to set Gunnar straight, else there'd be nothing left of their way of life. "Can I take this now?" he said referring to the sword he still held.

"Not just yet. It needs another polishing and a name."

Magnus could think of only one name, but he would not utter it. If the gods wanted him to have it, the blacksmith would name it true.

"I will name it Gramr," he said.

It was a name that came with a legend. A sword that could kill a dragon was not something to be considered lightly, but Magnus would accept the honour if the blacksmith felt it was right. After all, he'd spent all the hours hammering the steel to find its essence. Gramr it was.

Magnus smiled and nodded and handed the sword back to its maker and left the armoury. A quick stop into the tannery and he was the new owner of a tight, hugging pair of leather trews. They would no doubt loosen as they broke in, but for now every curve of the entire half of his lower body was accentuated. He was thankful that his tunic would cover the more revealing areas.

When he entered the hall again, it was filled with people. An aroma met his senses to which he was not accustomed. Normally, the hall smelled of burning peat and roasting fish or meat. This scent was familiar and called to him.

Magnus moved to the dais to stand near his brother. Turning, he caught sight of shimmering green fabric. The light cast in through the open doorway, prevented him from seeing any of the faces of his guests, but he supposed they must be the Scots the blacksmith mentioned. Very well, he'd stay and hear what his brother had to say, but he would not agree to anything.

"Magnus, there you are," Gunnar said.

"Do you remember Osgar MacAlpin from his visit a few weeks back?"

"Ja," he said. But he did not see that man in the present company despite the difficulty in making out specific features.

"This is his brother, Kenneth MacAlpin and his sister, Lady Elspeth. This is my brother, Magnus."

Magnus stepped down from the dais and shook Kenneth's hand, when he turned to Elspeth, he noted her eyes were cast down. There was something that appeared like defeat in her demeanour; a frown hung on her lips—her hair was flaming red.

"Say hello to our hosts, sister," Kenneth said.

At that point she squared her shoulders and looked directly into Magnus' eyes. If she'd punched him in the guts he couldn't have been more prepared for the strength resting there. "It is my pleasure to make your acquaintance, Magnus Haraldson.

"The pleasure is mine," he said. Her hair truly was the colour of embers and her eyes a bright green, her skin smooth and fair. She was stunning, there was no doubt about that, but there was something else about her he couldn't quite pinpoint. An essence hung in the air about her, as if the gods themselves approved. He then realized the scent coming from her—cloves.

"Shall we sit and talk our business?" Gunnar asked.

They sat at the long table; Magnus across from Elspeth and Kenneth across from Gunnar.

"As I was saying," Kenneth said, "MacDomnail and your sister appear to have made a good match. And my brother, Osgar speaks highly of you and your clan."

"And you would be interested in further aligning our families."

"Aye, I would."

Out of the corner of his eye, Magnus could feel Gunnar's eyes boring into him, but he seemed incapable of pulling his gaze from Elspeth. The door opened and with it a cool breeze drifted into the hall. Magnus shook his head and looked at Gunnar. His brother's face was drawn into a look of concern.

Magnus turned to the door to find his sister Vigdis along with Osgar MacAlpin. Elspeth turned at the same time and a heartbeat later was on her feet and in the arms of her other brother.

"What the hell do you think you're doing?" Osgar said to Kenneth.

"I'm taking initiative. Is that not what you suggested when last we met?" Kenneth said from over his shoulder.

He turned back to Gunnar. "My brother will take over

negotiations from here." With that he stood and made to leave.

"I thought you said you would never force anyone into these marriages," Vigdis said to Gunnar as she approached him. She swatted his arm then embraced him.

Magnus had had enough. "What in Odin's name is going on here?"

"Kenneth took off with Elspeth and has been trying to negotiate her for his own gain," Osgar said.

"Elspeth?" Kenneth said to her. "Do you want to tell them the truth or will I?"

"I will tell the truth," she said. "You could have hidden me away. You didn't have to make me—make me—"

"Make her what?" Osgar said and grabbed Kenneth by the tunic.

"I didn't make her do anything. I saw an opportunity to gain favour and I took it." He shook his head. "Remember, brother, 'tis you who want to get in bed with the Vikings."

"Not by prostituting my sister!" Osgar drew back to punch Kenneth who merely smirked and waited.

Gunnar was on his feet and standing between the two men in a flash. "Not in my hall. Kenneth, return to your ship and await your brother's orders. You and I have no further business. Osgar, come and sit. We will get to the bottom of this. Vigdis, prepare your chamber for our guest and take her with you. She will be your responsibility as long as she is here."

Magnus watched his sister try to guide a wide-eyed Elspeth from the hall.

"But you don't know what happened," she said to Gunnar. "'Tis not all my brother's fault."

"There will be plenty of time to explain. Right now I need to speak with your brother. Now go with my sister."

Magnus watched as she stared hard at Gunnar, as though

she had so much more she wanted to say. She met his gaze and once again it was like a punch in the guts. He didn't quite know what to do and before he could decide, Vigdis whisked her away to the back chamber beyond the hall.

~

The woman beside her was about the same height as she which was a relief from straining her neck around the men in the hall. By God, she was ready to tear her brother apart for his treatment of her once he'd discovered her on board his galley. Of course she wasn't supposed to be there, but he could have just hidden her until they returned to Alba.

"You must be weary from your travels. My name is Vigdis," she said in surprisingly clear Scots. "Would you like to rest? Are you hungry?"

"You are very kind and, aye, I would like to rest."

"Do you want to talk about your ordeal?"

Ordeal? Oh dear, she couldn't let this kind woman go on thinking she was completely a victim here. That wouldn't do. And if she hadn't been shut down by those damned men in the hall, everyone would have understood by now.

"I feel I must if we are to be friends," she said hoping she sounded genuine. The chamber was so welcoming and inviting with a crackling fire in the hearth and furs on the bed. Elspeth was so travel weary she couldn't wait to climb underneath the furs and fall into a deep sleep. But first things first, her new friend deserved to know the truth.

"My brother did not take me from my home; I hid away on his ship. The initial fault is completely mine and I take responsibility for it."

The petite blonde haired woman's jaw slacked. "Why would you do that?"

"Because I was tired of having to sit in a room all day long and stitch pillows and listen to idle gossip about people I do not like. I wanted an adventure. I've heard the stories about your sister, and I wanted to see a little of the world before I become as dull as one of the cushions and lose my desire for anything else."

The woman chuckled. "My sister can sometimes have that effect on people, but being a shield maiden has its challenges too. It's difficult to get either sex to take you seriously when you don't easily fit either mold and I know Saga has had her struggles."

"Not from what I hear. I'm told she can best three men at the same time."

Vigdis shook her head. "Whether she can is irrelevant. Saga has been training for battle since she was a young girl."

"I ken what you mean, but regardless, I wanted an adventure."

"And did you find one?"

"What I found was an angry older brother who would have likely thrown me overboard until he remembered my gift and the possibility of exploiting it for his own gain."

"What do you mean, gift?"

Elspeth sighed. There was no point holding anything back now. "I have a gift passed down to me from my grandmother. There are many healing methods that can be passed down through family members, but for some reason, my mother did not receive this one.

"My brother is jealous of Osgar and wants to establish himself as an important player in this grand alliance between the Scots and Vikings. He thought if he could curry favour with King Olaf, he could secure a more lucrative position in the upcoming talks. So, he offered to show off my gift to the King. The problem is that it doesn't work that way."

Elspeth shivered. She really was exhausted. A couple weeks sleeping on a pallet had taken its toll.

Vigdis pulled Elspeth toward the hearth and sat her in a chair then covered her in furs. The warmth was glorious.

"Stay here. I will bring you something warm to drink."

Elspeth stared into the fire. The heat and the darkness of the chamber pulled her ever so slowly toward slumber. She was glad she finally had someone to talk to. Her brother could be impossible, but she was never really in any danger. He was a brute, but he would always protect her. Wouldn't he? What would have happened if the Vikings had become aggressive and demanded more from her than her 'tricks' as one had put it. It wasn't her fault the visions could only be triggered if they had direct relation to her future, or so it appeared anyway. And try as she might, she couldn't get that through to Kenneth. Damned man. So stubborn and pig headed.

The chamber door creaked open revealing Vigdis and a maid servant carrying a pitcher, goblet and a platter of food. She sensed someone else close by, but could not see them in the door frame. But she was certain they were there.

"Is there someone outside?" she asked Vigdis.

Vigdis glanced over her shoulder and back and shook her head. "My brother Magnus offered to help carry the food and drink, but we declined. No one followed us in."

Magnus. That was his name. She'd seen him in Dublin and was shocked to see him again here. His presence stirred something within her, something she couldn't quite grasp or name. Somewhere in the recesses of her mind, she had an inkling she had a message for him, but that could not be since they had barely met. And yet her whole being told her otherwise. Aye, she had a message for him, but for the life of her she could not fathom what it could be.

Elspeth sat by the fire and consumed some meat and

bread, then downed a goblet of warm ale. She had no doubt Vigdis had more questions though she had no capacity to answer them. Between the fire, furs, and food, she was quickly slipping into a deep slumber. With the last strength she had, she crawled underneath the furs and snuggled down. So much had happened since she'd first tucked away on Kenneth's ship, not unlike her current curled up position. But she couldn't think about any of that now. She was safe and she was warm and she was about to get some much needed sleep. Before she drifted off completely, the vision of a tall, thick, blonde-haired man embracing her warmed her even more than the furs. Tomorrow she would discover more about this man, Magnus.

# CHAPTER THREE

Magnus sat back and watched as the two MacAlpin brothers squared off. Neither was a warrior in a way similar to his own kin, but these two could probably do some damage to the other with the right provocation. And it would appear their fair sister might be just that. He was certain she was one and the same mysterious cloaked figure from Dublin. And if the scent of cloves and the red hair didn't give it away, the tingling sensation at the base of his neck was surety.

Kenneth MacAlpin had already said his sister had stowed away in his galley and that wasn't altogether a wise choice on her part, but from there, the man should have turned around and brought her home. Why he would engage in a scheme to impress Olaf, Magnus simply couldn't reconcile.

"Tell us about her gift," Gunnar said.

"My sister has no gift, and I will not have her promoted that way," Osgar said and crossed his arms over his chest.

"She proved she has no gift," Kenneth said. "I tried to get her to see something for Olaf, but it didn't work."

"You should have never put her in that situation."

"What difference does it make? None of it is true in any case; it's all made up nonsense for women to feel they have some power over men," Kenneth said.

When Gunnar made to stand, Magnus placed his hand on his shoulder. There was no harm in Kenneth feeling this way. Both Elspeth and Freydis would be in less danger that way.

"I could not agree with you more, MacAlpin," he said to Kenneth. "Now weren't you about to take your leave?"

"Aye, I will leave you all to your silly fantasies about alliances and witches."

With that he left the hall. Osgar followed and closed the door behind him.

"Why did you do that?" Gunnar asked.

"Because it is safer this way. The man had absolutely no hesitation exploiting his sister and so he would give even less care to do the same with Freydis. My question for you now, brother, is what do we do with the MacAlpin sister? You seemed in a position earlier to offer her to me."

"You mistake me, brother. I saw the trepidation in her eyes. I knew she was not here of her own free will and I stand by my original statement when Giric MacDomnail first landed on these shores. I will not force anyone into an arrangement with which they are not in agreement. Not even you, though I wish you would consider making an arrangement sooner rather than later. We can use all the alliances we can get."

"I hope you are willing to put your own name into the sphere of arrangements, brother. A good leader does so by example." Magnus was only partly jesting. If Gunnar wanted to have more of his clan in support of his endeavour, he would need to prove it.

"There is only one woman for me, and she won't have me," he said quietly.

"And have you asked her?"

"I don't need to. Her absence tells me everything I need to know. And on that subject, the conversation is closed."

With that Gunnar left the hall. Not that Magnus wished any ill on his brother, but as long as he was pining for a particular healer, the focus of marriage on him was diverted.

"How fare you, brother?" Vigdis asked from behind him.

Magnus patted the bench beside him and waited for his sister to take a seat. "I am well, my little one. And how are you? How is our guest?"

Vigdis laughed. "It would appear it is my lot in life to tend to stubborn women."

"Is that so?" he asked. Though he didn't want to start the conversation with 'tell me every detail about her', now that the subject was broached, he'd ask away.

"What woman do you know who would hide away in a galley in order to find adventure because she was bored with her daily responsibilities?"

Magnus chuckled. "I can think of at least one."

"You'd be correct. This young woman admires our sister and considers her inspiration." Vigdis' eyes were wide as she shook her head. "How could she not understand the danger to which she had exposed herself? I will never understand."

Magnus kissed his sister's head. "It pleases me to hear that, Vigdis. You are wise beyond your years."

"Ja, and it comes from years of worrying about Saga. While Gunnar was busy being chieftain and you were off on adventures, who do you think had to drag her to Freydis every other day from getting into a scuffle with this one or that one?"

"You are mother to us all and I love you for it. And has our dear brother been pressuring you to align with a certain family through marriage?"

She sighed. "He has and I have told him I will decide when I am ready."

Magnus placed his arm around her shoulders and squeezed. "If you need a guard at any time, you call on me. I'll handle Gunnar for both of us."

A slight cough from behind them drew their attention to the back of the hall. Standing near Gunnar's chair was Elspeth. A tiny shaft of light lit a portion of her hair and Magnus swore it sparkled. Having only seen her in her black cloak, he hadn't seen the bright green plaid she wore over her green dress. The contrast with her hair was transfixing.

"Will you join us?" Magnus heard himself offer.

"Aye," she said quietly as she crossed the hall and sat directly across from Vigdis.

"Did you sleep well?" she asked.

"Aye, I did," Elspeth said glancing briefly at Magnus, but keeping her gaze directed at Vigdis.

There was a somber sadness resting in her gaze that made Magnus yearn to see how a smile might transform her expression.

"Are you hungry?" Vigdis asked as she stood. "Magnus and I were just about to share a trencher and a horn."

As if on cue, Magnus' stomach rumbled. Elspeth met his gaze and a tiny smile tugged at her lips. He was afraid to breathe. The sight before him was so delicate and perfect he never wanted it to change or alter from this exact moment.

Vigdis took her hand, urging her to stand. "Come let me show you the kitchen." Over her shoulder to Magnus she said, "We will return soon."

For several minutes after they left, he sat there staring at an empty spot, wondering what in Loki's name had just happened.

*E*lspeth watched as Vigdis directed the cook and servants to produce a small feast. This was the kind of work she was supposed to learn back at her home, but she had no interest. Oh, she was grateful for the tour, but she would rather see the rest of the village and learn more about Vigdis' brother than how they preserved their meat and fish.

"…we bury the fish in one chamber and pipe in the smoke from another so the fish does not cook from the heat of the embers…"

"I am sure I will enjoy it," Elspeth said, enjoying Vigdis' enthusiasm even if she didn't share a passion for the topic.

They returned to the hall not long after and she noticed Magnus had not moved from where they'd left him. She placed her platter of bread on the table and sat where she had before, more directly across from Vigdis than him. She didn't quite think he made her nervous, not particularly. Rather, tension filled her body whenever he was near. Like she had to tell him something but for the life of her she couldn't formulate any words to accompany the feeling. Even when the sight was upon her she only felt small tingles here and there along her arms. This reaction to him was all over her body and was unshakeable.

"Skol!" Vigdis said handing Elspeth a horn of ale. She enjoyed this sentiment and replied in kind recognizing it was similar to her own sláinte.

"Would you like to see our village?" Magnus asked her between bites of rabbit.

She met his gaze and smiled. How did he know she'd been waiting for just such an invitation? She nodded, not trusting her voice to betray the shakiness welling up inside her. The food was delicious, but the longer she sat there, the worse her symptoms became so the offer to change the scenery was welcomed.

"You'll need this," Vigdis said as she wrapped a large fur around Elspeth's shoulders. For such a large garment, it was surprisingly light, and the warmth enveloped her immediately.

"Will you join us, sister?" Magnus asked.

"I must see the cook as he had said earlier he needed my assistance with something," she said looking directly at Elspeth with a shy smile.

Elspeth had heard her brother had taken to a Viking, but didn't know until now exactly which Viking. And she could see why. Vigdis was petite and delicate, yet there was a shrewdness about her that was comforting. As though she could go to battle with the rest of them, though perhaps with a smaller weapon.

Elspeth's favourite was the dagger she kept hidden in her skirts. The handle was never far from her hand, and she'd practiced drawing it many times over the years. Osgar would be mortified if he knew she possessed it, so she'd kept it hidden from all of her family.

"What would you like to see first?" Magnus asked as they stepped outside from the shield of the longhouse. The sky was a bright blue reflecting the orange and red leaves that had yet to be pulled from their anchor.

She took a moment to enjoy the view from the longhouse toward the shore. The inlet was fairly small with a long wharf to which several galleys were moored. The sea was flat and calm, perfectly reflecting the surrounding hills. She breathed in the crisp October air filled with the aroma of smoke and salt water. She could get used to this view. Her home was a small castle, not nearly as large as MacDomnail's, but with ten main chambers plus a keep and the kitchen housed inside. The structure of this longhouse was incredible; it had taken her several minutes to recognize the roof was in the shape of a ship's hull.

Elspeth took it all in and rested her gaze on the man who waited patiently for her reply. By God he was handsome. Tall and thick with blonde, almost white hair and eyes like the north sky on a clear day. She wished she didn't feel so tongue-tied at the moment, because she wanted to tell him how excited she was to be in his village and how fascinating she found it all. But instead, she muttered, "Armoury, please," and waited for him to lead the way.

They walked in silence through the brush and along a well beaten path away from the beach. Her fur cloak snagged on a couple branches which threatened to challenge her balance once or twice, but for the most part she was able to keep pace with this great gentle Viking ahead of her. Or at least that was the impression she'd gotten so far.

"If you are tired, we can return to the hall at any time. You are a guest here and we want you to feel welcome," Magnus said from over his shoulder.

'We want you...', somehow she would have preferred 'I want you' to feel more comfortable. God, what was wrong with her? She was never this tight lipped.

"I am enjoying your village," she said. "I would like to see it all."

When he turned around with his brows raised, she smiled at him.

"So she speaks," he said with a grin.

"Aye, I do. My family would be shocked at my former silence." It was true, she'd never had a problem forming words before. Perhaps she'd caught some sort of bug on her voyages.

Magnus' brows knit for a moment. "You will tell me if you are unwell. Despite what some may think, we are not barbarians. We will not allow a lady in our care to be ill-treated."

Elspeth couldn't be sure, but she had an inkling that he

THE RAVEN

was making a dig about her brother. If he didn't know her part in that adventure, she would rectify that immediately.

"Please do not be so hard on my brother. I hid on his ship—"

Before she could finish her sentence, Magnus leaned down so close to her face, she could smell him and dear God, that was a jolt for which she wasn't prepared.

"I would never put you in harm's way. Never. Do you even fathom where he brought you? I know what your status as a lady entails. I may not be a Scot, but I know you are to be protected, not exploited."

His burst of anger was surprising as was his revelation of the expectation of her status. In truth, at home she would not be permitted to stroll through a village with a man unaccompanied. The thought had not even entered her mind until this moment.

He looked so concerned in that moment, her fingers itched to reach up and stroke his smooth face. That was another unusual feature of his—he was clean-shaven, and she'd not seen one other Viking man who looked like him.

"It appears I am safe now—uh—what should I call you?" She knew his name, but did he have a title to which she should refer?

"You should call me Magnus, my lady," he said with a grin. There was definitely an underlying implication there that she couldn't quite grasp, of that she was certain.

"Magnus it is. Well, Magnus, will you please show me the rest of your village before we lose any more of this glorious day?"

"The armoury seemed to capture your interest earlier. Would you like to start there or the tannery?"

Elspeth didn't want to sound greedy, but she wanted to see it all!

"The armoury sounds lovely, thank you Magnus."

She loved saying his name. It sounded strong and virile and made her want to stare harder at the tight leather trews he wore. She didn't know a man's legs could be so thick, and she didn't know the sight and scent of a man could scatter her brains so much.

Magnus winked at her and turned to lead the way again. Could he read her mind too? Before she could ruminate on him further, the clanging of metal drew her attention ahead.

Magnus led her into a long stone-walled and thatch-roofed building lighting several torches to illuminate the contents. Elspeth had seen an armoury before but none like this. She studied the axes, swords, and shields marvelling at the sheer size imagining the weight the largest axe must be.

"Would you like to hold my sword?" Magnus asked from behind her.

She turned too quickly and ran into his chest, letting out a breath she hadn't realized she'd been holding. The thick scent of leather enveloped her as she looked up into his gaze. He held her steady and grinned. Did he know the effect he had on her? He shifted and for a brief moment she thought he was about to kiss her and so she parted her lips and sucked in a breath. His eyes grew wide as he whispered her name.

"Ah there you are," Gunnar said from the door.

Elspeth shook her head and stepped back with heat rising to her cheeks. She was mortified by her wanton behaviour. She'd not been raised to tempt a man, but clearly she'd misunderstood his intentions and now he must think her a loose woman. Would the mortification never cease!

"We have business to discuss with MacAlpin that cannot wait," he said.

"We will be there momentarily," Magnus said, not taking his gaze from her.

Elspeth was pinned to the spot as long as Magnus stared

at her like that. So many thoughts ran through her head she wanted to form into words, but they all melded together and formed only one—the image of his lips on hers and her arms slung around his neck. She was wanton. Father Fothad would have a great deal of praying to do for her once she returned to Alba. Magnus Haraldson was just a bit more adventure than she had anticipated when she'd stowed away on her brother's galley.

She believed him wholeheartedly when he said he would never put her in harm's way, but who would protect her heart from succumbing to his irresistible—was there a word that could describe him? Her body felt what it felt, and her brain was muddled, but she had no words to define either sensation.

"Come, let us return to the hall. My brother will insist on a feast later and you will need to be well rested for it."

Magnus stepped back to let her pass and sucked in his breath as their bodies brushed against the other when she did. She walked on ahead only glancing back once to see him adjusting his tunic.

## CHAPTER FOUR

Magnus watched her walk ahead of him enjoying every step. His mind buzzed with the memory of her leaning toward him in the armoury. He'd known plenty of women in his time, and many were forward, but not this woman. She emanated a charm he was drawn to, but he wondered if she was even aware of it. Perhaps she was magic. In either case, he wanted to know more about her.

The hall was a buzz by the time they returned. Vigdis quickly whisked away Elspeth saying something about a gown. The latter glanced over her shoulder and smiled at him which made his breath catch in his throat. By Odin, she was beautiful! Few women in his time had ever captivated him quite like she did. He realized his damned trews were too tight. He vowed that before the feast, he would remove them and go bare legged. At least then he would be able to breathe.

"What is this business we must discuss with MacAlpin?" he asked Gunnar when he located him giving instructions to the cook. The latter looked mesmerized.

"Best you can do, then. This is an important feast, and we intend to honour our guests."

"Brother, what's going on?"

"We have much to discuss and celebrate," he said and clapped Magnus on the shoulder.

"Am I to guess? Or will you spit it out?"

Gunnar could be impossible sometimes. Magnus watched the grin spread across Gunnar's face. He was delighted about something.

"Oh for Thor's sake will you just tell me what's going on?"

"It appears our sister is to be wed," he said.

"Vigdis?"

"Aye, unless there's another sister you have that I don't know about. The very one will be married to The MacAlpin. They don't want to rush the nuptials, but are happy to announce their intentions while they're here."

"Saga will be disappointed to miss it," Magnus said.

"MacAlpin's sister will have to do for this feast. Vigdis plans to travel to stay with her sister over the winter months and have her wedding there in the spring. They'll return her for the supper and have our ceremony then."

"It will be lonely here over the winter with all the women gone."

"Aye, and that's the other reason I wanted to talk to you. I understand you have an attachment with Bjorn's sister Yrsa—"

"What? I most certainly do not! Who told you that?"

"She did, earlier when she came to tell me that she was certain you were about to propose to her but was afraid to disappoint me because she wasn't a Scot."

This was Loki's work. "Gunnar—"

Gunnar tipped his head back and laughed long and hard. The man had lost his mind, clearly.

"I jest!" he said. "I had asked to see her earlier to offer her a place in the kitchens. With Aslaug gone, the cook needs another hand. It's true, she did say she would accept to be closer to you, but I told her you were already spoken for."

Aslaug had been a good worker but had got herself caught up in Earl Einar's schemes and was banished from the village. Saga's husband had found her a place in a tavern on the mainland as far as Magnus knew. In any case, though extra hands were always needed, he wasn't so sure he was happy having Yrsa so close by. The young woman was Loki's spawn and where she went, trouble followed.

"You do not look pleased. Which part of my news troubles you?"

"All of it actually. Our sister is becoming betrothed to a Scot, you've betrothed me to someone without my knowledge or consent, and the young woman who will not leave me alone will now be closer to me than ever."

Gunnar put his hand up as his brows knit. "Our sister is happy, and you should be as well."

"I will speak to her and if I'm convinced this is truly what she wants, I will support her."

"As for you, I have made no arrangements."

"Good. I do not wish it. I will marry when I'm damned good and ready and I will not be pressured by you or anyone else," Magnus said. He thought he'd been clear enough over the past few weeks.

"As for Yrsa, I will make sure she leaves you alone."

"Thank you."

"Does anything else trouble you?"

There was a lot troubling him, but he wasn't sure exactly how to put it into words. Magnus didn't worry about Saga. Though she'd been initially opposed to marrying a Scot, she'd come around and for what it was worth, she could look after herself. Vigdis possessed a different demeanour altogether. Was it too soon for her to be considering marriage?

How well did she really know MacAlpin and the kind of husband he would be? Magnus would rip the man limb from limb if he didn't spend every second of his life tending to his sister's wellbeing and happiness.

"How certain are you of the MacAlpin?"

Gunnar looked over to where the man sat speaking with his own men and wearing a serious expression. He drew a deep breath. "I am as certain as any man can be. I have always looked at my sisters almost as if they were daughters, they being so young when mother and father passed. And you've always looked after them as well. Vigdis more than Saga of course, but you were there protecting them and teaching them too. I understand the concern and the need for us to be certain. But I am telling you, not only do I trust the man, but I also see your sister light up when he's in the room." Gunnar paused. "Not unlike how I've seen you light up with his sister Elspeth comes into your view."

Magnus eyed Gunnar for sincerity. He could glean no jest or false intent in his expression. And what did he think of the Lady Elspeth? He hadn't known her long enough to have formed an opinion. He was intrigued that was for sure and certain, but was there something beyond that? Was that even possible?

"Or how you used to when Freydis came by to patch you up? You should have married her years ago, you know."

Gunnar said nothing and Magnus knew better than to push on a subject when the man was quiet for that was when he was truly bothered.

"I will make you a deal," Gunnar said after a while. "We will feast for the next three days to celebrate Vigdis and her intended. I encourage you to get to know Lady Elspeth in that time and if you wish it, I will speak to the MacAlpin on your behalf. If you do not, I will not broach the topic of marriage with you for at least the remainder of this year."

What sort of deal was that? Magnus shook his head and grinned at his brother. The man was playing matchmaker and it appeared he enjoyed it until the tables were turned on him.

"Very well. On one condition."

"And what is that?"

"That the next time you see Freydis, you tell her that you are still in love with her after all these years and ask her to be your wife."

If Gunnar could have shot daggers from his eyes, Magnus was sure he would have. With a grunt and a glare, he walked out of the hall.

Magnus was quite proud of himself for shutting the man down. If anything were to happen between him and Lady Elspeth or any other woman, it would happen naturally, not as part of some bargain or deal. While he could openly admit to himself he was looking forward to spending time in her company, he was not ready to commit to her or anyone else.

Magnus set about to keep himself busy for the next while. He needed the distraction.

After a couple of hours, just as the light started to grow dim, the aroma of cloves washed over him. He knew its source immediately and the hair at his nape prickled. He didn't even have to look to know she had emerged from the chamber. He had only seen her dressed in the green gown and black cloak, and wondered if she'd brought more gowns with her. Though her dress was different from those his sister wore, he preferred her style of gown.

Magnus turned and caught sight of her. She had not changed, but his sister had braided her hair away from her face and placed a wreath of dried flowers around her head. She locked gazes with him, her green eyes holding all the expression of someone who is in new waters and unsure how to navigate. He would not have her in that state for one more moment.

Magnus moved to her and offered his arm. "Lady Elspeth, would you care to join me for a horn of ale, or would you prefer mead?"

∼

*E*lspeth focused on Magnus as hard as she could to quell the tingling sensations flooding her body. She'd never experienced anything so intense in her life and from the moment she stepped into the hall, everything around her seemed to shift, as though she were seeing it all through someone else's eyes. The corners of the hall flickered, and a dull ache crept up the back of her neck.

"Lady Elspeth, are you unwell?" Magnus asked. His voice sounded muffled.

Elspeth shook her head. "I need to sit," she managed to say. She was sure the episode would pass, and she didn't want to draw any attention from her new friend on her special occasion. When Magnus made to guide her to a chair at the head of the hall, she said, "No, over here."

He led her to the first table down from the dais. She looked up to see Vigdis standing near her brother and the chieftain. They were engaged in conversation and not currently aware of her issue. That was good.

"Lady Elspeth. Please tell me if I may get something for you," Magnus said as he held her hands and stroked her palms with his thumbs. The sensation was calming. After a time the flickering receded and the ache in the back of her neck subsided.

"Thank you, Magnus," she said. "I don't know what came over me, but it was like I couldn't speak or barely think."

"Does that happen often?"

"Not to this extent."

"Do you want to tell me about this gift?"

She eyed him for sincerity. Being cautious was sensible, but if these experiences were going to escalate, she'd need to trust someone.

"They started when I was a wee lass," she said and retrieved her hands. A different sensation had washed over her as he'd stroked her palms. It made her heart race and she felt warm all over from it. She clasped her hands together, her senses filled with too many sensations for her to process in that moment. "My mother told me I would call out the names of my brothers moments before they entered the room."

"That's quite a gift," he said softly. "And I imagine a bit alarming."

"Aye, 'twas at first for her. For me, I was used to it."

"Do you see things in your mind or are they impressions?"

"I see them as clearly as I see you right now. These images block out anything else around me."

"Your brother said you couldn't help King Olaf. Why do you think that is?"

"I have only ever seen things that are directly related to me. And I can usually tell when something is about to happen."

"Tell me about that," he said and reached for two horns and a pitcher from one of the servants passing by. He poured one and passed it to her then poured one for himself and sipped. He smiled at her. "Gunnar must be pleased with my sister's decision to match with your brother. He's brought out the good ale."

Elspeth sipped and enjoyed the clear crisp flavour as it quenched her thirst. Her world could be surprising sometimes. Just a few days ago, she didn't know much more about this Viking clan than the few things Osgar had said. Now she was telling her most guarded information about her gift to the chieftain's own brother. Not that there was anything intimidating about him. Well not to her at least. He was a tall and thickly built man, who had all the features of one who could have any woman he chose, though she didn't get the sense he was a skirt chaser. A female servant passed by and glared at her which prompted her to grin.

"What is it?"

How could she possibly tell him how her thoughts had turned?

"I was thinking of a time when I was small, and Kenneth had planned to jump out from behind a tree and scare me. I saw it in my mind and so I ran around the tree and scared him instead. He wasn't happy about that."

"Did he ever ask you how you knew?"

"He didn't"

"Tell me how you came to be on his ship."

She heaved a big sigh. "Aye, aye, I know that was not wise on my part, but I was bored, and I wanted to meet the Vikings everyone had been talking about. I knew Kenneth was planning to travel to Dublin and I wanted to go. It really isn't any more complicated than that."

She hated sounding defensive about it, but the truth was her brothers could come and go as they pleased and she was practically a prisoner in her own home.

"That doesn't sound unreasonable to me. Were it my sister, I would have taken her."

Elspeth studied his expression. There was absolutely no deceit there whatsoever, she would wager her life on it.

"Well now you've met several Vikings," he said with a grin as the same glaring servant came by with a platter of meats and bread and smoked fish. He gave her a quick glance and to Elspeth said, "Did we live up to all the talk?"

"We need to talk, Magnus," the servant said.

"Not now, Yrsa. I understand my brother has offered you a position in the kitchen. Isn't that where you should be?"

Elspeth gasped. Whatever the past or present relationship between the two, she didn't deserve to be spoken to in such a manner. She made to stand, but Magnus caught her arm. She looked at his hand and then him. Men were always the same, no matter from whence they hailed.

"Please don't go. I would like to hear more of your travels," he said.

"I must go congratulate my brother," she said. "It appears you have a more pressing conversation at the moment."

With that she drew her arm from his grasp and stepped over the bench. The servant gave her a smirk and lifted her head slightly as if in victory. Elspeth wasn't the angry or jealous sort, but she was also not interested in witnessing a private conversation between anyone. Surprisingly, as soon as she stood, her headache completely subsided and all the previous flickering around her vision disappeared. She was almost lightheaded with relief. Her morbid curiosity had her glance over her shoulder where she could see Magnus glaring at the poor servant girl; her expression was pitiful with her head bowed low. Elspeth had seen enough. She'd viewed enough of Kenneth's antics with the servants to have any interest in the goings on here. While she found this Magnus incredibly attractive and she was absolutely drawn to him, she was not prepared to fling herself into his or any man's clutches.

"There you are, my darling sister," Osgar said. "I thought you'd abandoned us for the chieftain's brother."

"Nay, Osgar. A moment of being caught up in the excitement of the moment, mayhap, but I am back to myself now," she said and straightened her skirt. "I believe congratulations are in order, brother. I have only known your betrothed for a short time, but may I say she has one of the kindest souls I have ever known."

Elspeth turned to Vigdis and embraced her. It was true, the lass didn't have an unkind bone in her body. Stepping back from the embrace she smiled at her soon-to-be sister. "Please take good care of my brother. He is not like any man I've ever known. Please be good to him."

Vigdis smiled back. "I will do my best."

The woman was a perfect match for her brother.

"May I join in on the well wishes," her brother Kenneth said from behind her. She thought he'd left.

"Aye, you can," Osgar said, "but our conversation about Elspeth is not concluded. You are lucky the chieftain was satisfied for you to stay, considering your treatment of her."

"I can speak for myself," Elspeth said, suddenly irritated with her brother talking about her as though she weren't there. "Kenneth, I am sorry for not asking you if I could join you on your travels, but you were wrong to try to exploit me to the Dublin King and arrange a match with this chieftain."

"You may think you are master of your destiny, sister, but one of myself or Osgar will be responsible for your future. I was merely taking advantage of the moment. But 'tis a moot point. You have no gift and so are useless to the king, and it appears there is no one here interested in matching with you," he said as he lifted his head toward the bench behind her.

Elspeth looked to see Magnus and the servant speaking closely and holding hands. She looked back and caught Vigdis' eye.

"It is not what you think."

"It is of no matter to me. As my brother said, there is no one here interested in me. Now if you will excuse me, my earlier headache has returned. I shall retreat to the inner chamber for a time to rest my head.

Before anyone could object, Elspeth moved past them and walked swiftly to the chamber and closed the door. She threw the wreath from her head into the corner and slumped into a chair by the fire. It barely crackled so she threw on more wood and soon the fire was raging. Its warmth did much to soothe the throbbing in her head. She was certain Vigdis and her brothers would understand if she did not appear any more this night. A knock at the door produced a servant with a huge platter of food, a pitcher and a goblet.

After she'd sampled the feast, Elspeth removed her gown and crawled under the furs. The fire would not need tending for hours and so she let herself slip into that cozy mindset where nothing else existed but a full belly, a crackling fire, and warm covers.

## CHAPTER FIVE

Magnus was beyond frustrated. While he understood Yrsa's feelings, it was completely unfair of her to present herself in such a manner that would make anyone believe there'd been anything between them at any point. He had to get Bjorn to talk to her and he desperately wanted to explain himself to Elspeth. He knew what it looked like and he could understand the disappointment in her expression.

Sweet Freya, he found her so intriguing. He wanted to know all about her gift. He wasn't sure if he believed in such things, but Odin's ravens told of many things to come. Could Odin's power have stretched to someone who did not revere him? The more he thought about it, the more he was curious. If only Freydis was here to ask. She'd been casting runes for years and seemed to have an insight like no other.

"You seem troubled, brother," Gunnar said. "Come and share a horn with me and join in celebrating your sister."

"Thank you," he said and joined Gunnar at the head table.

Magnus picked at his food as he scanned the hall. So many triumphs had been celebrated here in the years since his grandfather had settled on this part of Islay. The clan had thrived and though Gunnar considered Snorri Short-Beard a threat on the west of Islay, there was plenty for them both and then some. These lands of Alba were lush and had provided well all these years. Gunnar had long since set aside farmlands to the south for Magnus for whenever he was ready. The land would yield bounty there too, but was he ready for that?

He'd spent much of the last two years visiting all the islands along Alba's west coast and had even travelled as far north as Iceland. There was still so much he wanted to see and explore before he moored up for good. Once he was married, he would be responsible to provide for his family and any others who stayed with them. It was common for villagers to branch off with siblings of chieftains when their time came to cultivate their own lands. Magnus wanted Bjorn to join him and would secure a parcel of his land for his oldest friend. But he would not do so it if meant Yrsa would join him. This business with her had to end here and now and her father had to take responsibility for her once and for all.

"Your brooding is souring my ale," Gunnar said, rousing him from his musings.

"I am sorry, brother. I do not mean to dampen the festivities."

"You gave me an ultimatum earlier. Did you mean that?"

"Somewhat," Magnus said. "I mean I am not certain I'm ready to settle with anyone no matter how intriguing."

"And I vowed I would not force you so I retract my demands from earlier. I see how you are concerned. If it is Yrsa you wish, you have my blessing."

"Has Loki scrambled your mind? What makes you think I am interested in Yrsa?"

"Oh I don't know, perhaps it was the scene from earlier when it looked like you broke her heart."

"Gunnar. I am about to tell you something and I do not ever want to have to repeat myself. Yrsa has been pursuing me for a long time. I have never given her cause or encouragement. She is my best friend's sister and nothing more. Somewhere along the way she envisioned herself and me attached and no matter how many ways I tell her I am not interested, she ignores me and continues to imagine we are destined."

"So what was that all about earlier?"

"That was a jealous woman seeing me having an interesting conversation with another woman and finding ways to meddle."

"I know you Magnus. You have been casual with women before, but I have never known you to be callous with them."

"I have never mistreated anyone, Gunnar. You don't need to question this. If you want validation, speak to Bjorn. He will verify everything I have said."

"So what of Lady Elspeth? She was disappointed with what she saw."

"How do you know that?" Magnus asked.

"Because I saw it in her eyes. She is an expressive woman who sees much. Not unlike someone else with similar gifts."

"You think she has a gift like Freydis?"

"I am certain of it. I did not think Odin shared his raven's sight with those who did not follow our ways, but I am certain if she were here she would recognize it immediately. I am concerned about the younger MacAlpin. I fear if he suspects his sister does have power he overlooked, she would again be in danger from him. I do not believe he had her best interests or protection at heart."

"Will Freydis return before the snow?"

Gunnar frowned. "I do not believe so."

"Then I must bring them together."

"What do you mean? You cannot think to leave now and have time to return."

"I am proposing a one-way trip to return in the spring."

"You may do as you wish, but you will not be happy in a castle all winter."

Gunnar had a point. But connecting Elspeth and Freydis seemed like the right and necessary thing to do.

"I do not know any other way around it. I will have to return with my sister and the MacAlpin. Perhaps the winter storms will hold off until Yule to allow time for the return trip. If this is Odin's work, he will put me where I am supposed to be."

"I will send extra furs as gifts to our sister. No doubt she will be frustrated over the winter being unable to hunt while she carries the babe."

The thought of his warrior sister fat with child and still wielding a sword brought a smile to Magnus's lips. He would enjoy spending time with her, but mostly, he was compelled to protect Elspeth from possible danger. Or perhaps he was overreacting. But Gunnar seemed to have the same sense. Perhaps Odin was already working through both of them to protect this woman who didn't believe in Odin and Thor and Freya and Loki. Only Freydis and her runes would be able to make sense of this now.

"Do you think Kenneth MacAlpin was just being opportunistic or do you think there's more at stake here?"

"I have feared for Freydis for a long time, long before Giric MacDomnail sailed to our shores looking to make peace. I'd heard rumblings of lords and kings who would capture seers and force them to perform their gifts for their own gain. As Freydis would be the first to point out, it doesn't work that way. I was concerned about her going to the mainland, but also knew she would be safe as long as she was with Saga. I will say the same to you now. Keep Lady Elspeth and Freydis safe at all costs. Perhaps I am becoming a paranoid old man, but I cannot dispel this feeling that both women are in danger."

Magnus nodded and stood to stretch his legs. He was never one who could sit for long. He needed some fresh air from the joviality around him. While he was happy for his sister, his mind was too troubled to enjoy the drink this night.

He left the hall and walked to the wharf. The moon shone a bright streak of light across the bay. The sky was clear and there wasn't a breath of wind. The din of the hall fell away as he focused on the soft lapping waves of the beach. He sat there for a long time staring out at the water wondering how to approach Lady Elspeth without sounding completely mad.

~

Elspeth woke with a start. She sat up in bed and glanced around the chamber frantically searching for the sound of scratching that had awoken her. For a moment or two she didn't recognize her surroundings. She turned toward the hearth with its dying embers casting a red hue across the earthen floor. Not stone. She blinked and looked down to see the furs covering her body and then she remembered. She was on Islay with her brother and soon to be sister in a Viking longhouse owned by the chieftain of the clan.

She looked at the hearth again when the remaining log split and the halves rolled away from one another. Getting out of bed, she reached for the poker and another log. Once she had the fire raging again, she grabbed the top fur, wrapped it around herself and snuggled into the chair near the fire. The table with food and drink was within her reach so she topped up a goblet of mead and drank deeply. The thick liquid soothed and comforted as she swallowed. She'd always enjoyed the flavour of honey and silently thanked God for the person who had invented it.

She had no idea of the time and for how long she'd slept. Vigdis had not returned to the chamber so she assumed the festivities were still ongoing. Was there a bedtime for Vikings? She chuckled to herself. Considering how seriously they took everything else, she doubted it. Vigdis had said the feast would go on for three days and then they would set sail for the mainland.

Home. It would be a welcome sight. Not that she was in any hurry to stitch cloth, but she was ready to sleep in her own bed and fall into a familiar routine. If only this chamber had a window she could look out and see if it was yet dawn. She'd wait another while before checking in case there were only men about. Should they be well in their cups, they were company she would not want to keep.

Elspeth was not certain how long she sat there staring into the fire. Two goblets of mead and more meat and she again felt the heavy pull of slumber. She threw more logs on the fire and again crawled under the furs.

The next time she woke, someone was laughing beside her.

"And then I said, no, you surely jest, and he said, no you're jesting..."

Vigdis was half under the furs and facing her, with her eyes closed and a big grin on her face. Elspeth couldn't help but smile. Clearly the woman had drunk too much mead. Moments later Vigdis' soft snores prompted Elspeth to drag the covers over her more completely. Her gown would have to wait until morning.

Everything seemed so simple for Vigdis. Her sweetness seemed to make life so much easier for her. Mayhap she was wrong, but the same was true for her brother. Nothing overly complicated ever seemed to happen to him. His thoughts were always clear and he never seemed to ruminate over anything too long.

This match between them was surely sanctioned by her gods and his as well. Oh, how to have one's life so laid out. And was that what she wanted? The romantic side of her wanted the grand passion she had heard about between the shield-maiden and the MacDomnail. But surely that kind of wonderment between two people only came along but rarely. Well, mayhap twice if Vigdis and Osgar could be counted.

Elspeth sighed and turned over to stare into the fire. For a few brief moments she'd felt the tentacles of intrigue reaching out toward Vigdis' brother and could have sworn he felt the same. But it was folly to think that the man wouldn't have had some attachment, previous or current. Most men did, and that was the way of things which was what usually turned her off from anyone who came to speak to her brother about her. Each and every one came with some kind of history that was easily discovered; how she knew she wasn't sure, but it was likely an inkling stemming from her gift. When she finally did form an attachment with someone, she would be sure and certain of his loyalty.

Unable to sleep, she resumed her cozy nook in the chair by the hearth remembering the sea spray on her face and moments of feeling truly free.

"You sigh a lot," a sleepy voice said from behind her a time later.

"And you snore," Elspeth said with a chuckle as she turned toward her.

Vigdis sat up rubbing her eyes. "I should have removed my boots at least."

"You were mumbling until you fell asleep and you looked so peaceful I didn't have the heart to disturb you."

She smiled. "Thank you for that. I had a wonderful night and I suppose the mead and the excitement caught up to me."

"And I can think of no better reason to fall into a deep slumber," she said. She was truly happy for Vigdis and would be pleased to call her sister. They would always be close, she knew it in her bones.

"You were missed," she said, suddenly looking serious.

"I can't imagine by whom. I knew only you and my brothers. Nay, I was better off catching up on much needed sleep. Did you know my brother's galley does not have a proper bed? I slept on a pallet the entire time I was on board."

"I did not know that and you are changing the subject. Magnus was disappointed that you retired."

"I doubt that and I am certain he was able to find alternate amusement." Elspeth didn't like the sound of her own voice or the words that came out of her mouth. In that moment she was well aware she sounded like a ridiculous woman whose jealousy concerned a man over whom she had no claim.

"You couldn't be more wrong. Yrsa is the sister of Magnus' best friend. She's been following him around for years and he's been quite clear he is not interested in any sort of relationship with her except respecting that she's Bjorn's sister."

"I don't understand. I'm sorry, I shouldn't be saying anything. It really is not my business."

"Oh I believe you are wrong again, Lady Elspeth. I believe it very much is your business. Yrsa saw you two together as did the rest of us and became jealous of the intimate world you two were lost in for a short time. You two had the look about you that end up in stories told in song. Please do not doubt my brother or your moment earlier before Yrsa interrupted."

Elspeth didn't know what to say. She hadn't been angry,

or spiteful, rather disappointed, because in her heart she did feel that connection to which Vigdis referred. That it had been visible to others around them should be testament to its validity, but she still had doubt.

"Yrsa left shortly after you did with a smirk on her face. Magnus was miserable for the rest of the evening. He sat with Gunnar for a time, but then left the hall. I found him later sitting on the beach alone. I asked him if there was anything I could get for him and all he replied was 'more time'. Does that mean anything to you?"

In a sense it did. They'd just scratched the surface of getting to know one another. But the last thing she was about to do was try to interpret Magnus or any man's meaning.

"I have no idea," she said. "Mayhap he can clarify it for you in the morning."

"Mayhap, as you say," she said. "I admit, that is an odd word, but in any case it already is morning. You should get dressed and take a stroll down to the beach. I expect the scenery there might be appealing to you and *mayhap* you might find some clarity."

Elspeth grinned as Vigdis snuggled down under the furs so deep only a couple of her blonde curls poked out. "Goodnight," she said in a muffled voice.

"Good-night my friend. I will see you at the mid-day meal."

Elspeth donned her gown and the fur she wore yesterday, straightened her hair and threw a few extra logs on the fire for Vigdis. She left the chamber as quietly as she could and made her way to the hall. The place reeked of stale ale and farts. She held her breath as she made her way to the doors and only exhaled when she was outside.

The morning was beautiful and bright. She waited a few moments until her eyes adjusted to the light before scanning the beach. A lone figure sat facing the water. His blonde head was bowed low. Tingling started at the base of her neck again and grew stronger. She took a step toward him as pain shot into the back of her skull and brought her to her knees. Managing to cry out his name before she completely doubled over, she saw him running toward her from the beach just as everything went black.

## CHAPTER SIX

Magnus must have dozed off. He woke to the sound of a seagull screeching. Or something else high pitched. A cold breeze picked drifted from off the water bringing him fully awake. His mind identified the sound to be his name. He turned around and found the source on her knees and about to fall forward. He was on his feet in an instant and running to her. How long he'd been on the beach he couldn't say, but his tight muscles from remaining in one position for so long confirmed it had been quite a while.

On his knees he gently turned her onto her back and listened for her heartbeat. It was strong, thank the gods. Magnus scooped her up and brought her inside the hall and onward to kick open the door to Vigdis' chamber. His sister sat up rubbing her eyes.

"What's going on?"

"Lady Elspeth collapsed outside," he said. "Who has been healing the sick in Freydis' absence?"

Vigdis was on her feet and helped Magnus get Elspeth

onto the bed in an instant. She touched the woman's forehead and her cheek with the back of her fingers.

"She's not feverish."

"Sister, who can I fetch to help?"

"There's no one, Magnus. Freydis did not have an apprentice."

"That's not true," Gunnar said from the doorway. "She'd been training someone in secret for many months in the event her gifts were discovered. But, Magnus, you will not like it."

"Who?"

Somewhere in the pit of his stomach, Magnus knew who the person would be. He looked down at a pale looking Elspeth who remained unconscious and asked himself what choice he had.

"Fine, but you will tell her this is for healing only and that she will be watched."

"You will not have to worry about her," Vigdis said. "I will not leave Lady Elspeth's side." She went to the side table and examined the food and drink. "Who brought this to her last eve?"

"I had Sigrid bring it in," Gunnar said. "Why?"

"Just ruling out any external possibilities," she said.

"Wait, you think someone could mean to harm her? Here?" Magnus asked. The thought was incredible.

"I believe until we know what is going on with her, we must assume every possibility and rule them out one by one. I will take the goblet and trencher to the cook and have him examine it all for anything that could have tainted it. By the smell I do not think it soured, but let us be sure."

With that Vigdis gathered up the food and drink and left the chamber. Magnus sat on the bed and smoothed Elspeth's amber tresses from her face. She looked so peaceful at the moment, so ethereal as if her skin glowed from a source within. Perhaps it was just the light, but he could swear there were gold strands in her hair.

"Shall I summon Yrsa?" Gunnar asked.

"You will speak with her and be clear of her purpose here? I cannot handle one more word from her about a relationship with me. Do you understand? If she cannot help, we will board my galley and sail for the mainland today."

Gunnar nodded and left the chamber. Magnus pulled the covers around her tighter and tucked them around her to keep her warm. He hoped it was exhaustion from her travels, but he feared it was something no regular healer could manage. The thought of letting Yrsa anywhere near her made him cringe, but he did not believe the girl would harm Elspeth. She would surely know better than that.

Vigdis returned with Osgar who came to the side of the bed and touched Elspeth's cheek.

"She had episodes like this when she was a small child."

"What was the cause and what can be done for her?"

"No one knows the cause, not even she. But my mother used to call on an old healer from the village who would sit and sing to her. Old songs that I'd never heard before in a tongue I don't know."

Magnus knew what had to be done, there was no more delaying it. "Vigdis, prepare anything we will need for the voyage. I am sorry to leave your festivities, but I must get her to Freydis. I know in my heart she will be able to help."

"I agree," Vigdis said. "And we will suspend the festivities until we can return. I will join you and care for her on the trip."

"Aye, I agree too," Osgar said. "The sea is calm today. I will rouse the men and have them prepare the galleys. We should be able to push off in a few hours."

They both left the chamber again leaving Magnus alone with Elspeth. He sat there for a time stroking her hair.

Someone cleared their throat from the doorway. He knew who it was without even looking.

"You may enter. I trust Gunnar has told you why you're here?"

"He has. Magnus I'm sorry for earlier. I have no excuse and I hope in time you can forgive me. But for now, I must examine the lady. I do not have Freydis' skills, but I can tell if she was poisoned."

Magnus stepped away from the bed allowing Yrsa to move closer and examine Elspeth. She lifted her eyelids to peer into her eyes, touched her forehead, and lifted her hand out from under the furs to look at her fingernails. She listened to her breathing for a time. Yrsa held Elspeth's hand and placed her palm on the woman's forehead and closed her eyes.

She sat like that for a while and was still in that position when Vigdis returned a while later. His sister gave him a questioning look to which Magnus shrugged.

"She has not been poisoned," Yrsa finally said after what seemed like an age. "In fact, I can find nothing physically wrong with her. Freydis taught me how to listen to a person's body to find the source of sickness and I can tell you with certainty this woman is in perfect health."

Yrsa stood and approached Vigdis barely glancing at Magnus. "I can do nothing for her." With that she left the chamber.

Magnus was both relieved and further worried. He was pleased Yrsa would not be needed any further, but having no insight into what was wrong with Elspeth gave him an uneasy feeling in the pit of his stomach.

"I will gather what we need for our journey and you must do the same. There is no guarantee we will return here until the spring, Magnus. Pack what you can. I will sit with Elspeth until the galleys are ready."

Magnus nodded and left the chamber to head to the armoury. He hadn't unpacked his sea chest with his belongings from the galley as he spent most nights sleeping below deck. The ship's rocking usually lulled him into slumber whenever he needed rest so the only things he needed to stock up on were hand made from Ragnar the blacksmith.

As soon as he stepped inside he was struck by the memory of Elspeth and the aroma of cloves which was fast becoming a welcomed familiar scent.

He stared at the spot where she'd stood staring up at him with uncertainty and curiosity in her eyes. Magnus shook his head. He needed to stay focused.

With an armful of axes, Gramr, and a few smaller daggers, Magnus headed to his galley and stored them below deck with his other belongings. He usually sailed with a large crew to help navigate the northern sea, but for this voyage minimal would be best since he did not know when they could return.

Once his men were rounded up and preparing the rigging, he left the galley to check on Vigdis and Elspeth. To say he was shocked to see her sitting up in bed upon his return would be a gross understatement.

"How do you feel?" he asked as he came to her side and grasped her hand.

To his joy, she did not try to retrieve it, rather held on.

"I am feeling a little better," she said. "And looking forward to journeying home."

He couldn't agree more. Once she was in familiar surroundings, he was certain she could get these episodes under control and most importantly, be safe.

"Are you ready for another sea voyage?" he asked.

"Aye, Magnus, I am."

Magnus helped her out of bed and walked with her to his galley. He lifted her on board, a little surprised at how light she was. He was further surprised when she walked straight to the galley's prow and perched behind it, wrapping her arms around its neck. He'd thought to make the offer for her to spend the journey below deck, but clearly she had other ideas. Shaking his head, he retrieved two large thick furs and wrapped them around her and grinned. She had courage, he'd give her that.

*~*

Elspeth closed her eyes and leaned forward loving the fresh salt air on her face and the occasional spray from the sea. The waters were calm with little swell making for a pleasant journey thus far. She loved how the galley rocked to and fro and was convinced she was meant to be a sailor.

She'd always felt happy when near water. Nana Besse, the old woman from the village who used to visit her, told her how each person was connected to one of the four elements, wind, water, earth, and fire. In Elspeth's rare case, she was connected to all elements and must respect them for a time would come when she must call on them for aid. The wise raven would guide her when the time came.

The story had always intrigued her, not that she believed it, but it made for some interesting fantasies as a wee lass. She used to envision herself riding a giant raven and conjuring up sea creatures to join her army in the fight against the powers of darkness who threatened to conquer their lands and claim all the maidens and lock them in a tower for all time.

Aye, the imaginings of a wee lass were best left in the recesses of her memory. The present was far more pressing, like how she was currently on board of the galley belonging to a Viking warrior to whom she was convinced she had some connection on a level she could not fathom. That same warrior offered a safe haven in the storm twice now when she'd needed it. How exactly did he quell the turmoil in her mind and body when the episodes were upon her? And why were these episodes not followed by visions like she normally experienced?

She sincerely hoped the Viking healer could provide insight. Vigdis spoke quite highly of her and was convinced they would become fast friends. Elspeth hoped so. She wasn't comfortable around people who had anger in their hearts. They made her feel uneasy and it took time to wash the feeling from her soul. Mayhap that was why she didn't like stitching with the other ladies. They gossiped and were overall relatively miserable in their own existence. Elspeth always left their company feeling drained.

"How do you fare?" Vigdis asked from beside her. She'd drifted off not long ago and had curled into Elspeth's side at the prow. She sat up and stretched.

"I am very well. I do so love the sea."

"You look rested and at peace," she said.

"Aye, I am when I'm aboard a galley sailing the seas."

"You've the sea in your blood."

"You're not the first person to tell me that. Though my brother did not believe so when he eventually discovered me aboard his galley."

"I cannot imagine. How did you remain undetected?"

"I hid below deck for the first day, but the seas came up on the second day and as I tried to get my footing, I accidentally knocked over a barrel. One of the crew saw me and started screaming. It took a punch in the face and a tankard of ale to convince him I wasn't a sea siren."

Vigdis tilted her head back and laughed so hard, Elspeth couldn't help but to join in. Thinking back, it was rather mirthful. The crew member had given her a wide berth the rest of the voyage and when they arrived at Dublin, vowed he would not step foot on the ship with me on it again. And so Kenneth released him to find another ship."

"You were not offended by the accusation of being a sea siren?"

"Of course not. Such creatures have a purpose as do we. I always felt they were there to keep sleepy sailors more alert," she said with a grin.

Vigdis looked out toward the land on the horizon. "Will you be glad to return to your home?"

"Aye. But I do not regret my adventure. And I am pleased to have finally met you."

"And I you. Your brother thinks very highly of you."

"The feeling is mutual. Osgar and I have always gotten on well. 'Twas Kenneth who stuck out as being different. Not that he was ever excluded from anything, but somehow being born second never seemed to sit well with him."

"It is similar for Magnus. He has Gunnar's shadow looming over him and sometimes he does not want to be told what to do."

"Not while I am captaining my own galley, little sister," Magnus said from behind them.

"How long have you been standing there?" Vigdis asked and looked over her shoulder with a grin.

"Long enough to know I shall always check below deck for sea sirens before sailing from now on."

Elspeth turned. His eyes crinkled at the corners and a grin tugged at his lips. His face could express brutal fierceness or subtle kindness. The duality was no doubt mirrored by the many sides of him she'd experienced thus far.

"I assure you, I will not be stowing away in any galleys in the future. 'Tis too damp and dark below deck for my liking. I'll take the clear sky and wind in my face any day."

"I will note that," he said with a grin and turned back to the crew, yelling orders about the sails and rowing.

Within a short time, they docked in Prestwick. She loved the bustling market here. As soon as the galley was moored, she practically ran down the gangway and approached a vendor selling all manner of trinkets for one's hair.

"Have you ever been to Edinburgh?" Vigdis asked. "I wish to visit to view the fabric markets."

"Then we shall travel there together in the spring. If 'tis fabric you seek, I can show you a small shop here in Prestwick, but the best selections are by far in Edinburgh. Come with me whilst my brother secures our transportation."

Elspeth took Vigdis' hand and led her a few steps toward a shop on the main thoroughfare of Prestwick. Magnus was not far behind them and she looked over her shoulder a few times just to make sure he was there. His size and the furs strapped around his upper body made him an imposing sight. So much, the villagers give him a wide berth. If anyone wanted to take issue with him, it would be easily apparent considering most people appeared to avoid him.

"The horses are ready," he said to her after Vigdis had filled her arms with her purchases.

Together they returned to Osgar. He'd secured three horses and Elspeth could ride so she moved to the smallest of the three.

"You may ride with me if you wish," she said over her shoulder. The invitation was intended for Vigdis, but before she could protest, large arms had encircled her waist and her body was lifted onto the largest of the horses. Magnus was behind her moments later.

"I can ride," she said to the large block of man behind her. It was a few hours' ride to her home and she wasn't sure she approved of the proximity.

"I will not have you falling off your horse when I've

sworn to protect you. Until you are in Freydis' care, you will ride with me. Besides, you'll be warmer here." His last words were practically whispered into her ear. Tingles, good ones, spread from her neck all the way down to, well, as deep as tingles could go.

Elspeth settled onto the horse as well as she could. The blankets and the man behind her would certainly keep her warm, she didn't doubt that for a second. And there was some validity to his reasoning. She seemed to have lost control over her functions when these episodes were upon her. What had caused their intensity she couldn't even fathom.

"It is many hours to my home. I look forward to showing you our castle. It is not like the one where your sister lives now, but it is almost as nice."

"And I look forward to seeing it. Our tour of my village was cut short, but I hope to show you all of it someday. But for now, we will ride to MacDomnail Castle. Freydis is there and I wish to see my sister again."

While she was intrigued by this Freydis, and she wanted to meet the shield maiden, Elspeth longed for her home and her chamber. Magnus appeared determined that the healer would know exactly what to do to help her. Mayhap she was just tired from her travels. Did everything have to come down to some message from their gods? She supposed she was about to find out.

# CHAPTER SEVEN

Magnus recalled the first time he'd ridden double on a horse with a female. He was but fourteen summers and she was around the same age. He supposed he may have only invited her to see how how body felt against his, and they only really had a couple horses fit for riding considering they lived on an island. She'd only been too eager and the ride ended in his first kiss.

Now he was a man fully grown and with every step the horse took, her body pressed tighter against his. Magnus shifted to better position his resulting desire. He wanted to pull the hair away from her neck and nuzzle there and smiled when she tilted her head to the side as if she could read his thoughts.

What was it about her that seemed so in tune with him? These episodes concerned him. He'd only known her a short time, but already he felt protective of her. Attraction aside, and she was captivating from her flaming hair to her pouty lips to her petite frame and full breasts, he wanted more from her than just a tumble.

He'd been attracted to plenty women before. His time in

Iceland had been wild and the women there quite free with him. But this was different. With this woman, something tugged and pulled from somewhere beyond his physical self. But how could that be? He was a Norseman—a Viking. She was a Scottish lady who prayed to the Christian God. His sister and her new husband had found a way past the differences in their cultures, but did that mean the same could happen for himself and the enchanting woman whose bottom was pressed hard against him?

"Are you cold?" he asked her, trying to break the pattern of thoughts that could lead him to finding a secluded spot to explore every inch of her.

"Nay, I am quite warm, thank you."

Her words contradicted her when a shiver ran through her easily apparent through the layers of their clothes.

"You're shivering." Magnus wrapped his arms tighter around her and tucked her head under his chin.

"I don't know what's come over me," she said. "I feel light-headed and feverish, though I know I am not ill. My whole body is tingling and I cannot seem to stop it from happening."

They'd only been riding for a short time, but somehow he sensed she needed a break.

"We will catch up," he said to Osgar as he pulled on the horse's reins and slid off the horse. He reached up to helped Elspeth down, keeping his hands on her hips until she gained her footing.

"Thank you," she said and moved away from him.

She smoothed her skirt and walked toward the other horses on foot so he did the same while holding onto the reins. They walked together like that in silence for a time. Magnus wished he could read her mind to glean her thoughts. Was she bothered by him, or attracted? He'd always been a direct sort of person and was a little surprised that he did not wish to be that way with her. He shook his head. What a ridiculous way to think. Thor's breath, this woman had muddled his brain.

"Do you want to ride again? You do not have to share a horse with me if you do not wish. I am sure my sister will ride with either myself or your brother."

She looked up at him with a furrowed brow and a frown. She looked ahead to where Vidgis and Osgar were trotting slowly back to him.

"I will ride with your sister," she said and called out to her. "Do you mind?"

"I do not mind at all. I am not a great rider so would welcome the help," Vigdis said.

Elspeth mounted behind her and held the reins. The two women were similar in size so it didn't appear difficult for her to control the horse. She'd said she could ride and Magnus was impressed that she didn't exaggerate. Elspeth kicked in her heels and galloped on ahead of them.

When he mounted and approached Osgar he said, "There's much more to your sister than meets the eye."

"You have no idea. I swear she is a laird in a woman's body sometimes. She can manage our home, ride horses, and settle the accounts as well as I can."

"How bad are these episodes of hers?" he asked as they settled into a fast trot enough to keep the women in view but to also converse outside of their earshot.

"She's had them her whole life, but they are worse since she left with Kenneth. I don't know what's making them worse but I am as worried as you."

Magnus looked at the man. Were they all mind readers?

"I can see in your expression, you are troubled. Do you really believe your seer can help her?"

"I do. Freydis is a woman of many talents not only with

medicines, but she casts runes. She has the confidence not only of my brother and me, but of the whole village."

"Then I will reward her with whatever she desires if she can help my sister."

"She will not take coin. She has often refused gifts we have brought back from raiding, saying her gifts are greater than gold and have no earthly value, or some such thing as that."

"A true wise-woman."

"She is more than that. You will see for yourself when we reach MacDomnail Castle."

"Aye. And thank you for your blessing for mine and your sister's betrothal. I will take good care of her."

"I do not doubt that for a moment," Magnus said. "My sister has a kind soul and a sharp mind. If she is convinced you are the man for her, I would never question it. I know better than to stand in the way of anything either of my sisters wants."

"Aye, I can believe that. The elder of the two will not be gainsaid. There are times when I have truly pitied my friend, MacDomnail."

"You and me both. I do look forward to seeing how she is settling into life in a castle. I imagine she has the dress maker scouring the country looking for enough leather to make trews that can expand as her belly does with the growing babe."

"It would not surprise me."

Magnus hesitated asking the next question. He did not know either man well and he'd sort of injected himself into the well-being and care of Elspeth, but he had to know.

"Tell me if your brother is a danger to your sister."

Osgar looked at him and nodded. "I wondered if you had already made up your mind about him."

"I am a man who will act when I need to, but I would rather have knowledge first."

"Aye, very well. Our family has always played down my sister's affliction. There are some who are convinced they are otherworldly gifts, while others are convinced it is a sickness of the mind." Osgar shifted his position on the horse.

"And which do you believe."

"We are Christians, Magnus. We believe in the holy father. There is no room in the Christian faith for gifts from enchantresses or pagan gods."

"I believe in pagan gods as does my sister."

"Aye, and I do not question your faith. Vigdis will marry me in my church, and if she wants I will attend a ceremony of her choosing. She has already said she will pray regularly with Saga in the prayer house Giric is having built for her. I have no quarrel with either undertaking."

"But?"

"But my faith is my own. And if you're asking me if my sister's affliction is a gift from one of your gods, my answer would have to be that is not possible."

It was a fair approach. Magnus had known plenty Vikings who had converted from their beliefs to the Christian God and he had decided long ago to leave them to it. But he was not so closed-minded on the subject. Magnus had seen enough of the world outside of his village to understand there was a great deal about the world he'd yet to learn.

"And you do not worry that we are about to put her well-being in the hands of a pagan who firmly believes in otherworldly gifts?"

"I do not, if it will bring my sister relief. But I will also pray in my chapel for her."

"And your brother, which way do his beliefs fall?"

"My brother is more concerned with personal glory and wealth than who is the true creator."

"Then he is the worst sort of danger to her."

"I am glad you see it that way," Osgar said. "That is why I plan to speak with MacDomnail about Elspeth staying on for the winter. She will be safer in his castle with his guards."

"She could be equally safe in my village."

To that Osgar did not respond. Magnus didn't push the issue, but firmly planted Kenneth MacAlpin as a threat in the back of his mind. The man would not come within ten feet of Lady Elspeth.

~

She was not one to covet what another had, for she was well aware how fortunate her circumstances. But every time she visited MacDomnail Castle, she swooned just a little. Her own home was not that much smaller, but this castle always felt grander somehow. From the large keep to the towers overlooking the lands below, she appreciated every stone inch.

"Should we wait for our brothers?" Vigdis asked.

"Nay. I am known here and anxious to meet your sister and the healer."

They dismounted in the middle of the bailey once a stable hand approached them and made their way into the keep. It would be soon time for the evening meal and as the kitchen was connected with the keep, the delectable aroma of roasting rabbit filled her senses.

"Sister!" a loud voice boomed from just inside the hall.

"Saga!" Vigdis called and ran into her sister's open arms.

Elspeth watched as the two women held the back of each other's necks and touched foreheads. No words were needed when such a bond was on display. Elspeth was a little envious since she had never felt that bond with another woman.

"Saga, this is Osgar's sister, Lady Elspeth. Elspeth, this is my sister, Saga."

The woman was like no other Elspeth had ever seen. She was tall and blockier than any other woman around her. Her arms were curved and muscular, evident from her sleeveless tunic. Instead of a gown, she wore what looked like leather trews much like the ones Magnus wore. Though his held a different sort of fascination for her.

"You do not look like your brother," Saga said.

"Aye, but you look like yours."

"You think me fat like Gunnar?" Saga said and took a step forward.

"Stand down, sister," Magnus said from behind Elspeth. "She meant you look like me. The gods surely smiled on you when they blessed you with my looks."

Saga's entire demeanour changed from the first word. So it was not just Elspeth whom he could disarm with his charming manner.

"Brother! I did not expect to see you return so soon. I am pleased you are here," she said and embraced him the way Elspeth often embraced Osgar when she was a wee lass.

The bond between siblings in this family was unshakeable. There was no doubt in her mind. Though she was quite close with Osgar, she regretted not having a similar relationship with Kenneth. But he was just so unlikable. Why did he have to be that way?

"I am pleased to meet you, Lady MacDomnail."

"Thank you," she said and smiled. Her expression, while before was striking in ferocity, now enhanced the incredible beauty of her Norse heritage. She truly was a sight to behold. "But please call me Saga. I do not feel like a lady, though my marriage dictates that I am."

"And I wish you to call me Elspeth. I have heard much

about you and have been looking forward to meeting you. Is it true you have bested four men at one time in battle?"

Magnus looked at her and grinned. Rolling his eyes, he said, "Do not encourage her, please. She will tell you she bested ten and four." As he said this he put his arm around his sister and kissed the top of her head.

Saga pushed him away with surprising ease. "I have bested many men in battle, but all my strength is reserved for the babe I now grow in my belly."

"How do you feel?"

"I feel well. Freydis says I need to rest more, but I do not believe my babe would want me to become fat and lazy."

"That will not happen even if you do rest. You may be active, but you should not be practicing your battle exercises while you are with child," Freydis said from the doorway.

A heartbeat later, Elspeth turned and locked eyes with the woman. The hall spun around her and a great pressure began in her head. The woman at the threshold of the hall turned white, her eyes wide and her mouth agape. Crackling noises grew around her as if the stone walls were about to split apart. She could hear muffled voices, but could not make out any words. The woman's mouth was moving and she moved slowly toward her. Strong arms lifted and carried her out of the hall and up the stone steps away from the woman.

Saga opened a door and Magnus brought Elspeth inside and placed her on a bed. She covered her with quilts and sat beside her. The chamber still spun a little, then started to calm.

"Is she unwell?" Saga asked Magnus.

"She has been having episodes for the past few days," Vigdis said from the doorway.

The room spun around her again and somehow Elspeth didn't have to look to know the healer had entered the chamber.

"I will have to examine her, but I have to tell you that I am suddenly feeling a little unwell myself," Freydis said.

"Then you will come with me," Saga said to the healer. "Vigdis, stay with Lady Elspeth. I will return once I see to Freydis."

Saga and Freydis left the chamber. Magnus sat on the bed and took Elspeth's hand in his. The warmth was soothing and comforting.

"Can you describe what you feel?"

"Everything is spinning," she said and tried to sit up, but curled onto her side when that didn't help. "It became worse when the woman entered the hall. I can feel her somehow."

"What do you mean, you can feel her?"

"It is hard to explain. I can feel her inside my head. As though we share the same thoughts."

Elspeth must be losing her mind. There was no way such a thing was possible. These episodes she'd been having, were they the start of some new aspect of her gift? She was always careful about how she thought about the odd things that happened to her. But this was different. She was convinced the woman, the healer, had a direct effect on her symptoms and she needed to find out why.

She tried to sit up again and this time the spinning settled more.

"Where do you think you are going?" Magnus said as he placed his hand on her shoulder.

"I need to speak with that woman. She must know why I feel this way. She is the cause of it."

"Why do you not wait until you are well again," Vigdis said. "Once you eat and drink something, you may regain your strength and then you can speak with Freydis."

"I don't want any food or drink. I can tell you I felt her in my head and I need to know why."

"Let me go speak to her," Magnus said. "Freydis is the

most giving person I have ever known. If she is in your head, there is a good reason for it. She would certainly not be trying to harm you."

"I do not think she is trying to harm me, but I know she felt it too."

How could she explain this to either of them? There was only one person who could understand what she was trying to explain and she was with the shield maiden. Nay, she was not overwhelmed, nor exhausted, nor ill. For the first time in her life, she knew with every part of her existence there was a reason for every sight, every episode, every inclination.

While she firmly believed Magnus wanted to protect her, keeping her from learning some much-needed truth was not helpful. Elspeth stood up and placed her hands on her hips.

"Do you both plan to keep me in this chamber or will you help me find the healer?"

She watched as Vigdis and Magnus looked at each other. The latter shrugged.

"We will help you," Vigdis said. "But you will stay here with me and Magnus will go find Freydis. But I will tell you now, I understand this is important to you and I agree, there's some connection between you both, but if Saga thinks Freydis is at risk in any way, she will keep her from you."

Elspeth didn't doubt it. She didn't want harm to come to either of them. She wanted answers and she was hell bent on getting them.

## CHAPTER EIGHT

Magnus left the chamber reluctantly. He didn't want to be anywhere but by Elspeth's side. The episodes were frightening enough, but this talk of being inside someone else's head was another level of concern. Was the stress of her affliction muddling her brain? He didn't know and prayed to Odin that Freydis might have some answers.

He didn't have to go far to find Saga and Freydis. They were arguing in one of the chambers just down the hall.

"I need to see her!" Freydis said as she placed her hands on her hips.

"Not if you're putting yourself at risk you're not."

"I am not at risk. She is not harming me and I am not harming her."

"I certainly hope not," Magnus said from the doorway. "Because I will not let you come within ten feet of her if she drops like that again."

"Magnus, thank Freya. You must tell me everything you know about her."

"She is MacAlpin's sister. She is beautiful, smells like

cloves, and has episodes that make her faint. Oh, and her brothers think she might have the sight. She said she has always known things before they are about to happen.

"She stowed away on her brother's galley about a month ago and he brought her to Olaf of Dublin to sell her sight abilities to him. Apparently it didn't work. After that, he tried to convince Gunnar to arrange a marriage for her."

"Marriage to—?" Saga asked.

"Kenneth MacAlpin would not have known Gunnar had a brother, so I can only assume he would have given her to any Viking to claim an alliance."

"How does that benefit him?" Freydis asked.

"I do not see how it does anything besides make him think he is acting on behalf of the security of the clan before his brother can have the opportunity."

Saga shook her head. "Schemes! You men and your plans. I have no patience for it. Was the girl harmed?"

"No, she was not harmed. At first I thought her fainting could be from exhaustion or from the ordeal of her brother's treatment of her. But now I do not know what is the cause. She is convinced you were in her head, Freydis. We both know that is not possible, so what is going on?"

Freydis' eyes went wide and she paled. "I need to sit and think for a moment," she said as Saga led her to a chair by the hearth. "It's just not possible," she said after a time. "She is Christian?"

"She is according to her brother."

"I do not know what the gods intend here," Freydis said. "I have cast many runes for many purposes, but I have never had to ask them why they have blessed one who is not of our heritage with the power of a Volur."

"She's a what?"

"I cannot say for certain, and I will have to think on it. It appears Odin has blessed this woman with one of his ravens. She may be able to see into people's thoughts."

Magnus took a step back and closed the door. "You must keep such thoughts to yourself, Freydis. Did you not hear what I said about her brother? If anyone, and I mean anyone believes that, she could be in a great deal of danger."

"But what if it's true? We have to learn what is Odin's plan for her?"

"Hang Odin's plan! I will not let her come to harm."

Freydis stood and Saga stepped in between them. "Listen to me both of you. Freydis, sit down; Magnus, you sit here."

Magnus knew better than to object to his sister's demands. He watched Freydis' expression. He had never seen her so agitated. The woman had always appeared completely in control of any situation whether it was when healing someone's wounds or managing his stubborn older brother.

"Freydis. How certain are you about Lady Elspeth's abilities?"

"As certain as I am sitting here."

"I will not have her exploited," Magnus said.

"Why are you her protector?" Saga asked.

"I cannot tell you how, I just know that I have an undeniable urge to keep her safe."

"Ah ha! I tell you, it is Odin's plan."

"Odin doesn't not have a plan for Elspeth, or me."

"Odin has a plan for everyone—"

"Who believes in him," Magnus finished.

"Apparently not," Freydis said. "Magnus, listen. I understand your need to protect her, I can feel it rolling off you in waves. I believe it, but do you not question how strongly you feel about a woman you just met?"

He had been questioning that very thing, but he would have never considered that it was Odin's doing. He had never believed Odin troubled himself with the small immediate actions of individuals, rather with bigger issues.

"I want to understand what is at work here so I can help her. Do you want her episodes to continue?"

"No, I do not. But I'm asking you to be careful with what you say and to whom you say it. Her own brother would sell her for far less than what you're suggesting and he's just one man with limited power. A true Volur like you are suggesting would be a target for every power-hungry man in the world. I will not have her put in such harm's way."

"I agree with Magnus. You do not know of the darkness that can live in men's hearts. I have seen it myself in Einar. Can you imagine what he would do to her if he thought for a second she could help increase his wealth?"

"That man is Loki's spawn," Freydis said. "I know that much. Very well. I will consult the runes, but first I must speak with her."

"How do you know you will not feel ill again?" Saga asked.

"I know what to expect now. When I first felt her power, I fought against it. The next time, if she tries to see into my mind, I will let her. I may be able to better understand her as well."

It all sounded too fantastical for Magnus. The thought of a person seeing into someone else's mind was illogical and impossible. Yet Freydis was convinced it was possible and happening to the very woman who seemed to hold him hostage in every sense of the word. For he was convinced that he could not leave her side now even if he wanted to. Perhaps he was a part of whatever plan was in place for Elspeth. Perhaps their destinies were linked. What was he thinking? Did he really believe that was possible? Of course not. But what other explanation could there be?

"Did you say the lady smelled of cloves?" Freydis asked after a time.

"She does. It's in her very essence I'm convinced. Is that important?"

"I use cloves and other herbs before I cast runes. Cloves help attract positive outcomes and encourage sight. If she smells like cloves, she must carry some with her."

"She does wear a vial around her neck. Perhaps it is in there."

"What sort of vial?" Freydis asked.

"I haven't examined it closely. But noticed it when I was looking in that general area," he said not exactly comfortable sharing that much information about his desires for Elspeth.

"General area," Saga said. "You were staring at her breasts and happened to see a vial around her neck." Saga crossed her arms over her chest and shook her head. "You men are all alike when breasts enter the room."

"I was not being disrespectful to her, if that is what you are implying. Regardless, she wears a vial around her neck and that may be the source of the aroma."

"It could be," Freydis said. "I will need to speak with her to find out if she performs any incantations."

"Then let us return to her. I had a difficult time trying to get her to stay with Vigdis, so I believe she is just as anxious to speak with you."

They left the chamber and walked down the hall to where he'd left Vigdis and Elspeth. He knocked on the door then entered. She was sitting up on the bed with her eyes wide and her skin pale. Perhaps this was a bad idea. He turned to prevent Freydis from entering the chamber, but before he could, she skirted around him and approached Elspeth. Her demeanour immediately changed. Her expression softened as she was fixated on every move Freydis made. When the latter sat beside her and clasped hands, both women gasped.

He may not know what Odin's or anyone else's plans were, but he was certain, something much larger than anyone in this chamber was in control here.

~

*E*lspeth closed her eyes hoping the spinning would stop. The hands that held hers were seared onto her skin as if they were bound there. When she opened her eyes again, she didn't recognize her surroundings. The healer was beside her, but they stood in a dark forest with shafts of light coming through from above. Before them was a small wooden dwelling with no walls, just posts keeping the roof up. A solitary figure sat crossed legged on the floor watching them. When he opened his eyes, they glowed bright white.

A rush of fear coiled around her heart and she closed her eyes again just as she pulled her hands away from the healer. She sat back on the bed and wrapped her arms around her knees and gently rocked herself for comfort.

A firm hand touched her shoulder. She didn't have to look to know it was Magnus. She placed her hand over his and squeezed, unable to find the words to thank him for being there.

"No more touching," he said. "And maybe you can sit over there."

Elspeth opened her eyes as Freydis left the bed and sat by the hearth. Vigdis had lit it a while ago and the warmth now generated around the chamber. For a moment all she could do was stare at the woman. She'd never experienced anything like this in her life and though she needed answers, the intensity of it all was quite overwhelming. Her mind was unable to process sharing thoughts with another person, despite witnessing it first-hand. The phenomenon was certainly nothing she would believe if someone else described it to her. But that shared experience was real. She didn't have to ask the woman to know it was true. Now what did it mean?

"How do you feel?" Freydis asked her.

"Like I am in someone else's body right now."

"What happened?" Magnus asked.

"We were transported to another realm. I suspect it was Vanaheim."

"But how is that possible?" Vigdis asked. "You were sitting right in front of us."

"I do not know. And I did not recognize the being there."

"That was not your god Odin?"

"No, it was not," Freydis said, now wringing her hands. "That most certainly was not Odin. But why would you ask if it was he? What do you know of Odin?"

"I know nothing of him, but the name is in my head and I do not know why," Elspeth said. Mayhap she should go to the chapel and pray. Mayhap all this was happening because she snuck onto her brother's ship and this was her punishment. She was supposed to be obedient and this was what happened when one wanted adventure that wasn't meant for them. Well, she'd gotten more than she'd bargained for and it was time to beg forgiveness.

"I wish to visit the chapel," she said. "I am overwhelmed by all of this and I wish to pray."

"What is happening here has nothing to do with your Christian God," Freydis said.

"That's enough," Magnus said. "If she has had enough, this ends now."

"Do you not want to get to the bottom of what is happening to you? To me? To both of us?"

"Aye, I do," she said and stood up. "My body that is being invaded by these images, and I want it to stop, not encourage it to grow stronger. I do not know who that person was in that vision, but I do know that I was afraid. I do not have your powers to heal, and I do not know your gods, but I do know that God will protect me and I want to go pray to him."

Elspeth left the chamber with Magnus tight to her heels. She knew this castle well enough to navigate to the chapel quickly. There was no priest inside but there were candles alight so she sat on a bench and bowed her head. She immediately felt at peace. Her whole body hummed with it as if God had wrapped his arms around her body.

She sat there like that for an age. She didn't pray, rather she enjoyed the peace and comfort as a brief respite from the chaos she'd experienced over the last several days. She couldn't deny there was something going on and that it was larger than she, but she was having difficulty believing Norse gods had any hold over her or were working through her. That wasn't possible in her mind. And to what end? Was this a test of her faith?

"You can sit with me, if you like," she said.

Immediate shuffling from behind her made her smile. Had he been waiting for an invitation all along?

"How do you feel? Has your god spoken to you?"

"I feel at peace here," she said. It was difficult to explain to him. She didn't need God to speak to her to feel his presence.

"I will sit with you as long as you like," he said.

"Do you understand any of what is happening here?"

"I do not. Freydis seems to think this is part of Odin's plan, but I do not understand how that could involve you."

"Nor I. That is what I have been contemplating."

"Freydis said you were transported to another realm. What did she mean? What did you see?"

"We were in a forest. There was a platform with posts holding up a roof and a person sitting in the middle. When he opened his eyes, they were bright and shining and I was afraid."

Magnus wrapped his arm around her and pulled her close to him. His strength was such a comfort, she was almost certain she could quell all her fears simply by standing beside him.

"Did the person speak?"

"I didn't wait to find out. That was when I broke from holding Freydis' hands. I was too afraid of what he might say or ask and I am not sure I even want to know what it means anymore."

"What do you want to do?"

"I want to go home. I want to sleep in my own bed and eat at my own table, and stitch boring fabric with boring people and forget any inkling I ever had to go on an adventure. Mine has been filled with frightening events and I am of the mind that I am better off tucked away like the delicate thing I always resented."

Oh how naive she'd been. All those countless hours envisioning herself sailing around the islands of Alba meeting new people and learning new things. She never dreamed she'd ever be in danger not only from a family member, but now from someone's else's gods. It was all too preposterous to imagine. Nay. She would give up and go home and spend the rest of her days doing absolutely nothing useful like she was supposed to. Let someone else have all the adventure, she was finished with this one.

"I will return you to your home at first light," he said. "And do not be afraid of adventure. It often finds you when you are not looking for it as well. You are not being punished for hiding aboard your brother's ship."

"I'm not?"

He chuckled deep in his throat, the sound a soothing song for her soul. "We are not always meant to know the why of things. You have a gift and I believe it has a purpose. I am here and I will protect you from harm so you do not need to be afraid. If it is your true wish to return to your home on the morrow, I will ensure you arrive safely. And if you wish to remain here and explore what Freydis believes to be true, I will protect you here as well. I do not know why, but I believe that is my purpose."

Elspeth had no words for him. Part of her wanted to explore this fantastical turn of events, but the other part of her wanted to crawl under the heavy quilts on her bed and stay there for the rest of her life.

She was sure Magnus was somehow sent to protect her. Mayhap that was the message God had sent her that she could only see here. To trust in him, that he would keep her safe.

Elspeth drew a steadying breath and stood. "I shall try to get some sleep and decide in the morning what it is I want to do. I thank whichever of our gods sent you to watch over me. I feel safe when you are near."

Magnus stood and kissed the top of her head. She would rather it have been on the mouth, but she would accept it either way. Together they walked back to the keep and when they entered the hall it was to see only Saga and MacDomnail seated at the table. They joined them and she ate a little, but her belly was not content to process much in the way of food. Saga looked at her pointedly a few times, but thankfully said nothing. Elspeth was not sure she could handle any kind of confrontation with anyone at the moment much less this woman.

After she finished her meal, a servant led her and Magnus upstairs. She entered one chamber and he was directed to the one across from hers. She was glad to know he would be close by. Without removing anything other than her boots, Elspeth crawled under the covers and closed her eyes, willing precious peaceful sleep to sweep her away from the madness her life had become.

# CHAPTER NINE

Magnus paced outside Elspeth's chamber door. He'd been awake since dawn wanting to go across the hall and sit beside her bed while she slept to convince himself she was unharmed. If they were still on Islay, that's exactly what he would do. Here was different.

"Is she awake?" Vigdis asked from the top of the stairs.

"I do not know. I do not want to disturb her if she is resting, but I want to be sure she is well."

"Then we will knock and see for ourselves," she said and raised her fist to the door.

"'Tis open," a voice called from inside.

Vigdis opened the door revealing Elspeth who was dressed and sitting by the fire.

"Do you need anything, Lady Elspeth?" Vigdis asked.

"I am a little hungry," she said.

"Come, let us break our fast with the others in the hall."

Magnus was confused. Elspeth appeared as though nothing from the day before had occurred.

"Did you rest well?" he asked her.

"Aye, I slept through the night and am feeling much better this morning."

"Are you certain you want to dine in the hall with the others?"

"I am," she said. "I do not wish to stay in this chamber all day. Besides, if I'm to understand what is at play here, I must face it head on."

"So you have decided to stay and speak with Freydis?"

"I have."

"What if you discover something that is upsetting or counter to what you believe?"

"Then I shall face that too."

She walked past him, leaving him no choice but to follow. He'd been so worried about her throughout the night, he scarce slept. Now to find her refreshed and eager to discover what was happening was a welcome transformation from where she'd been the night before in the chapel. Either way, he'd promised to stay with her and that was exactly what he intended to do.

When they entered the hall, those gathered stopped eating and watched as she crossed to sit beside her brother. He kissed her on the forehead and filled a trencher and goblet for her.

Magnus sat beside Saga and across from Elspeth and Vigdis sat on his right. Magnus watched her devour her bread and meat for a while and when he was convinced she really was feeling better, filled his own trencher with chunks of rabbit and wild boar.

"Where is Freydis?" he asked Saga.

"She has been at her dwelling since last evening. She said once she cast her runes and had some answers she would return here to speak again with Lady Elspeth."

"I am eager to speak with her too," she said between bites of food and sips of ale.

"I will send for your gowns today," Osgar said. "I believe we should remain here until—"

"That is a very good idea," Saga's husband Giric said.

"Until what?" Magnus asked. He didn't miss that Giric tried to cut Osgar off. If there was something going on, he had a right to know what it was.

"I said, until what?"

"Word has spread about Lady Elspeth and Freydis," Saga said. "It appears one of the servants overheard some of our conversation yesterday and told the others. We've had four people leave us saying they won't return whilst there's a pagan witch in the castle, and those who have remained give us all a wide berth."

"Is Freydis in any danger?" Elspeth asked. "If the servants are afraid of her, they might try to harm her. She needs to be protected."

"No one is afraid of Freydis. She's been here as long as I have and they know her. It is you they fear."

"Me? I am neither pagan nor a witch." Elspeth dropped the food she was holding and sat back to wipe her hands.

"I want my question answered," Magnus said again to Osgar. "You said until, and I want to know until what."

"Until the danger has passed. This castle is better defended than mine and MacDomnail has a stronger compliment of men to watch who enters and leaves the castle and grounds."

"How long must I remain here? I mean no disrespect to you both," she said to Giric and Saga, "but I do not wish to be a burden to anyone."

"You are no burden," Giric said. "Your brother is practically my brother and as such I consider you family. I would offer protection to you the same as I would my own siblings. No one will harm you here. And if I am assessing correctly, you appear to have not one, but two Viking warriors looking out for your wellbeing. There are not many who could boast such an honour."

Magnus and Giric had gotten off to a bit of a rough start all those weeks ago when he'd sailed to Islay to bargain peace with Gunnar. He'd come to know the man as honourable and eventually respected his sister's decision to marry him.

"Thank you for your compliments, MacDomnail. I have promised my protection to Lady Elspeth and I intend to remain with her until I am convinced there is no threat."

"I thank you all for your kindness," she said. "I do not believe anyone would want to harm me, but I will not oppose the protection either. But I do feel that Freydis should be protected as well."

"I agree with her," Magnus said and looked at Osgar. "You agree there are those who would exploit a person believed to have any kind of power they could gain for themselves. I warned of talking about such things openly and considering her own brother tried to exploit her, I do not think for one moment he would not try the same with Freydis."

"He wouldn't dare," Saga said and stood up from the table. "If anyone touches one hair on her head, I will rip them limb from limb."

"Easy, love," Giric said beside her. "I will send someone to bring her here now."

"I will go myself," she said.

"You will not," Giric said. "Osgar, where is Kenneth?"

"I instructed him to return home and run inventory on our lands. It's a large task that he normally does well and without argument."

"Then you best travel there yourself to fetch your sister's belongings to ensure he is there. But do not tell him why your sister will be staying with us."

Saga's hands were on her hips as she glared at her husband. Magnus chuckled to himself. The man must be made of an incredible amount of patience to have taken on his sister.

"I'll go," Magnus said. "Though I will require a guide as I am unaware of her location."

"I will accompany you," Giric said. "We will take some of my men and a cart for her belongings. I believe my wife has long since wanted her friend to move within the castle walls anyway. Now we have a reason to quell any protest."

"Make sure she leaves nothing behind so she has no excuse to return," Saga said. "That woman is as stubborn as—"

"You?" Magnus asked and ducked just as Saga swung her arm to hit him. He had missed her dearly, but he knew when to stay away from her right fist.

"Come let us make our way to the village," Giric said.

Magnus glanced at Elspeth. He felt awkward for a moment, almost as though he wanted to embrace or kiss her, but instead he nodded and followed Giric out of the keep and across the bailey. Giric motioned for four guards to accompany them and located a cart for Freydis' belongings. They mounted two horses and passed through the gates saying nothing.

Magnus had come to admire Giric's approach to issues. He was tempered and thorough, but was quick to act when needed. Magnus had checked himself a few times since meeting the man. In contrast, he'd always been quick tempered and that had worked up to a point when his foes had been clearly outlined before him. Now he fought an invisible enemy from a direction he could not fathom. And he would fight for her. No matter if he had to travel to Jotunheim and battle the frost giants. She was his primary focus right now.

*A*fter the men left and the servants cleared the table, Elspeth paced the hall. She hated fearing her brother, but she needed to keep her wits about her. Something extraordinary was happening to her that made her question nearly everything she'd ever known and she absolutely understood the danger in which that placed her.

The thought of servants fearing her was upsetting. She'd never hurt someone who threatened her, couldn't even bring herself to harm a beetle, much less someone who worked for her. She'd had good relationships with everyone who served her and her family and had never raised her voice or said a cross word to anyone.

"Your pacing is making me dizzy," Saga said with a grin.

"I am sorry," she said and joined her on a seat near the hearth.

"You have no reason to apologize," Vigdis said. "You have a great deal to process and it is only natural you are worried."

"I feel very badly about your servants, Saga."

"Do not worry about them. It's been adjustment enough having me as their lady; there's only so much that is unfamiliar we can expect them to accept."

"Saga!" Vigdis said placing her hand over her mouth.

"I am only partly jesting, sister," she said and shrugged. "You recall how fearful some of them were of me when I first arrived. These people are superstitious over the least little thing. And I have no idea what is going on here, but it is far beyond anything any of them or I have ever witnessed. All I am saying is that I am not surprised."

"I will help in any way that I can," Elspeth said.

"There is no need for that or for you to worry about it. Giric will hire more people from the village or Prestwick and we will be manage."

"May I ask if Freydis had any insight last evening?"

"She did not and was quite anxious to return to her dwelling to cast the runes. She said she would need to be alone in order to do so," Vigdis said.

Elspeth drew a deep breath and let it out slowly. She didn't know what to think about any of it. And while she was grateful that Magnus was the kind of man who would go to see the woman here safely, she couldn't help but feel the loss of having him nearby. Every part of her yearned for him as though he were her lifeline in this stormy sea of confusion.

"Tell me again about the man you saw," Vigdis said. "You said he was sitting. Could you make out any of his features?"

"Nay. I could only make out his glowing eyes. I was so afraid at that moment I just wanted to run away."

"Freydis did not feel fear from him," Saga said. "She was convinced he was a sage and had a message for you both. She feels your destinies are connected and that you are a Volur."

"And what is that?" Elspeth asked.

"In our world they have magical abilities like seeing into the future and healing the sick. In your world, according to my husband, you would be called a witch."

"I am not able to heal anyone."

"But you have seen things before they've occurred."

"Aye, I have many times since I was a small child. But I still say this is not possible because I am Christian. Will all my respect, I must emphasize that I do not believe in your gods."

"You do not have to believe in our gods to be influenced by them. It does not work the way you think. There is a reason Odin has blessed you with one of his ravens. It is a great honour that you should accept," Saga said a little more firmly than Elspeth cared for.

She was not trying to insult them, she was merely trying to explain her predicament. It was not that easy to even consider that everything she believed was either not true, or only a portion of reality.

"You have faith in your gods and I have faith in my God. It is possible that even if what Freydis suspects is true, that I have some kind of power, that we may disagree on the source."

Saga opened her mouth and closed it again when Vigdis placed her hand on her leg.

"You are correct, Lady Elspeth," Vigdis said. "How could we possibly know if this gift is from Odin or your God? And perhaps that is not the question to be answered at this moment."

"What do you mean?"

"I mean perhaps the more important question is what is the purpose of the gift? What are its properties and how are you to use them?"

While that may be true, what if she was not able to glean answers to any of the questions they posed? What if she never fully understood what was happening, or why, or how?

"There's only one thing I'm certain of right now," Saga said after a while.

"And what is that?" Elspeth asked, welcoming any clarity.

"I am certain my brother is more taken with you than I have ever seen him with anyone."

"I see that too," Vigdis said. "From the first moment we arrived on Islay, Magnus seemed unable to tear himself away from you. Surely you must have magical powers, for you have enchanted him and I never thought that would happen." Her soft smile and kind expression made her all the more believable.

But was it true? Could they really see the connection she had felt for Magnus almost from the first moment she'd met him? The more she thought about his tall muscular frame and piercing blue eyes, the warmer her whole body became.

An image of his tight leather trews flashed across her mind and her cheeks grew hot.

"I see just the mere mention of his name makes you flush," Saga said. "You are not the first to find my brother attractive, but you are the first to conjure such devotion from him. If I were to guess, and I am no Volur, I would say you are two halves of one soul."

Elspeth didn't quite know what to say in response. She was certain of what she felt, but had no idea if those feelings were in any way reciprocated. She was a little hurt when he didn't want her to ride with him the day before and so had thought he was not interested in her. But his declarations of protecting her and staying with her in the chapel told of a different story. She'd been so wrapped up in her episodes, she supposed she could have missed any indication from him that he felt something for her.

"There is one way to find out," Saga said.

Realization dawned on Elspeth and she shook her head which made Saga laugh.

"And I believe you just proved how you feel about him too." Thankfully she didn't add anything to that statement.

Elspeth wanted Magnus. Both physically and otherwise, he was hers, she was sure of it. But the thought of voicing that to him was daunting. Her belly did a million flip flops at just the thought of him touching her or kissing her. Having grown up thinking that at some point Osgar would make some sort of arrangement for her to secure their lands and wealth, she'd never fantasized about love and romance. Not that she didn't want it—of course she did. But she was surprised that these feelings were upon her and she hadn't been looking for them.

"Saga will not embarrass you, I promise," Vigdis said.

"I will say nothing if it is your wish. But I believe that if two people look at each other the way you do, they should be able to talk openly about it free from shame."

"It is all a great deal to process at the moment," Elspeth said.

She appreciated the insight and encouragement from his sisters, but her world had just sped up to a degree she was not able to comprehend and she desperately wanted to catch her breath.

"Oh look, there's Magnus now," Saga said looking at the entrance to the hall.

Elspeth turned her head quickly to find an empty door. Saga's boisterous laughter filled the hall as she turned her attention back to her. The woman was an enigma. She was a warrior, wise and clever, free spirited, and filled with mirth. Aye, Saga the shield maiden did not disappoint Elspeth's anticipation of meeting her. The woman had lived up to every expectation Elspeth had of her from the moment Osgar told of the marriage.

Magnus would return soon enough and she would feel better when he did. Freydis would help her understand her gift and she would reconcile her faith with whatever she learned. She had to remain positive that all of this was happening for a good reason and that all would be well.

CHAPTER TEN

The woman was a terror when she dug in her heels. Oh yes, his brother would have his hands full with her if they ever smartened up and realized they were meant to be together.

"Saga said to pack everything since you will not be returning," Giric said.

Magnus grinned and stepped out of the cottage with an armful of glass jars and bottles of various substances. He had no idea what they were, but he was firmly aware that they smelled awful.

Freydis didn't appear to care that Giric was laird and master here and she was supposed to go wherever he told her to go. Clearly the man kept forgetting he was not dealing with the ladies of the castle anymore.

But there was one lady of the castle who was never far from his thoughts. Elspeth was not docile nor meek or in contrast, aggressive, but her demeanour was different. She was more like Vigdis than Saga, yet there were times he'd seen a ferocity about her when she set her mind to something. He had to admit he liked that about her. He'd never been so taken with anyone in his life and he was not at all upset or concerned.

The thought of Gunnar having arranged a marriage for him had made him want to drive his broadsword through something. But the thought of that someone being Elspeth was not worrisome at all. Rather, he would welcome that. He placed the box of bottles in the cart and scratched the back of his head. Freya must have conjured up that thought. Either that or Loki was playing tricks with his mind.

He barely knew the woman, how could he possibly be thinking of claiming her? But the second the thought entered his mind, somewhere deep inside him he knew it to be true. She *was* meant to be his. He knew no other truth to match in his entire existence.

"…and another thing," Freydis said following Giric to the cart, "if you think I will be dining in your hall like the other ladies, you may think again. I am a free woman and I shall eat wherever I please."

"Freydis. This is for your protection. I hope you can see that. You are not being punished."

"It certainly feels like it. I told Saga from the beginning, I would remain here to aid her as long as she is with child. But my conditions were that I could live in the village on my own."

"That was before," Giric said.

"Before what?"

"Before Lady Elspeth's brother decided to draw attention to anyone in this area who has the power of sight," Magnus said to her. "You understand the threat, Freydis. You always have. Even Gunnar was always careful about you when we had certain visitors and played down your abilities."

"Leave Gunnar out of this."

"I will not if you continue to be difficult when all we are trying to do is keep you safe," Magnus said. Freydis was like a sister to him and he would not see her harmed any more than he would Saga or Vigdis.

She turned on her heel and mumbled something as she re-entered the cottage. She emerged a moment later with an armful of clothes and closed the door behind her.

"This is all I need to take right now. If I need anything else, I will come for it, and I will take someone with me if that makes you feel better."

Freydis climbed into the cart and arranged some of her belongings then sat cross legged and pouted. Magnus shook his head and mounted his horse.

"Has she always been like that?" Giric asked.

"As long as I've known her."

"I pity her future husband."

"That may very well be my brother."

Giric tilted his head back and laughed. Magnus chuckled as well. Gunnar seemed to find mirth in another's discomfort in a playful way and so it seemed fitting he would have to tread lightly in his own personal relationship.

"Your brother would have his hands full with that one. Why are they not together?"

"We all thought they would have married a couple of years ago, but they had a disagreement and have been dancing circles around one another ever since. Gunnar has been a little lost since she came to live with you and Saga. Perhaps her sour mood is a reflection of missing him as well."

"Mayhap you're right. We have other healers and a midwife we can call on to help Saga with the babe when the time comes. Freydis can return to Islay whenever she wants. She would be as protected there as here and so the only person standing in the way of that decision is herself."

"I suspect that is the reason for most of that woman's turmoil." While he was jesting, he could never understand why Gunnar and Freydis had not simply settled their differences.

An image of red hair floated across his mind's eye. If he was even remotely convinced Elspeth felt for him as he did for her, he would move mountains to claim her. No argument or living arrangement would keep them apart. Of that he was quite certain.

The closer they rode to the castle, the more his guts tightened. Even just a few short hours away from her was too much. He wanted to show her that being away from her was likely to make him miserable. How that was even possible, he had no idea. And he really didn't care. All he knew was that she had not left his thoughts since the moment they met and his enchantment with her grew with each passing second.

Magnus wasn't sure how much of her time he was permitted in private, if any. But he would speak to her and he would let her know how he felt. Not just that he wanted to protect her from harm. But that he wanted to know her in every sense. He shifted on his horse. His damned trews were still tight and every time he had even the smallest thought of kissing her delicious mouth, he thickened and unfortunately the leather was not yet broken in enough to have any give. The result was painful ride to the castle.

Before long, he was riding through the gates, dismounting, and tossing the reins to the stable hand. Magnus strode into the hall to find only his sisters there.

"She's in her chamber," Saga said with a strange grin on her face as she nodded to Vigdis. He didn't know what was so funny and he didn't care.

Magnus took the stairs two at a time and hesitated outside Elspeth's door. His arm was raised to knock when she opened it and drew him inside. He had no words for her. He looked upon her beautiful face, deep within her eyes and placed his hands on either side of her face.

Magnus leaned down and brushed his lips across hers. He loved the way her small hands felt on his body as she slid her arms around him and drew him closer.

"Is this permitted?" he whispered to her.

She smiled and reached up to return his kiss. Magnus drew her toward him and deepened the kiss. He played with her lips then urged her mouth open with his tongue. Once inside he tasted her sweetness and he was lost to everything but the sensations flowing through his body from their connection.

She pressed her breasts against him and he was undone. Magnus reached down and lifted her body and pressed her against the wall. He hooked her legs around his waist and pressed his erection against her skirts. Sweet Freya, he wanted to slide his hard cock inside her and pleasure her until she couldn't take anymore. Her hands were wild in his hair and she pushed her body back against him.

"I want you so badly," he said in a hoarse voice when he broke free from the kiss to catch his breath. He kissed her chest and her neck. "Tell me you want me as much."

He didn't need to hear the words; her body told him everything he needed to know. But he wanted to hear them anyway.

"I want you Magnus. I want you like you want me," she said softly.

The soft tone of her voice tempered his desire. He pulled them away from the wall and walked to the chairs by the hearth. He placed her in one and sat in the other. Magnus raked his hands through his hair and stroked his hands over his face. He needed a moment to cool his thoughts. Never could he have imagined that she would respond to him the way she had. No woman had ever responded to him like that and he was a little overwhelmed by the force of their mutual desire.

He drew a deep steadying breath and smiled at her. For the first time in his life, he had no idea what to say.

～

Elspeth studied his flushed cheeks and wide-eyed expression. He shifted on the chair a few times and she almost giggled with an understanding of the part of him that was causing his discomfort. So that was at least one question answered. She wasn't sure how she could have broached the topic with him and now couldn't think of any way that would have been better. She was aware of the silly grin that rested on her face and for the life of her she lacked the ability to adjust her composure.

"That was unexpected. I hope you are not upset with me," he said. "I would never want to disrespect you or have anyone view you any differently because of my desire for you."

The way he said desire with a rasp in his voice sent a thrill through her body. She wasn't even sure she could trust herself to speak. The only thing she knew for certain was that she wanted to climb onto his lap and kiss him again. She stared at his mouth and couldn't help licking her lips to remember the taste of him.

"Elspeth you cannot look at me like that," he said in a whisper. "I want you too badly."

She gazed into his eyes and saw raw truth resting there as though she could see into his very soul. Her heartbeat thudded in her ears. Or was it his? She was convinced she could hear his even though they sat apart.

"I can feel you," she said. She didn't know any other way to say it.

He stood and walked to the chamber door and placed his hand on it as if he couldn't decide what to do.

She moved up behind him and wrapped her arms around his torso. He sucked in his breath quickly. God's breath, he felt so good. Magnus turned and wrapped his arm around her and rested his chin on her head.

"We should go to the hall. I am not certain it is proper for me to be up here so long with you like this."

"I know, but how can something that feels like this be wrong?"

"It is only wrong because we are not joined in marriage."

"Is it that way for you too?"

"For the most part. I will not treat you with any less respect than I would expect of my sister's suitors. Come, let us go to the hall before our desire rises again."

From any other man, that sort of language would have been mortifying to hear. But somehow coming from him, she didn't mind it. In fact, she rather enjoyed being the cause of his discomfort.

They walked together to the hall. She would have loved to hold his hand and tell everyone how they felt, but the moment she entered, her head tingled with the familiar signs of the Viking healer's presence.

Because she knew the feeling, this time she did not fight it, rather allowed it to wash over her. She drew strength from Magnus as she walked to the table to sit beside Freydis never breaking eye contact with her. Already she was aware of the tension in the woman. She seemed upset or angry about something, and there was something else—deep and desperate longing and sorrow.

"That's as much as I can take," she said then Elspeth could feel nothing from her.

"What happened?" Magnus asked.

"I spent a sleepless night last night trying to figure this out. I have come to the conclusion that you have the abilities of a Volur and you have been gifted with Odin's raven. There can be no other explanation though my runes did not confirm it. How you reconcile that with your own God is something you will have to explore yourself. But I have no doubt that you are able to see into a person's very soul if they are willing. To be honest, I also think that with some practiced effort you may also be able to break into a person's mind even if they were not willing."

"I do not wish to force myself upon anyone. Were you willing just then?"

"I was and I tried to connect with you. I do not know if it would work on anyone else."

"I will try it," Magnus said.

Elspeth turned to him. Was she prepared for what she'd find if she probed his mind? She certainly was not willing to do so in front of anyone.

"I don't think that is a good idea," Freydis said, thankfully.

"We do not yet understand the full extent of her abilities and whether or not any harm could result from it. It would be like giving your sharpest sword to a small child. I do not mean to offend you, Lady Elspeth, but the truth is until we spend more time together, I will not understand the full extent of your gift."

"I am not afraid of it anymore."

"I cast runes until the sun came up and I saw nothing of this in them. I saw much about every person in this hall, but absolutely nothing of you. It is as though our gods do not even see you and I do not understand how that can be."

"Is it because I am Christian?"

"Not at all. I saw Saga's husband in her runes long before he ever landed on Islay. You do not have to believe in Odin for him to have a role to play in your destiny."

She supposed that made sense. She had faith in her own beliefs and that there was a higher purpose at play, and that could include any of the people in the room, not just the Christians.

"How do you suggest we proceed?" Magnus asked.

"Very slowly," Freydis said. "I would like to understand every experience you've had like this and maybe in a few days' time, we can try to reconnect with the seer of Vanaheim. I know you were frightened, but he is harmless, a visionary whose only purpose is to share information to Volur."

"Does that mean you are one as well?" Elspeth asked. This was all so strange to her.

"To a certain degree yes, but I do not have the level of power you have. I am able to cast runes and see messages from the gods, but I cannot look into a person's mind or know if someone is about to enter a chamber."

Put like that Elspeth felt a little freakish. If someone had told her a few weeks ago that she would be having this sort of conversation she would have laughed at them and called them mad in the head. Now she was not only accepting what she was being told, she was the subject of the conversation.

For the next few hours, Elspeth detailed every time she'd predicted someone's arrival or an impression she felt when something bad was about to happen. She told Freydis about her Nana Besse and how she'd tried to help her.

"Is that why you wear cloves around your neck?"

"Aye, Nana Besse said cloves would help me see good things more clearly."

"She is right that cloves have good magical properties. She was a wise-woman?"

"Aye, she was. She passed away a few years ago and I often wish I had more time with her, especially considering how this has all escalated."

"Did she ever tell you if there was a source of your gift?"

"She said it was a gift from the Celtic Goddess Brigid. I

admit that I didn't really pay much attention to that part of her teachings which is something I now regret. I dismissed her reasoning because I thought it was blasphemous and so I didn't even want to listen to her speak against God."

"Your faith is strong and you should never apologize to anyone for it. You may find yourself drawing on it for strength."

"She has me for strength," Magnus said.

Elspeth turned to him and smiled. That was a certainty. She had no doubt he had enough strength for both of them. She didn't need to probe him to believe that his heart was true and his honour was intact. And though he had said he would volunteer to let her know his mind, she would rather find out her own way over time. Knowing all his secrets up front would prevent them from learning about each other together and strengthening their bond from there. Nay, she would not probe him or anyone else. A person's secret thoughts were meant to be theirs alone and they had a right to keep them. Elspeth vowed then and there she would never enter a person's mind again no matter the reasoning.

# CHAPTER ELEVEN

Magnus had been listening to Freydis and Elspeth for hours talking about the latter's past experiences. In his mind they didn't appear to be making any forward movement, rather returning to the same point over and over again. How could Elspeth be chosen by Odin for any purpose?

He stood and stretched his back as he moved to the hearth for a change of position. He never had much patience for sitting around, and though this was important, he felt idle and unproductive.

"How was your meeting with King Olaf?" Giric asked from beside him.

He'd almost forgotten all about it. With everything that had happened with Elspeth in the past several days, the looming threat from Athelstan seemed eons away from priority.

"He will join forces with us."

"You do not sound convinced."

Was he certain of Olaf's alliance? Was he certain of

anyone's? A memory flashed in his mind and he moved back to the table.

"I need to interrupt for a moment."

He waited for both women to look at him and nod.

"Lady Elspeth, do you recall specifically what it was King Olaf wanted you to see for him?"

He couldn't believe he'd forgotten that piece. He really must be losing his focus as he was usually much sharper than that. Clearly this woman had gotten to him in a way he hadn't imagined. That was a first.

He waited as she looked down at her hands and furrowed her brow. "'Twas personal in nature," she said.

Personal or no, it could very well affect their reasons to trust or not to trust Olaf.

"I too would like to know more about your meeting with him," Giric said.

"Did you feel threatened?" Freydis asked.

"Nay. My brother told the King that I have the special power of sight and that I could answer any question he had. He laughed at first until I looked in his eyes. A great number of images flooded my brain and I closed my eyes to block them out. It was too much."

"What did you see?" Magnus asked and sat beside her, placing his hand over hers. He didn't want her to be afraid or uncomfortable, but this was too important.

"I saw a great battle. I don't know where he was or who fought whom. I could smell blood and I could hear swords clanging."

"But that was not what he asked you about," Freydis said.

"Nay. He wanted to know about our King's daughter and if they would be a good match."

Magnus knew it! The man had been holding back on him and Gunnar with the level to which he understood the Scottish king's plans. Constantine had already planned to partner with Olaf, long before the man beside him had approached. He didn't like this way of warfare. He preferred knowing the enemy and facing them full on. This sideways approach was not honourable. He would be damned sure to inform Gunnar before any additional alliance discussions occurred between any of them. The problem was that Gunnar would be fine to talk and talk and talk. Magnus knew betrayal when he saw it and he didn't trust Olaf now as far as he could throw him.

"And what did you tell him?" Giric asked.

"I told him I could not see him or a woman."

"Did he ask you if you saw anything?"

"Nay. He seemed distracted by someone leaving the hall and sent us away. My brother was angry with me and so we went straight to the ship. He grumbled the whole way about false gifts and there being no way for him to get ahead."

Magnus understood what it was to be second born. He'd stood in Gunnar's shadow his whole life and disagreed with him on many occasions including the most recent business with Short-Beard. But the thought of outright defiance to the extent of harming the clan or any of his siblings was not something he could even fathom. He would stand between either of them and harm without a second thought. The interesting aspect of Elspeth's experience with her brother is that it allowed them some inadvertent insight into King Olaf's priorities. He was clearly more concerned with King Constantine's daughter than he was with Athelstan. That could mean a few things. Perhaps he really didn't see the English king as a threat because he was in league with him. Or perhaps he was overly confident in his own defences. Either way, Magnus now questioned trusting him.

"Is this the witch?" a voice boomed from the doorway.

Magnus tensed and turned toward the door. A man of lesser stature than himself strode toward the hall table in

Elspeth's direction. Giric met him halfway and in a couple strides, Magnus was there as well.

"Donnan," Giric said. "What do you think you're doing?"

"I have heard all about the witch and want her gone from this castle immediately. She will bring hellfire and damnation upon us all. Whoever heard of a Christian witch speaking to Viking gods? It's the worst kind of blasphemy and I won't have it here. And it's high time the Viking witch was burned for her offences to God as well."

Magnus grabbed the man by his tunic and lifted him off the floor. "You will not speak about either woman in that way, or I will remove your tongue from your filthy mouth."

"Put my brother down," Giric said in a surprisingly calm voice.

Magnus didn't move. It didn't take a seer to understand the dishonour that lay in this man's soul. He would not allow him one inch closer to either Freydis or Elspeth.

"Magnus," Giric said. "I said put him down. You are not Laird here and I am ordering you to put him down."

Magnus looked at Giric with Donnan still aloft. "And what do you intend to do with him if I release him?"

Magnus wasn't interested in any more talking. And he was tired of the implications of an invisible threat to these two women. Now he had a face to put with the threat and he planned to ensure the man was dealt with appropriately.

"I will ensure both women in my hall are properly protected. Now put down my brother." This time his voice raised.

The man he held while wide-eyed, smirked at him. He needed a lesson he'd not soon forget before he threatened someone Magnus cared about again.

Magnus released Donnan who dropped to the floor.

"This is why I told you we should have never let filthy Vikings into our hall."

Magnus took another step forward but before he could grab the man again, Giric grabbed him from underneath the shoulder and lifted until Donnan had no choice but to stand.

"You will not insult my guests or my wife. Do you hear me?" he asked as he shook him.

"Aye, I hear you. You're as stubborn as you've ever been. You won't be satisfied until you have us all slaughtered in our sleep."

"You will leave this hall and not return until you have some civility about you," Giric said.

That wasn't enough for Magnus. There was something about the unhinged look in the man's eyes that said he was not a threat because he wanted to exploit the women, he was a threat because he feared them. That was worse. Fear caused men to lose their wits resulting in unpredictable actions.

"We will not remain in this castle one more moment while that man has access to it," Magnus said. He had no idea where he would go, but he would not stay here if Elspeth and Freydis' security could not be assured.

"My brother is no danger to anyone," Giric said. "He likes to stir trouble, but he would never harm the women."

"Are you certain of that? Would you trust your Viking child in his care?"

"Saga is not due for many months. Donnan will have plenty of time to reconcile his mind to our marriage."

"And in the meantime, his words poison your servants. Do you not see from where the fear stems? You've lost servants. Do not tell me you have not considered your brother sowing the seeds of hatred and loathing against your wife, Freydis, and anything having to do with us."

"I agree with him," Freydis said. "Do you not recall when you introduced Saga to everyone? Who was the most upset? I will remind you," she said. "It was not the servants, they were in awe of your wife. Nay it was not until Donnan put ideas in their heads about her being dangerous that any of them grew concerned. I have been pacifying those concerns for weeks and now I see they've stirred again. I am telling you, your brother is the source of rumblings in your castle amongst the serving staff."

Giric shook his head and strode out of the hall. Magnus turned to Freydis and Elspeth. They should leave. Right then and there, they should go somewhere, anywhere away from this place and any place that still held danger. But where could that possibly be?

~

The fire spread warmth, but her bones were like ice. Hours of Freydis' probing and the accusations from the laird's brother were enough to wear on anyone. Elspeth wasn't sure if she needed rest, nourishment, or Magnus' strong arms around her. As if he sensed her thoughts, he pulled a chair toward her and sat with her near the hearth holding her hands. Strength seemed to seep from his body and into hears, as if blood flowed from his veins into hers.

"You need not worry," he said in a deep, low voice that made the back of her neck tingle.

"I know that. This is all a little overwhelming."

"Do you feel that it is helpful?"

"Aye. I do. I have a better understanding of what I see now."

"How so?"

"Freydis and I have determined there is always some kind of trigger to my visions and the more closely the future event is linked to my wellbeing, the stronger the reaction. She and I are connected because we share a similar gift, though she is convinced mine is much stronger."

"But what is the source?"

Elspeth smiled. That was the part that would give her comfort when her emotions eventually caught up to what her mind was trying to process. "The source may not be as important as I originally thought. Whether Freydis believes it is from Odin, or I believe it is from God, the result is the same. It is a gift we must figure out together and use wisely. Mayhap Odin and God are working together," she said with a grin. She was not one to possess blind faith, but she was certain her current situation had a reason and until she understood it fully, she was content to continue to work with Freydis.

"If you are sure you wish to continue, I will help you in any way I can. But if you wish to leave here, I will make that happen for you."

"I believe you. Perhaps our paths were meant to cross as well."

She didn't want to say too much, but there was no doubt that Magnus' presence gave her comfort and strength she did not possess when he was not near.

His smile was warm and the lines around his eyes crinkled. His expression could be welcoming or deadly and she counted her blessings she was on the receiving end of the former. What did she really know about this man besides an invisible connection that she couldn't define or understand? But it had been there right from the start. Now that she was more in tune with her body's triggers and warnings she was better able to determine a safe forewarning from that which denoted danger.

Freydis left the hall with Giric stating she would meet with her again later on. The woman looked drained and Elspeth hoped she would be able to contribute more to their sessions going forward. She understood enough about how tired she was and could only imagine the toll such an effort took on Freydis.

"I would like to leave this hall," she said to Magnus.

"Where would you like to go?" he asked with a light tug on the corner of his lips.

"Do you think it safe to go for a ride?"

"No. I agree with Giric there. You are safer within these walls. But I have an idea."

Elspeth had an idea too, but she was not about to tell him that, nor was she about to let her mind linger down paths that would lead to her ruination.

"What do you have in mind?" she asked, not trying to sound wanton, but somehow he grinned as his eyes drifted from her mouth down across her breasts and slowly back up again.

"What I have in mind is different from what I will suggest," he said in a low voice she knew was meant only for her.

Heat rose to her cheeks. How was it he could enflame her body with a simple look and a few words?

Elspeth opened her mouth to speak but the heat in his eyes stopped her. His thumbs stroked her hands and she reacted as if they were bellows swelling her flame. She squirmed on her chair to ease the tension that built between her legs. His eyes grew wide and he released her hand and stood.

Magnus stepped away from her and raked his hands through his hair. God's breath, he was magnificent! Through his tight tunic his back rippled with corded muscle and she didn't doubt for a moment he could fling her over his shoulder and have her anyway or anywhere he wanted. And she'd let him. Elspeth shook her head and stood to smooth her skirts. She didn't know what God had intended for her when it came to her visions, but she was certain he did not intend for her to become wanton.

She pushed thoughts of his hard body aside, no easy feat with said body so delectably on display before her. "We should explore your idea," she said, obviously not meaning ripping one another's clothes off and ravishing each other until dawn.

Magnus turned to her and chuckled. "You will be the death of me," he said.

"What does that mean?" she asked.

"It means we will make a visit to the armoury and see which weapons are most suited for a woman of your strength and stature." His smile faded. "There may come a time when despite all my efforts, you still have to defend yourself."

Elspeth thought about Saga who was quite accomplished with weapons. Word had spread quickly about the lessons she conducted with the servants at MacDomnail Castle. Any new staff here were expected to go through training in order to learn how to at least protect themselves. And what about Vigdis? Was she trained in battle too? The thought of learning how to wield a sword versus stitch a pillow almost made her laugh.

The air was warmer than usual for late afternoon during the fall harvest. Elspeth and Magnus made their way across the bailey and to a long stone structure. Elspeth had never been inside before, though she'd spied the building many times when crossing the bailey to approach the keep.

Magnus appeared to know where he was going and so she followed him to the structure and inside. He lit torches along the inside which revealed more weapons than Elspeth had seen in her entire life. She'd never been interested in them, though her brother possessed an armoury, she never bothered to look inside. Now she wished she had for there were items there she did not know what to call.

"If you had to choose just one," she asked him, "which would it be?"

Magnus took his time touching the various swords and axes until he came to a long rod with a metal ball on the end. Spikes protruded from the ball. He turned to her with a wide grin.

"I like this one."

She'd never seen the like in her life. "What is it?"

"It's called a mace. I prefer to call it 'destroyer of my enemies'. Would you like to touch it?"

She wasn't sure if he was jesting or not and preferred to think he was, though he did seem to be quite enamoured with the object. "Perhaps you and destroyer would like some time alone?" she couldn't help but ask.

Magnus tilted his head back and laughed, a deep rich sound that resonated through her body. She could spend many pleasant hours listening to him talk or laugh; she wasn't fussy.

"I apologize. I am in admiration of good workmanship. But these are tools, and are only as good as the one wielding them."

That made sense. If one didn't know how to use the ball with the spikes on it, what was the point in owning it?

"Come, look at this one," he said and drew her to a series of swords that were thinner and longer than the one she'd seen him carry. He lifted it up and gazed directly into her eyes then spent a moment or two finding a particular spot where he could balance the whole thing on his finger. "Weight balance is critical in sword play," he said, never breaking eye contact with her. With a flick, the sword swirled in the air then landed in his confident grasp. He pointed the blade downward and directed the handle toward her.

Did she really want to learn how to use a sword? She kept a small dagger in her skirts and imagined she could use that if given the opportunity. But in reality she didn't quite know how to use that either.

Elspeth reached into her skirts and pulled out the dagger. Magnus' eyes went wide then narrowed. "Has that been there the whole time?"

"Aye," she said with a grin.

"I believe I shall have to pat you down, Lady Elspeth, for my own safety."

Her heart flip flopped in her chest as he placed both the sword and her dagger on the table beside them. Magnus' hands encircled her waist and drew her tight to his body. His hands slid down to cup her buttocks causing her to suck in her breath. They were alone, she was unchaperoned, and his hands were on her again.

# CHAPTER TWELVE

Magnus had to get his wits together. It seemed like every time he came within two feet of this woman he wanted to devour her and that would not do. But perhaps one little taste wouldn't hurt. He leaned down and brushed his lips across hers and groaned when she slid her hands up his chest.

Pulling back, he met her gaze. Her cheeks were flushed and her lips parted. Loving her would be so easy.

"I apologize again. It seems that's all I am offering you these days," he said and turned to pick up the dagger and sword. He handed both to her and reached for his broadsword.

"Let us remain focused, shall we?"

He was grateful she didn't respond because he truly didn't know what he would do if she said go ahead and bend me over the table. He shook his head. Those thoughts would no doubt get them both into trouble.

When she still didn't say anything, he turned to her. Her eyes were wide and didn't seem to be focusing on anything in particular.

# THE RAVEN

"Lady Elspeth, are you unwell?" he asked and touched her arm.

She seemed to break from the spell and regarded him and her surroundings as if she didn't know where she was.

"I—"

"Please, sit here," he said and pulled over a stool. "Tell me what is happening."

Elspeth placed her hands on her head and closed her eyes. "Danger," she whispered.

"Here? Now?"

She nodded.

Magnus went to the doorway of the armoury. He'd left it open a little and now looked through the crack. Men trained with swords, a young boy pushed a cart full of vegetables, and some men kept watch at the gate. All appeared normal by his estimation. He'd been granted a full tour of the grounds and defences when Saga had first come to live there. Giric was more than generous with sharing the purpose of each man present and even shared some of the castle's few weaknesses. So by his informed estimation, there was no current threat—not that he could see, at least.

Turning back to Elspeth he was surprised to find her standing directly behind him and staring at the door. Unblinking, she stayed like that for a few moments and appeared to break free from the spell. Fear crept into his heart. She looked around her and met his gaze with a furrowed brow.

"How did I get here?"

"Lady Elspeth, I believe we should return to the keep. We can resume your training on the morrow." Magnus collected her dagger and returned the sword to its proper place.

He opened the door wide enough for her to pass through and when he stepped out, something caught the corner of his eye. MacDomnail's brother leaned against the forge that was on the other side of the armoury. Was he the threat? Magnus scanned the man's height and size. Unless he was a master swordsman, there was no way he would get to Elspeth.

Donnan spit on the ground and slowly walked toward them. Magnus clenched his jaw when Elspeth reacted by standing a little behind him.

"What do you want?" Magnus asked.

"I live here. I don't have to want anything. I can go wherever I want. And I can do whatever I want."

"You're upsetting Lady Elspeth. That is something you are not permitted to do."

"Oh aye is that so? And are you going to stop me if I want to speak with her?"

"I will."

"Do you see all these men?" he asked and pointed behind Magnus. "If you so much as look at me the wrong way, they will be on you in a heartbeat. I cannot imagine even a mighty Viking like you can take on twenty men."

"And if you so much as look at the lady the wrong way, you will find out soon enough just how easily I can best twenty and one men."

Donnan's eyes went wide for a moment before he masked his obvious discomfort at Magnus' claim. He might struggle with the number, but he'd fought men with far more motivation than these. And he didn't believe for a moment they'd do anything to support any abuse of Lady Elspeth. No, this man liked to throw his weight around to make up for the fact that he was weak, both of body and of mind.

"You are rather fearful of that which is new to you," Magnus said. A true test of strength lay in one's adaptability. Change was inevitable, he'd learned quite recently through his sister's marriage, but preserving oneself and one's standards through that change was what separated true men from weaker ones such as the one standing in front of him at the moment.

"I do not have to explain myself to you," he said and spit on the ground in front of Magnus' boot. "You both will bring demise to our family. My father is rolling in his grave." Donnan pointed his finger at both him and Elspeth. "Vikings and witches do not belong here." He walked past them and glared especially at her. "You better keep your door locked at night while you are here. I am not the only one who thinks you bring evil into this place."

"Are you threatening her?" Magnus asked and stepped in front of him. He was fast losing patience with the man. Understanding he was being baited only quelled his rising anger so much.

"Like I said, I live here. I can say and do anything I want."

"Is that what you think?" Giric said as he approached from behind Donnan. The latter jumped at the sound of his brother's voice.

"I believe your brother may need an education, MacDomnail," Magnus said. "He is of the mind he can threaten Lady Elspeth and that he will not be held accountable. This is the second time he has attempted to upset the lady. I hope that you will now take some action to protect us or we will not remain one more moment."

"Good! I don't want you here. No one wants you here. And take your filthy Viking sister with you. No one wants her here either!"

Magnus took a step back. If he'd learned one thing since meeting Giric MacDomnail, it was that he was fiercely protective of his wife. He moved to the side with Elspeth and waited for the explosion. He didn't have to wait long. Giric's right fist slammed hard into Donnan's jaw sending the man flying through the air and landing on his backside. For a moment no one moved.

Somewhere above a raven's *kraw-kraw* drew Elspeth's attention skyward. Magnus looked up to see several ravens circling overhead. He'd never seen them do that before. The behaviour was more commonly viewed from eagles and hawks.

"They heard my call," she said.

"See! I told you she's a witch! No one can speak to ravens! You have to get her out of here," he said to Giric as he rubbed his jaw. "She will be the ruination of us all!"

Giric motioned for a couple of his men go to Donnan. "Take him to the hall and stay there with him until I join you."

After the men collected Donnan and practically dragged him away, Giric turned to Elspeth. "I do not know if it will be safe for you here. Donnan is my brother and I will not banish him. While I do not agree with his opinions, I feel he will try to influence the staff and that will put you in harm's way."

"I understand," she said.

That wasn't good enough for Magnus. "So what, we are just left to our own devices? What about all the talk about us being better protected here than anywhere? Better than her own home, you said. I have a feeling my sister will have a different opinion, MacDomnail."

"I know what I said and I do not like it any more than you do."

"And are you afraid for Saga's well-being? He has lumped her with us as being unworthy of being here."

"I will deal with Donnan and Saga. For now we need to keep our wits about us and figure out where you can go. And I mean it when I say, you have my full protection and as many men as I can send with you to help keep you undetected."

"So it is into hiding, then." That was marginally better. At least they wouldn't be subject to the brother's abuse. Magnus had some patience, but that would wear thin quickly if he had to listen to that man day and night.

"Lady Elspeth, do you agree we must leave?"

She was still looking up at the sky. "Aye. We must leave. There are few places we can go at the moment, but there is one."

"And where is that?" Giric asked. His voice had softened and he now rubbed the hand he'd used to flatten his brother.

"It is a very old place. You do not know it." She turned to Magnus then. "Come we must make haste. It is a long journey and we will need to pack provisions."

Magnus looked at Giric and shrugged. Perhaps the ravens were speaking to her. Perhaps it was Odin's protection or her Christian God's. Either way, if she had a solution he was willing to hear it.

~

With one last look at the sky, Elspeth turned toward the keep. The more she trusted her instincts and visions, the stronger they became. She could clearly see an abandoned tower house and was certain not only was it within a day's ride, but that she'd not seen it before. And without any additional information that what she'd seen in her mind, she knew exactly how to get there.

She was well aware of the man walking beside her and the questioning glances he threw her way. But she was not yet ready to describe anything that was running through her mind at the moment. She scarce understood it herself, let alone explain it to anyone else. But suffice it to say, the ravens had spoken to her and she understood them. As mad as that sounded even in her own head, she would swear on her life 'twas real.

Once inside the keep, Elspeth walked up the stairs and

straight to the chamber in which she had slept the eve afore. Osgar had not been gone long enough to return with her belongings and so she had no additional gown or undergarments to pack and would have given anything at the moment for a bath, but she would have to make do with what she had. Food was the most important thing on her mind at the moment. They would have to pack enough for a few weeks at least. And the moment *they* popped into her head, the door closed quietly behind her.

She turned to see Magnus leaning beside it. "Please tell me what we are doing? Are you certain you know of a place that's safe?"

Elspeth drew a deep breath. He'd stood by her this long, if a little madness didn't send him running for the hills, she vowed she would never doubt his loyalty.

"You will think me mad in the head."

"I will not," he said in a quiet voice.

It was his unwavering stare and the small smile he offered that convinced her. Since she'd decided to trust her instincts, they would expand to include this man. She'd felt comfort and strength from him from the moment they'd met and he'd given her absolutely no reason to doubt him now.

"I have seen a vision of an abandoned tower-house. I have never known of it before this day, but I have seen it and I know how to get there. We will be safe there."

"And how do you know this?"

Why did he have to ask her that? Why couldn't he just agree and help them be on their way? Why? Because she sounded like she needed a padded chamber or an exorcism. She understood all too well why the MacDomnail's brother had reacted so. Most sane people would never entertain a person who claimed they could speak to animals much less one as revered as a raven.

"I was told."

"By whom?"

She hesitated and looked down at her hands. He walked toward her and lifted her chin with his fingers so she had to meet his gaze. Kindness and patience rested there.

"The ravens," she whispered and waited for him to burst out laughing or call for the guards to take her away. So much for not doubting him.

"You firmly believe that?"

"Aye, I do."

"Then I do too," he said and stepped back. "How long is the ride and how long will we need to stay there?"

Elspeth nearly gasped. That was it? He would trust her instincts too. Her pulse picked up a little and she smiled at him. He blinked a few times and smiled back. She didn't have the words to express her gratitude. Without someone else to help her, she would never admit the like to anyone.

"We should prepare to be there a while," she said. "There is a storm brewing and I do not know the extent of it yet."

"I will help you understand," he said. "Should we tell Freydis? And is she in danger?"

"She already knows. She shared that vision with me." It was all so incredible. Elspeth had no idea how she could be so certain of something that had absolutely no logic or explanation. Freydis was in a different kind of danger, one that only she and her heart could resolve. But she was not about to tell Magnus that. Freydis' private feelings were not for anyone to know and Elspeth was not entirely comfortable knowing as much as she did.

"Freydis is not in danger from the MacDomnail's brother nor any servant here."

"Then why are you being singled out?"

That was a question she could not answer. Mayhap Donnan was more threatened by her because of her status. Perhaps he felt that someone of Freydis' standing could be contained whereas Donnan held no power over Elspeth. Either way, she was certain Freydis would come to no harm from him.

"I do not know. But we will leave here and ride hard to the tower-house. Freydis will quell any concerns Saga might have at us leaving in this manner."

"Very well, I will secure all the provisions we require and horses. MacDomnail said he will provide us some men for protection as well."

"We do not need them where we are going," she said. "We will not be found."

Magnus nodded and left the chamber. Elspeth sat near the hearth and stared into the fire. Visions of the tower-house floated across her mind's eye. She could see the path clearly now. The entrance to the wood in which the tower sat was about halfway between MacDomnail Castle and her home. Unease crept into her belly at the thought of those woods. Nana Besse had said they were haunted and to never go there. Not that as a child she would have, and it was curious that the woman would single out the place to a wee one.

But she'd done more than that. Nana Besse had described the entrance as a wooded gateway with vines curved around two large, curved trees that met at an apex several feet high. *Do not enter this place alone.* She'd gone on to say that the tower had belonged to a wealthy laird many years ago who had succumbed to the advances of Glaistig who'd haunted these parts preying on lonely men. Elspeth didn't believe in Nana Besse's old tales, but the tower house was clearly in her mind's eye now and the more she ruminated on it, the more she was certain she did in fact know the place of which the ravens spoke.

Elspeth leaned forward and rested her elbows on her

knees, then her face in her hands. She rocked as she watched the fire consume the embers, feeding its insatiable hunger.

Was she going mad? Mayhap she was merely drumming up old memories as an explanation for her episodes. That would mean Freydis was as mad as she and that was not the case. Nay, she must trust herself now more than ever. And if the Glaistig was real and set her faery sights to torment them, Elspeth would send her to the depths from whichever realm she hailed.

She thought of the Father's teachings. She'd been brought up to believe that forgiveness was divine and that devout people went to Heaven and the damned went to Hell. While she still believed that, some part of her couldn't help but wonder if that was only part of the story. What if there were many other places a person could go beyond this world? What if there were countless realms where one could find oneself and what if the tower house was one of them?

There were no answers at the moment, but one thing was certain, she was about to find out what being hidden away in a tower with Magnus would entail. Could she keep her hands to herself when all she wanted to do when he was near was to touch and kiss him and more?

## CHAPTER THIRTEEN

The cart was packed to the brim. Giric had not hesitated to provide them with enough provisions for the winter. And Magnus had never needed to have more blind faith in anyone in his life. He didn't know where they were going. He didn't know how long they'd be there, and he didn't know how he could protect Elspeth without any additional information. Blind faith indeed. He prayed to Odin that he would have the courage for whatever lay ahead. Men he could best when in battle. But these were invisible foe and he possessed no weapons to fight them. If Elspeth were to fall ill from her episodes he had no skills to help her. Before he left he needed to speak with Freydis.

He located her in the kitchen yelling at the cook. Did the woman have to be so disagreeable all the time?

"Freydis, I must speak with you," he said, intentionally interrupting her. The cook's grateful smile not lost on him.

"I know all about it," she said and placed her hands on her hips. "And I do not appreciate being blocked out of knowing exactly where you're going."

"Blocked out how?" Now she sounded mad in the head.

"Lady Elspeth will not let me see her visions of the direction to the tower house."

Magnus pulled her to the side and away from the cook whose brows had shot nearly up to his hairline.

"Keep your voice down. You know how dangerous it is for Lady Elspeth right now."

"I understand the danger," she said in a raised whisper. "I am more aware than you think."

Magnus regarded her defiant stance. She was quite vexed about something and he had an inkling what it might be.

"You don't like that you're not in control."

"That's not true. I have only been trying to help and I do not appreciate being blocked."

"Has it occurred to you that she might be trying to protect you?"

"Protect me from what? I saw the vision. It was an abandoned tower. I know about it so why can I not know where it is or join you there?"

"Because she believes that you are safer here."

"And how would she know that?"

"That's the question isn't it, Freydis? How do you know any of this is real?"

"I just do."

"And you cannot accept that perhaps she does as well?"

Freydis folded her arms across her chest. Thor's teeth, she could be the most stubborn woman.

"What am I to do?"

"You are to do what you said you would from the beginning which is to stay with my sister until she doesn't need you any longer and then return to Islay. I can say with certainty that you are missed there."

Her whole demeanour changed. She dropped her arms to her sides and her expression softened. She opened her mouth as if to speak and closed it again. Magnus couldn't tell her what to do, but she really should return to Islay before the winter. And he understood the need for control. He'd felt it slipping from his grasp at times since he'd met Elspeth. But somehow his course was entangled with hers. Their paths were now linked and he'd had to give up thinking he was in control of any of it. None of them were.

"I came to ask if there was anything I should do for Lady Elspeth should she fall into an episode again."

"There is nothing you can do, but keep her from walking off the tower's ledge or into a pool," she said with a small smile tugging at her lips. "Keep her safe and make sure she feels safe. Talk to her, listen to her. Don't be afraid of anything she tells you and don't doubt her. Her gift is powerful and if she fights it, she will be harmed. The forces working through her will not be held at bay. She must embrace all of it and all will be well."

The thought of some unseen force controlling the will of the woman he—what? Loved? Is that what this was?

"And in Odin's eyes, you two are already married."

"What?"

"You heard me. You have been brought together as part of the larger plan for her. There is no shame in your feelings for one another. They are real and they are blessed by the All-Father. I saw it in my runes."

"What else did you see?"

"Naught that I will discuss with the likes of you," she said with a broader grin now. "Take care of her, Magnus. She will need your light in the dark days ahead."

Dark days, indeed. With battle looming and a possible English invasion, Magnus did not envision himself hiding away. But those battle plans would have to be left to his brother, Olaf of Dublin, the Scottish king, and Giric MacDomnail.

"Take this," she said and handed him a smooth flat stone

with a marking on it. She strung a string of leather through the small hole at the top and tied a knot at the end. He bent low so she could place it around his neck. "Algiz will protect you from anything you cannot see with your own eyes."

He wasn't sure he was ready to put his faith in a small stone, but because it meant something to Freydis, he would accept it. "Will it protect Elspeth too?"

"She is protected in other ways. The forces working through her will see to her safety in the other realms."

Magnus didn't like the sound of that. Other realms held frost giants and fire giants and elves and dwarves. He wasn't interested in leaving her in any of those places without him being present to defend her.

Without warning, Freydis hugged him. He looked down at the top of her head with his arms held aloft.

"Hug me back you big oaf. I do not know when I will see you again."

"You make it sound like one of us will not survive this," he said as he wrapped his arms around her and squeezed.

A moment later she pulled out of his embrace and without another word left the kitchen. Magnus was left scratching his head. She was troubled, of that he had no doubt. But he couldn't spend another moment worrying about her cryptic messages. He needed to collect Elspeth and get on the road.

As he was leaving the kitchen, the cook approached him with something wrapped in a cloth. "Some warm bread for your travels," he said. "I like your lady. I would like her to be safe as well."

Magnus took the bread and nodded at the man. He'd heard far more than Magnus cared for and when he was outside promptly gave the bread a hard toss across the bailey. Unless he had a very good reason, he wouldn't be trusting anyone easily for quite some time.

Once the cart and horses were completely secure he turned to retrieve Elspeth only to find her walking toward him wearing a dark hooded cloak like the one he'd seen her wear in Dublin.

"Do we have weapons?" she asked as she lifted the corner of one piece of canvas to spy inside the cart."

"We do."

"And will you train me in swordplay when we reach our destination?"

"I will."

"Very well. I am ready, Magnus. Let us begin our journey."

"You are certain you do not wish to wait until your brother returns with your belongings from your home?"

"I do not wish to wait, nay. I have spoken with your sister and left a message with her as to what he will need to know. She agrees that the less anyone knows, the better for all involved. She is not happy we will be leaving here, but she understands the necessity."

"Then let us ride whilst we still have plenty of daylight."

Magnus helped her onto her horse then mounted his. The cart was tied to his horse so their travel would be slow but they should be able to make good travel time that day because of the dry roads.

Once outside of the bailey, the gates were closed behind them. He never felt so separated from everything he knew in his life. Even when he'd travelled, he always had someone with him and he always knew the rules of the world. Or so he thought. This journey was unlike anything he'd ever encountered and though the pathway for Elspeth was clear, it was not so for him.

He watched as she occasionally looked overhead as if looking for something. Did she think the ravens would guide them to this tower? And what would he do if they suddenly appeared and led the way? He'd likely fall off his horse is what he'd do. Believing something and seeing it with one's own eyes were two different things.

~

They'd been riding for what felt like days, but could only have been a few hours. Elspeth scanned every tree she could think of until her eyes were tired from the effort. Though she could see the path clearly and had no doubt she was going in the proper direction, she was not sure of the distance to the gateway. She'd travelled this road many times and had never seen anything like what Nana Besse had described that she could see so clearly at the moment in her mind.

"Are you certain it is visible from the road?" Magnus asked.

Thankfully he hadn't been badgering her about it, but it was a valid question and she truly didn't know the answer.

And then she did.

Ahead and to the left the trees looked different. They were more curved and as they approached it was clear that vines had woven their way around two curved trees. Beyond lay more thick forest, but it did in fact resemble a gateway or doorway of some sort. She was about to find out if she was having delusional memories coupled with a complete mental breakdown, or if, in fact, she was the source of an incredible gift.

"This is it?" Magnus asked.

"Aye. You sound disappointed."

"I expected something bigger," he said. "And with shiny stones around it. Something worthy of the gods. Not a few curly sticks and more woods."

Laughter erupted from her. His jest wasn't really that

honourous, but perhaps the tension had gotten to her for now she was doubled over her horse gasping for breath.

"Are you ready to go through?" he asked when she settled down again.

She wiped the laugher induced tears from her eyes and nodded. As she approached the trees her neck tingled. Softly at first then so much so to the point of burning. She drew a steadying breath and relaxed her shoulders. The tingling immediately settled. She had to remember to let the sensation flow through her, else she could be on the ground unconscious.

As she passed through the threshold, calm settled over her. It was as if all the cares of the past few days and weeks disappeared and she was truly safe. She looked behind her to see Magnus's reaction, but he was nowhere to be seen. She dismounted and looked all around but could't find him anywhere. Fear coiled around her heart when she realized she could also no longer see the gateway.

What if there was more than one destination once one crossed over? What if Magnus was somewhere else entirely? Her heart raced as she walked around the horse three or four times thinking that he would be on the other side, but nothing. She focused hard on him as if willing him to appear before her.

After several agonizing minutes she heard her name. Now she had truly lost her mind. But then it grew louder and she recognized it as Magnus'.

"I'm here!" she called to him.

A few moments later he came into view trotting along with the horse and cart in tow.

"What happened to you?" she asked. "You were behind me and then you were gone."

"I swear to Odin, I watched you walk underneath those trees and disappear. I walked through behind you and you were nowhere to be found. I called and called until finally, I heard you reply."

"This makes no sense. How could we be together and then separated like that?"

"I was hoping you could answer that question. Do you know the direction to the tower from here?"

She looked around and then closed her eyes. When she opened them she was sure she knew exactly which direction to go. Elspeth mounted her horse and kicked the horse's sides to get the animal moving. They trotted along together for a couple of miles then the woods cleared onto a broad meadow in the centre of which stood a tall stone tower. It was taller even than the towers at MacDomnail Castle and she was in awe that no one had taken up residence in this place.

They tied up the horses and entered through the main doorway. Magnus lit a torch and located several unused ones on the walls. The inside was much larger than Elspeth had imagined. The outside was deceiving and drew the eye upward which made it easy to overlook the structure's wide base.

They explored the main level to reveal a reasonably sized hall with a large stone hearth together with a table and chairs that looked like new. The adjoining kitchen had another large hearth and a broad wooden-topped bench for food preparation. Wooden bowls and trenchers, and iron cooking pots were all clean and stacked neatly at the end of the bench. A block revealed several different knives. When Elspeth took one out to view it she was surprised to see it was still shiny.

Exactly how long had this place been abandoned and how was it possible there was no dust on anything?

As she continued to explore the kitchen, Magnus brought in firewood and started the fires in both the kitchen and the hall. The sun was beginning to set so she decided to bring in some of the provisions and stack them in the kitchen for ease of access. She had been taught how to manage her brother's household and so knew how to properly ration food they could not replace easily like spices, and other food that they could easily replace like bread and meat. She glanced over at Magnus and smiled thinking of him bringing home rabbits or a wild boar for her to cook.

She brought in enough of the food and wrapped the covering over the cart tight so as to not attract vermin and closed the door behind her. They found candles and before too long were seated at the table in the hall with a roaring fire and a nice meal of bread, meat and cheese that had come from MacDomnail Castle.

She looked across the table at Magnus. He looked tired. She felt tired. They had not discussed sleeping arrangements and she had not explored the upper levels for bed chambers. He had disappeared abovestairs earlier she suspected to light fires up there as well.

As soon as the food and drink hit her belly, she could feel the need for slumber. Her eyes began to droop and she smiled when Magnus dropped the knife he'd been using to cut his meat.

"You are tired," she said.

"We both are. Perhaps we should clean up in the morning and find a place to rest."

Her belly flip flopped. Did he mean they should find a place to rest together?

"I have lit fires in the chambers above. We can retire whenever you are ready."

Elspeth took his trencher and hers and brought them to the kitchen. He followed with the goblets and the ale. They covered the food and drink and left the kitchen to blow out the candles. Magnus took one and bolted the outer door then took her hand and led her up the winding staricase.

"Do you think there is something odd going on here?"

"Odd as in we appear to be in an enchanted tower where no one can ever find us, or odd that you have not asked me where you are to sleep?"

He said the last part with a grin as he squeezed her hand.

"A little of both, I suspect."

"To answer your question, yes I do think, despite the incredulity of our circumstances, the fact that this place appears to be well cared for though there is clearly no one about is, as you say, odd."

Once they reached the top of the stairs he opened a door that led to a short hallway. There was one door on each side.

"Take your pick," he said as he stood to the side so she could peer inside. He'd lit not only the fireplace but also candles so she could see all the attributes of the chambers. One was decorated in soft blue satin and contrasting heavy velvet. A four-post bed was topped with various sections of both fabric that covered the bed and wrapped around the posts. Across the hall and in a similar style, the colour of the chamber was crimson red. Something drew her to the warm colour immediately. She touched the coverlet which was stitched with gold thread in the pattern of a thistle and a unicorn. Aye, if there ever was a sign that this chamber was for her, those two symbols were it.

"I choose this chamber," she said to Magnus.

She was a little disappointed when he left, but her heart picked up several notches when he returned and closed the door behind him.

"Then I will sleep here too until I am certain of this tower's security."

She watched as he pulled the covers back on one side,

then the other. When he was done he came to her and placed his hands on her shoulders.

"All will be well," he said. "Tonight we sleep here together and tomorrow we talk."

Elspeth was relieved and disappointed both at the same time. But he was right, they were both exhausted and tomorrow would be time enough to discuss sleeping arrangements.

## CHAPTER FOURTEEN

The pain in his neck woke him. He'd stirred earlier when Elspeth had scooched a little too close, probably for heat, but he lacked the strength to lie that close to her without wanting more. He got up and stoked the fire, placed more quilts from the chest at the base of the bed on her, then dragged a chair over to the bed. He tilted his head back to see if sleep would bless him.

He'd been used to catching a little rest here and there any time he was at sea. The waters in and around Scotland's west coast were unpredictable and one must always remain alert —this was a different kind of restlessness.

What was he doing here? Really, did any of this make sense. He watched the figure in the bed and tried to think of a time when he did not feel so completely tethered to her. That feeling was so strong and overwhelmed any other that he had no idea what his feelings were before these.

"Is it morning yet?" a meek voice asked struggling to emerge from underneath the quilts.

He chuckled. She might not have needed all the extra

blankets, especially with the roaring fire, but he would not see her cold or uncomfortable.

"Aye, it is just past the dawn. You have no need to rise yet, my lady. I will light the fires below and let some heat warm the place before we go belowstairs to break our fast."

She rubbed her eyes and lay down again. "What is this place?"

"I do not know. Did you sleep well, at least?"

"Aye, I did. And I did not dream which is unusual for me. Most mornings I wake up exhausted from the legends playing out in my mind all night," she said and smiled at him. "Do you ever dream?"

He could honestly never remember a time when he had. His sisters had talked of them all the time, but when he went to sleep that was it.

"I do not."

"That is good and bad, I suppose," she said and sat up fully. "I mean, sometimes a dream can make you think about a happening in a different way. Like if you had a disagreement with someone and you dreamed about the conversation in a different way, you may wake with a different perspective."

He'd never thought about it that way. But then again, Magnus never, ever regretted his actions. While he might be quicker to act than was sometimes required, he trusted his instincts at every turn. That was why he'd followed his gut feelings where she was concerned, and though he might question what was actually going on, he would stay the course. Too bad he didn't dream; perhaps they would provide him some insight.

"You do not have to get up yet, if you do not choose. I will go and light the fires now. After we eat, I suggest we start your training."

He had taken off his damned leather trews the night

before and while he was comfortable in his tunic, the sight of her just roused from sleep with her hair disheveled around her shoulders and that sleepy look in her eyes, made him want to crawl into bed with her and provide a better reason for her hair to be tangled.

"I will help," she said and threw the covers back then hopped onto the floor. She smoothed her skirts and started to braid her hair. Magnus was transfixed. While having her hair bound in the braid was far more practical with what they would be doing that day, the sight of her hair being put away saddened him a little.

What was wrong with him? This place must be having an effect on his mind. Either that or he was losing it altogether.

Magnus arranged the logs in the hearth so they would burn more slowly. He damped down the flue while Elspeth fixed the bed and dragged the chair back to the hearth.

"Did you sleep in the chair?"

"I did."

"But why?" she asked.

He looked up at her. Was that disappointment in her tone?

"Because you apparently like to have the bed to yourself and practically kicked me out of it," he said with a grin. There was no way he would tell her it was because he wanted to bury himself inside her sweetness for a year and a day and bring her to heights of passion she never knew existed.

"You jest. I do not hog the bed."

"You do. Truly, I do not know how your future husband will manage."

"It is possible in my slumber I was looking for him," she said with a grin, but the air in the chamber shifted.

Magnus' pulse picked up a notch, his heart beating loud enough he was sure she could hear.

"Elspeth," he whispered. "I am trying to be proper here."

She moved to him and placed her hands on his chest then looked into her eyes. "I do not know what is happening to me," she said. "There are thoughts in my head and sensations in my body I do not understand. And they only happen when I'm with you."

She should have said something else—anything else than to admit her attraction. His strength to quell the intensity of his desire waned. He had no doubt she fought it too, though she may not fully understand the extent of her admission.

"They are in my mind and body as well."

"Is this the way of husbands and wives?"

"For some. The lucky ones. But Lady Elspeth, we are not married and I will not bring shame upon you."

She laughed then. The sound resonated through him and made his loins tighten as if she'd stroked him.

"Why do you find that humorous?"

Her smile was warm enough to melt the ice in the North sea.

"I just recalled something I saw in Freydis' mind when we shared our thoughts."

"And what was that?"

"She is convinced you and I are already wed. That God and your Odin have made an accord where you and I are concerned. We need not perform a ceremony. In their eyes, 'tis already done."

"She said as much to me as well."

Elspeth moved closer to him, her gaze tracing the outline of his face then locking with his. She placed her hand on his face. Magnus held his breath, he really didn't know what to do next.

"Do not worry, my Viking protector. I do not believe her either."

She patted his cheek and moved past him to the chamber

door then opened it and moved out into the hall. Her soft footfalls a gentle echo off the stone walls.

Wait. She thought he didn't want her? He'd been holding onto his desire so tightly he was about to burst into flames. Perhaps it was best to let her think so. That might make it easier to be in her presence without wanting to rid her of her clothes and spend the next year in this place learning every inch of her body and her mind.

He grinned as he finished with the fire and left the chamber. How would she react if she saw into his mind? Would she be afraid of the images she saw there of the carnal things he wanted to do to her body, of the many positions in which he'd have her, and the powerful release he would ensure came over her as many times as she could stand?

Magnus shook his head as he descended the stairs to the main floor of the tower house. Today he would push his lustful thoughts aside and focus on exploring the remainder of the area, ensuring they were fully capable of defending themselves should danger present itself, and begin Elspeth's training. She needed to learn how to best use the dagger and she needed to learn how to use a sword.

He found her in the kitchen stacking splits to start the fire there and so he left her to it and went to do the same in the hall. Before long both fires were roaring and Magnus went to the kitchen to help prepare the morning meal. Elspeth had already laid out bread, meat, and cheese and something was starting to bubble in a small pot over the fire. He watched her from the doorway and admired the ease with which she went about her tasks. She'd said something at one point about stitching pillows. Nay, this was not a gentlewoman meant to be stowed away and protected. He entered the kitchen and grabbed a platter to bring into the hall. She nodded and followed with a second and a pitcher. The more he thought about it, the more he was sure she was meant to possess all the gifts she had and more. They'd find out soon enough if those gifts extended to defending herself as well.

~

Elspeth ate as much as her belly could handle. She worked hard to ignore the raging ache in her body brought on by the man sitting across from her. There were things in her head and her body that did not match up with what Freydis was so convinced to be true. And there were times she was sure Magnus shared her desires, but this morning's revelation was quite in contrast.

Nevertheless, she had been guided here for a reason and if he was not it, she would not rest until she discovered why.

"You are hungry this morning," he said, sitting back in his chair and wiping his mouth with a cloth. She'd found some neatly stacked by the plates. She'd never seen anything like that before and so thought it could be used practically in the absence of a cloth for the table.

"Aye. I am looking forward to training today. How shall we begin?"

Magnus leaned forward and clasped his hands together on the table. "I think we will begin with that dagger of yours. Many of the same principles of attack and defend apply whether your weapon is a knife, sword, or axe. The difference is in the person's agility, strength of mind and body, and intent.

"I have little strength, but I think I am agile and I am not certain what you mean by intent." Elspeth was fascinated by the thought of there being more to battle than just, well battling. She'd hoped to broach this topic with Saga. Truth be told, she wanted to know everything that woman knew and develop skills in the same manner. It was not enough for her to expect someone else to protect her. She wanted to be an active participant. Her pulse picked up a little at the thought of battle training with Magnus. She would have no difficulty focusing on his every word and move. Nay, it would be impossible for her to do otherwise.

"You have more power than you think," he said.

Did he mean for battle? Or something else? Her gut told her that he meant power over him, and this was one of those confusing moments. And so why couldn't she just ask him what he meant? Why? Because she wasn't sure she was ready for the answer. Her feelings for him were so potent that she was not sure she was ready to hear they might not be returned. Nay, she would stay focused on her training with him and let the questions be for another day.

When she was finished with her meal, they repeated the cleaning up ritual including securing the food from vermin, though Elspeth was surprised she'd not seen any evidence of a field mouse, rat, or even pigeon. That was unheard of for every kitchen had some sort of issue to deal with. Perhaps the years of inactivity had meant the critters had moved on. She would keep an eye out over the next few days in case the aroma emanating from the tower attracted them again. She threw the cutting knives in the boiled water, something her cook always did without fail, though he never explained why. She would fish them out later to dry before using them again.

Elspeth followed Magnus outside and toward a clearing to the side of the tower. She took in the tree-line that encircled the area and marvelled that the tower appeared to sit directly in the middle. She'd never seen grounds that were so perfectly kept before. Wildflowers dotted the base of the tower in a beautiful blend of blues and purples despite the lateness of the year. And further to that, the air was warm as if a summer's day.

"The first thing you need to think about in defending yourself is how to find an advantage. As you said, you may not be strong, but your size should make you agile. So let's test that."

Elspeth made to take out her dagger, but then Magnus reached for it. "You will not need an actual blade for these lessons," he said. "You may turn out to be quite skilled, and I do not wish to be sliced apart," he finished with a grin.

She turned the dagger's handle toward him and offered it. He placed it aside and after a few moments of searching, produced a stick around the same size.

"Here," he said. "Hold this as you would a knife and point it at me."

Elspeth did so and had to admit to herself, she felt a little foolish standing there pointing a stick at this big hulk of a man.

"I see what you're thinking," he said. "How could you possibly combat me with a stick? The truth is without an advantage, you can't."

"So that's it then?" she asked, a little annoyed at his approach.

"Not even close to being it," he said, "but the truth is if you do not know how to use the knife, it is as useless as the stick."

Magnus advanced slowly. "Stay still and watch my movements."

He came toward her and when her gaze moved to his body, he motioned with his fingers to stay focused on his eyes. Once she locked gazes with him, she realized that she could still see his movements clearly. His right hand moved to grasp her right wrist and she instinctively pulled the stick back to protect it. What she hadn't seen while focused on his right hand was the foot that had reached out to slip between her legs and hook her right leg forward causing her to fall to the ground.

He grasped her right arm and lifted her up again with

ease then stepped back and approached again, still painstakingly slow.

Elspeth did this dance with him several times, each time she tried moving the stick to a different point on her body and each time failing and landing on her backside then being lifted back into position. She tried everything she could think of to avoid being tripped, but each time he succeeded.

"What is the point of this?" she asked after about the tenth time.

"This is your lesson. Tell me what you have learned."

That she was terrible at battle training? She wasn't sure what he wanted her to say. She took a step back and thought about the set up. He came at her the same way every time and she did not possess the size or strength to stop him. A small flash went off in her mind.

She got into position again and watched as he approached. This time when he reached for her arm, she jumped out of the way and jumped behind him. Because he was so big, he couldn't turn fast enough before she placed the stick into his side. Surely a dagger in his ribs would cause some serious damage.

Magnus dropped his arms to his sides and turned toward her and chuckled. "That was a good move," he said. "The only problem is that you didn't run away. Your wound will not kill me, I can still harm you."

"I understand," she said, "but next time you will expect me to stab you where I just did."

"I will anticipate that possibility, but you must always keep your mind working to find those places within your reach that can do more harm. Battle is as much mind play as it is sword play. You must quickly assess your advantages and disadvantages. I can help you build some strength, but your biggest advantage when defending yourself is your size, agility, and how quickly you can remove yourself from the situation."

"You mean hide somewhere?"

"I do. The moment someone of my size is able to contain you, your chances of finding an escape reduce. You must go for the eyes, or neck if you can get your weapon close. Your greatest chance of survival is to not get caught."

She thought about it and while she had to admit, she'd sort of thought she could be capable of defending herself in time, she could never match his sister. The truth was the woman was nearly a foot taller and possessed five times the strength. Magnus was right and she needed to be clever in how she approached her lessons. She needed to be as stealthy as a wildcat. The only other thing that remained to explore was how she could use her gift to her advantage. Maybe she would look into a person's mind in the future after all.

## CHAPTER FIFTEEN

Magnus drank deeply. He'd donned his trews earlier as they would provide protection while training but had long since removed his tunic in the heat. Elspeth had proved more than capable of responding to his instructions and was showing progress even in understanding the places on a body that were more likely to cause the greatest damage.

She took the cup from him and poured some ale. She turned away when he dunked his head into a barrel of rainwater. He flicked his hair back over his head then flicked off the excess. She now sat on a bench near where they'd trained and sipped from her cup. Her cheeks were flushed and she'd removed as much of her gown as she could leaving only her shift and the gown that had been pinned to it.

"We have had a very good first day," he said.

"We have. I am learning much from you, Magnus, and I thank you for it." She opened her mouth and closed it again.

"I feel like there is something you want to ask me," he said, not sure if he should probe her deepest thoughts, but curious as to what could be going through her mind.

She paused mid drink then placed the cup on the ground. She gestured in a sweeping motion toward the clearing. "This," she said. "All this is well and good and will help me at least feel like I have some chance to survive should I ever be in a situation where I am threatened."

"But?"

"But what is the purpose of all of this if I cannot use all that I possess to my advantage?"

"Are you referring to the gifts Freydis spoke of?"

"Aye, I am. What is the point of having them if I cannot use them to save myself or someone else?"

"What makes you think you can't use them?"

"What do you mean?"

"I mean you should understand them enough by now to know how. The tools I have were learned and practiced for years. They are physical tactics that I use, as you say, to protect myself and others. I am far better with an axe than a small sword because of my size and strength. You must use whatever tools are at your disposal and understand all the ways you can find an advantage."

She stared hard at him for a moment then narrowed her eyes. For a split second she appeared angry. In the next moment he could hear, no feel her heartbeat. She was sitting ten feet from him, but he would swear she was underneath his skin. A pulse-beat later and it was over.

Magnus bent over for a moment feeling dizzy. He sat on his arse on the ground for a moment and stared at her.

"What in Odin's name did you do?" he asked. His whole body trembled for a moment before he felt steady again and could stand.

She turned pale pursed her lips as if she didn't know what to say. He could see her trembling so moved to sit beside her. He placed his arm around her and pulled her close. Though their bodies now touched, the sensation was nothing like what he'd just experienced.

"Elspeth, tell me what just happened," he said as gently as he could.

"I swore I'd never do it again," she whispered.

"Is that what Freydis was trying to show you how to do?"

"Aye. I saw things in her mind that I should not have seen."

His heart raced. Was she really telling him that she'd just entered his mind? Surely it was not possible, but what other explanation could there be? He had been rendered completely helpless for a moment so much so it had landed him on his backside.

"What did you see in my mind?"

She looked at him quickly. "I didn't see anything. I promise, I would not look because 'tis not my place." She wrung her hands and frowned, her eyes wide.

"Do not worry yourself. I pushed you to explore this gift. I would not hold it against you if you did see what was in my mind."

"You wouldn't?"

"I would not. There is nothing in my heart or in my mind that I would hold secret from you."

"May I?" she asked and placed her hands on either side of his head. She touched their foreheads together and closed her eyes.

Magnus kept his open watching the concentration on her face. He meant what he said, there was nothing in him he would not share with her and maybe it was easier for her to see what he felt rather than voice the words.

Pressure on his head forced him to close his eyes. A split second later he experienced the same sensations as before only this time they were less forceful, as if she slowly opened the door versus flung it open.

He could feel rather than hear her questions. They were about her safety and if she was truly mad or if this was real.

He smiled and wrapped his arms around her as if to reassure her not quite knowing how else to answer for he was sure his voice would not sound if he tried.

A small sense of another question encircled him. A different sort of query that needed no words, rather a form of beckoning squeezing his heart. His beat harder as did hers as if they kept in time. In that moment there were no questions or answers, only the sensation of one heart recognizing another and in an expression of relief for finding its missing part.

It was too much and not enough at the same time. Where he'd originally felt paralyzed by her entry into his mind, now he realized he could move freely with her still there. He also learned that he could probe her mind too.

Magnus quickly scanned what he needed, he had no idea how, and made his decision. Freydis was absolutely without a doubt correct about them. They were two halves of one being and no power in the world or in any realm could shake that—he needed no further convincing.

He stood and lifted her into his arms. She held on tight and kept her eyes closed as he strode into the tower house and up the stairs to the chamber they'd shared the previous night.

Placing her on the bed her lifted her chin to tilt her head back. "Open your eyes, my Valkyrie. For you have certainly come to sweep me away."

Elspeth opened her eyes and stared into his eyes. Though the mental link was broken for the moment, their souls' connection was not, his heartbeat and hers were solidly linked together for now and for all time.

Lifting her further onto the bed, Magnus lay by her side and stroked the loose hair away from her face. He bent low and brushed his lips across hers. Her arms encircled his neck and pulled him closer. He deepened the kiss and slipped his tongue inside to taste her. There was no turning back now. She'd offered, or had he offered? It truly didn't matter anymore. They'd both offered themselves and they'd both accepted in an unspoken ceremony he wondered had ever existed anywhere before. And it did not matter.

Elspeth's hands tugged at his shoulders until he was above her. He wedged himself between her legs and lifted her skirts for better access. Leaning on one elbow then the other, he unpinned her skirt and waited while she shimmied out of it. He stroked her leg and drew tantalizing lines up the outside of her thigh and up her belly to cup her breast. She sucked in air when he flicked her nipple. Her body squirmed beneath him as he shimmied her shift up and over her body. She now lay fully naked beneath him and he absolutely refused to rush this moment.

Magnus let her hook her toes into the waist of his trews and tug them downward. "You're crafty," he whispered and sucked hard on one nipple, marvelling at how quickly her body bucked upward and she gasped.

He shifted so he could kick off his trews then settled between her legs tasting her breasts, kissing his way downward.

She squirmed and bucked beneath him as he stroked her inner thigh then brushed the backs of his fingers across her slick heat before driving a finger inside. She gasped and tensed around him. He loved witnessing every sensation she experienced. She was built for this sort of pleasure and he wanted to make sure she experienced the full extent of its possibilities.

Magnus found the source of her desire and rubbed hard while he thrust two then three fingers inside her pumping harder and harder until she tensed and tightened around him. Her body twitched for what seemed like ages until she finally settled again. Her cheeks were flushed and her hair was tangled half in and out of her braid, she smiled and motioned him upward into a deep kiss. He took that as a signal that she was more than ready for more.

~

Elspeth paused and gazed deep into Magnus eyes. She could have closed them and still known what lay within. Never had she been so unsure of someone else's desires or even her own. But the moment they connected, everything clicked into place as if all the pieces of a puzzle had lain in various places then came together at once.

He leaned down and kissed her, more softly this time. The explosion her body had just experienced was like nothing she ever knew could exist. And she'd shared it with him. In doing so, she understood his need. The resulting effect awakened hers again. She marvelled at every ripple of his muscular back and loved the feeling of his hard body pressing onto hers.

The thick member that pressed hard against her thigh begging entry was now all she could think about. She wanted him as deep within her as he could go, pulsing, throbbing, driving them both to another climax.

She lifted her legs over his back and pushed against his erection. He gasped and drew back a little. "We must go slowly at first," he said.

She didn't have the patience. She was consumed with her need of him.

His hard tip stroked her sending delicious thrills through her body. She arched toward him and this time he pressed into her. His girth quickly filled her with a pressure that made her breath catch. He pushed deeper and she held her breath waiting for her body to adjust, praying that it would. Part of her ached for more of him and part of her protested the invasion. He stopped moving.

She opened her eyes, not even realizing she'd closed them and watched his pained expression above her. She reached up to touch his cheek and drew him down to kiss her again. He slowly pulled out of her and pushed all the way back in again, releasing some of the pressure and reawakening her desire. While he kissed her, he drew back and thrust slowly forward again a few times, each time increasing in forcefulness and speed. The sensation brought about renewed urgency within her. Like she was running toward something she did not understand or could not see.

As her desire built, his body tensed above her as if he chased the same invisible prize. The faster he thrust, the more she wanted from him, nay demanded from him, as if the need had awakened a side of her she never knew was there. Before she could think to stop herself, she entered his mind and linked their passions. Powerful waves built around them as he drove himself almost madly into her. Elspeth held onto his shoulders, her whole focus on the man who claimed her very being with his hard, unrelenting thrusting as if he was branding his name onto her soul.

The crest of the wave was in sight. She clung on tightly to him and he thrust hard one last time, so hard she slid across the bed. Wave after wave started in her spine and washed over her. Their bodies pulsed and twitched as their climax peaked and settled. Elspeth was boneless as Magnus collapsed onto her. Though he was much bigger, his body was a comfort in quelling the storm that had raged through her body.

She had no words or sense of the enormity of what they'd shared. After a time, he slid out of her body and lay by her side, pulling her in close to him. He tugged and shifted until he managed to pull a quilt over them. She wasn't sure how long they lay there or if she slept, but it appeared that time did not pass, for when they eventually stirred, the daylight appeared the same as when they'd first awoken. Or was that simply in her mind?

Her thoughts took on so many different turns that she wasn't sure if she was dreaming or awake. The soreness between her legs and the naked man watching her quietly beside her were the only certain things that proved what had just happened was real.

"You look worried," he said after a time.

"I am not," she said and turned toward him. "Are you?" she asked, not really knowing what to say.

He smiled. "Worried? No. Spent? Ja."

She smiled at the thought of their vigour. For in the height of it she was just as enthusiastic as he. Wanton indeed. But somehow she was not embarrassed by it. Nothing that felt that good could possibly be wrong.

"I am sorry," she said.

He lifted his head a little. "For what?" he asked and shook his head.

"For looking inside your mind again. I did not ask and in truth, I am not even sure I had a choice."

He chuckled and pulled her closer and stroked her hip. His tantalizing fingers drew circles up and down her thigh and across her bottom. Tingling started low in her belly and spread. She was surely spawned from a demon if she was capable of feeling like this again.

"I am very glad you did. For it allowed me to know your heart as well. I have never experienced anything like what we have. I do not know if anyone has."

"What now?" she asked.

He pressed his fingers into her hip and drew her close to his body. His hard erection rested on her thigh. She smiled.

She wasn't sure if her body was ready for his so soon, but she was more than willing to try.

Magnus rolled onto his back and lifted her atop him. As she slowly slid onto him he reached up and cupped her breasts. She lifted her body up and down taking him in and out of her as she placed her hands on his chest. This way she felt him even deeper than before and the control she had was driving her mad with need all over again. Magnus pinched her nipples and drew her forward for a deep kiss. He thrust upward to match her pace and a few moments later flipped her onto her back, pummelling into her again. She arched upward to take everything he had to give as her climax crested and tore through her body. She shook and quaked as he drove harder and harder into her. As he thrust deep one final time, a second wave crashed over her making her almost lightheaded. She breathed her way through it and stared hard into his eyes as he strained above her.

Magnus rolled over onto his back, breathing heavily and chuckling to himself.

"What is so amusing?" she asked.

"Not one thing," he said. "But I think that I may too need some battle training if we are to continue at this level of our desire."

Elspeth propped herself up on one elbow and regarded him. He was a magnificent man with a strength she'd never seen matched. There was something of wonder in his voice as he'd stated his point that she agreed with wholeheartedly. They'd been given something unique and incredible and she prayed to God that nothing ever prevented them from keeping it.

"Can we stay here forever?" she asked.

"I wish it were that simple," he said. "But I wonder if this place is only here for us right now because we need it."

Not that she didn't think him capable of deep thought,

she hadn't realized just how much he had been wondering about the meaning of all of this as well.

"Then we had better make the most of it while we can," she said trying to lighten the mood.

"That is true, and at the moment, I feel I could eat an entire wild boar."

She nodded and grinned. They dressed quickly and went belowstairs leaving the bed dishevelled and perhaps knowing they wouldn't be out of it for long. In the kitchen she prepared a trencher they could share while Magnus stoked the fires. They ate their meal in the hall and sat quietly staring into the fire. Every now and again she would catch him staring at her with a solemn look upon his face. She didn't want to know what he was thinking and so would not hold his gaze. If he thought they would not be allowed to keep what they had then she didn't want to hear it. Not now, not after what they had just shared. Surely neither of their gods would be so cruel as to give so much and take it away.

# CHAPTER SIXTEEN

Time seemed to not exist in this place. Magnus' days were filled with training Elspeth and his nights filled with loving her. Knowing they could not stay there forever, his heart grew heavier each morning as he watched her sleeping. With no word from either Gunnar, Giric, or Osgar, he had no way to find out if the danger had passed or if they could return.

And then what? They had both agreed that in their minds and hearts they were wed, but what would her family say? He didn't expect any issue with Gunnar as he'd been pushing Magnus in this exact direction. A simple sacrifice and ceremony would take care of that. And he suspected her family would not object either. Osgar clearly had his sights set on Magnus' sister so he likely would not oppose their union.

Magnus reached over to pull the quilts up over Elspeth's shoulder; she stirred a little and turned over on her side. As quietly as he could, he slipped out of bed and dressed. He stoked the fire and with one last look at her, he left the chamber, careful to make as little noise as possible.

Belowstairs he completed the same ritual he had for what,

days? Weeks? He honestly could not say. This time of year the leaves should have all turned their amber and orange and red colours. Instead, when he looked out through the small window in the kitchen, the trees all appeared to hold their summer colours.

Once the fires were raging he unbolted and opened the main door of the tower. An elderly man with a great long white whisker and hair that stuck off to the sides, stood there with his fist raised as if to knock. Magnus stared at the man unable to reconcile how he came to be in this place.

"I can see that you were not expecting me, lad. But as I have travelled far, I would appreciate you letting me pass so I can rest my weary bones."

"Who are you?" Magnus asked, managing to find his tongue.

"I am the owner of this tower," he said. "I admit, I was surprised to find it occupied, but I am a generous sort. I do not mind sharing what I have."

Magnus' mind buzzed. Elspeth had not seen this man coming, or if she had, she hadn't said anything. And while it was true, the place had appeared well cared for, she was certain its occupant was long deceased. Something niggled in the back of his mind, but he pushed it away.

"What is your name?" Magnus asked.

The man tilted his head to the side. "You do not know who I am?" He shook his head. "Let me pass, lad. 'Tis a brisk day and I am weary from my travels. Magnus stepped back and let the man pass, noticing how the trees now had all shed their leaves and a fair dusting of snow had fallen on the ground. He turned around to see where the man had gone but he was nowhere in sight. Instead, Elspeth sat at the table with a goblet raised to her lips.

"Will you not join me?" she asked.

What in the name of Loki was going on? Magnus turned

back to the door and the wintery scene outside. His mind buzzed with confusion. He closed the door and bolted it again.

"Where is he?" he asked Elspeth as he approached the table.

"Where is who?"

"The old man who just came inside. He said he owned this tower."

Elspeth almost dropped her goblet. Her eyes grew wide. "Magnus what are you talking about? There is no one here besides you and I."

"I left you sleeping abovestairs. How came you to be here with the table already set?"

"Magnus we came downstairs together hours ago. Really, now you're scaring me. What is going on?"

That was a good question. He recounted his exact steps since opening his eyes that morning including every detail right down to the leaves on the trees and the snow on the ground.

"That makes no sense," she said. "The leaves have been turning for days and the snow started last eve."

Magnus didn't like it. Something was off at the moment and he didn't like the uneasy feeling creeping into his heart.

"We must leave here," he said. "I do not feel it is safe any longer."

"But why? Because you had a bad dream?"

"I was not dreaming, Elspeth. I was completely awake as sure as I am talking to you right now."

"Magnus, please. I feel at ease here. It is like this place is protecting us, I am not certain how that is possible, but I believe it to be true."

"And I believe the forces at play here are not entirely benevolent." As soon as the words were out of his mouth he heard a crash in the kitchen.

He raced in to see what was going on and found a pitcher on the floor with its contents inching across the stone.

"What happened?" Elspeth asked from behind him.

Magnus' arm began to sting. He raised it up to see scratches for which he couldn't account. Elspeth held his arm up for her inspection and frowned.

"How did you get this?"

"It just happened." Magnus could deal with any man who was a threat to him or her, at least he could see them coming. This madness was something he could not fight. And it appeared Freydis' rune offered him no protection here.

"We are no longer safe here," he said. "Grab your cloak. We leave now."

When they entered the hall again there was no fire in the hearth, no food on the table, and the place looked like it had been abandoned for centuries.

"We need to get out of here now," he said and led her to the door.

He unbolted it and they stepped outside. The cart they had brought with them was still fully stocked and resting by the door. Their horses were tied up where they had been the first day of their arrival. There was no snow on the ground.

"Magnus, I do not understand."

"Neither do I," he said and turned back to the tower. It looked decrepit and the exact opposite of the place they had viewed before.

He hooked up the cart and helped Elspeth mount her horse. As they trotted away he dared one look back to see the figure of the old man and a larger feminine figure behind him cloaked in green peeping out from behind the tower. He waved and they disappeared.

Magnus had seen enough. Whatever danger lay ahead he would face it with full force. He wondered if he'd dreamed everything they had shared up to that point. Perhaps he'd hit his head upon entry and had one of Elspeth's dreams. But that was not possible. They had been there for weeks. They'd trained and laughed and loved.

Leaves crunched beneath the horses and cart. Magnus wanted to ask Elspeth what was going on, but she appeared just as solemn as he. After a time they located the main roadway and as soon as they stepped onto it, a large raven let out a loud *kraw-kraw* just above them. Its voice was deep and almost urgent as it flew in the direction away from the arched trees and MacDomnail Castle.

"It is flying toward my home," she said. "We must follow it."

Magnus needed a minute. This was all a bit too much. He dismounted and stepped off the road on the opposite side from the gateway.

"Are you unwell?" she asked after dismounting and coming to his side.

"How can you ask me that? With what we just witnessed."

"I do not possess any answers either," she said.

"So you experienced it too? I did not bump my head and dream it all?"

"Nay you did not. We were in that tower for many days, probably weeks." Her cheeks turned bright pink.

He hoped she remembered their lovemaking the way he did.

"Did you see the old man?"

"Nay, I did not. And I have no explanation for the man or your arm, or any of what we just saw back there. But I have trusted the raven thus far and I will continue to trust it. We must ride to my home and there we will try to figure out what has happened to us."

Magnus nodded and waited for her to mount her horse then mounted his. He followed her slow trot as his mind blazed with questions. His world had shifted much in the past few weeks in a wonderfully positive way and he now felt that a part of that had been ripped from him—from them. Was it possible the whole thing had been as she had said before, an enchantment? Did they still feel the same way about one another or was that as false as the warmth in the tower?

Focusing on the raven's path allowed Elspeth to put aside the ache that had settled into her heart. Thankfully Magnus was behind her and so would not see the tears flowing freely down her cheeks. Her body felt hollow, as if her soul's well had been full to brimming and suddenly emptied. And she couldn't find the words to express to him what weighed so heavily upon her, but they needed to talk about it.

That morning when she'd awoken, she'd found him sitting up in bed staring into the fire. When she asked him if he was unwell, he didn't even respond to her, rather dressed and went belowstairs. From there everything became murky. When he'd started talking about an old man, she thought he might be going a little mad in the head, but then they went outside and the place changed as if they'd never been there to begin with. She had no answers and had no way to find them. She was lost on this path with no guide except the fat raven that hovered above and slightly ahead of them, gliding as if it did not have a care in the world.

Elspeth drew in a deep breath trying to fill her lungs with clean pure air and expel the doubt resting in her heart. She discretely wiped the tears from her eyes and looked back at Magnus. His head was bent low and his gaze cast downward. He looked miserable. Was it possible they had been bewitched? The hopeful part of her envisioned this bereft feeling a natural result of the enchantment being lifted. What was she thinking? Now she sounded mad in the head. Perhaps they had fallen off their horses and bumped their heads. The thought made her chuckle.

"You find something amusing?"

She moved to the side and waited until he was alongside and grinned at him. "I just had a thought of both of us being knocked out and sharing the same dream, then getting up as if nothing had happened and moving along on our merry way."

The sides of his mouth curled a little, then spread. He was magnificent when he smiled. The ache in her heart dissipated in that moment. As if one happy look from him could be all the healing she would ever need.

"When you put it like that, this whole business is a bit unbelievable."

"Perhaps we should not tell anyone, for they may put us both in padded cells," she said and laughed a little harder.

Magnus chuckled. "I want the cell with the window so I can watch the seasons change," he said which sent her into more fits of laughter.

She thanked God there was no one on the road for they would have probably run the other way if they saw them there laughing like children on the road with a cart full of provisions that they had most certainly eaten from but was now full.

"Can we agree on one thing?" he asked quietly.

A knot formed in her belly. She was not ready to lose any part of him or the moments they had shared in the tower. But it was not fair to silence his voice either. He had a right to say whatever he wanted even if it crushed her soul.

"Aye, what is that?" she tried not to sound bitter, but the trepidation was almost overwhelming.

"What we did, what we had back there—"

She held her breath as he searched for the words.

"That was real wasn't it?"

The uncertainty in his voice and in his expression was more than she could handle and the tears that she thought were held at bay surfaced and spilled once again onto her cheeks. Before she could say anything, raw pain washed over his face.

She had to reassure him quickly. "Aye, Magnus. 'Twas real."

He locked gazes with her as he dismounted. He reached for her and drew her into his arms holding her in an embrace from which she never wanted to be released. He had felt just as bereft as she.

"I do not know how I could carry on if only I had experienced all those moments with you," he said and kissed her hair.

She leaned back and cupped his face with her hands. "We did share every moment together whether they actually happened or it was only in our minds, 'twas real."

She thought about the obvious physical way to find out, but thought better than to bring that up whilst they were in the middle of what was normally a busy roadway.

"Come let us finish our journey," she said. "It is still quite a way to my home and I already feel the effects of the ride."

He nodded and they resumed their travels. The time passed quickly as they passed rolling fields awash with faded growth from the harvest. The trees had all turned colour here and splashes of bright purple showed the resilience of the mountain heather that should have long since lost its bloom. For some reason it had always held on longer around here. Perhaps there was something in the very earth that allowed life to thrive and grow. Was it possible that the tower and surrounding lands contained some ancient magic that somehow seeped into the ground over time?

Nana Besse had warned her not to go to the tower alone and she was relieved she hadn't. She now had an understanding of the danger residing there. Time and age meant nothing in a place like that.

So lost was she in her musings of the events that had taken place she was surprised when she looked up and saw the flat stone roadway leading to her home. Somewhere in size between the tower and MacDomnail Castle, MacAlpin Keep had two towers flanking the main stone house. The kitchen, armoury, cellars and gardens were all behind the main keep, but the part she loved the most about her home was the courtyard leading to the gardens.

The front of the keep was constructed with security in mind with wooden palisades and a gate house, but once they passed through, the beauty of the home became apparent with all the shrubs and trees dotting the walkway to the keep.

Once through the gates, they made their way to the stables and ensured their horses would be well cared for. She was pleased to see that Magnus seemed to want to take in every aspect of the place. She was proud of her home and she couldn't wait to show him all it contained.

"Come with me inside," she said. "I will show you the keep then we can explore the grounds."

"There you are!" Osgar said coming around the side of the armoury. "I thought you were going to wait for me to bring your belongings to you. I was finishing packing everything up."

Elspeth needed a moment to think about what he meant. She then recalled he had come here to collect her gowns so she could stay at Castle MacDomnail for her safety.

"It was not safe there," Magnus said.

Elspeth was grateful he spoke up for she truly did not know what to say.

"What happened?" he asked. "Have you been harmed?"

"No. But the threat was there. MacDomnail's brother took issue with some things he the servants overheard relating to Freydis and your sister."

"That man would not dare lay a hand on my sister. Surely Giric threw him out."

"He did not," Magnus said. "Rather he told us that it would not be safe for us to stay any longer."

Osgar looked at her and then Magnus. "I do not believe it. I have never known Giric to behave in such a manner."

"It is true," Elspeth said. "Donnan threatened me and Freydis and Giric would not turn him out, rather offered us provisions and sent us on our way."

"Provisions?" Osgar asked. "Why would he do that when you obviously would come here?"

Elspeth regretted the words the moment they were out of her mouth. She'd never been adept at falsehoods and she would not be able to lie to Osgar if he seriously pressed her and from his furrowed brow and frown it appeared he was about to.

"When we left, we were not sure in which direction to go," Magnus said. "We were still unsure of the intentions of your brother as well, considering the circumstances."

"My brother is not here," Osgar said. "I am, as of yet, unaware of his whereabouts."

Elspeth had not thought about Kenneth. And considering all that had happened, and now with her bond with Magnus, she did not fear him any longer. She knew him well enough to understand his level of cowardice. He would be terrified of Magnus and that would be enough to quell any opportunistic ideas.

## CHAPTER SEVENTEEN

Magnus watched as Osgar took in the information he was given. The man was clever and honourable, he would give him that, but he would not stand for a repeat of the events at MacDomnail Castle. And considering Osgar's recent activity, it was becoming apparent that neither Elspeth nor Magnus had spent any longer that a few moments at the tower house. How in the name of Odin was that even possible and how were they to pretend nothing had occurred between them?

Elspeth reached for his hand and he shot her a look hoping to remind her that their secret must be kept, at least for now. She seemed to have understood the message and flicked her hand halfway to his as if to swat away an insect.

"Are you all right?" Osgar asked her.

"Aye," she said and walked along ahead of them.

"I suspect my sister has had an exhausting time of it over the past few weeks."

Magnus thought of the many times they'd let their desire run freely and smiled to himself. She probably did need some rest, though for a different reason than what Osgar thought.

And he had to stop his train of thought again. Did any of it actually happen? Was she a maiden still? He shook his head. His mind ran circles around itself and he could not make sense of it one way or the other.

"And now I must ask you the same question," Osgar said. "Are you all right?"

"I am well. I am also worried about your sister. I have become protective of her lately."

"Aye, I could see that at MacDomnail Castle. I'm told your brother is interested in making an arrangement for you."

The man didn't mince words. Was he that eager to be rid of his sister? The thought made his jaw tick. One wanted to exploit her and the other wanted her married off. He supposed he should be grateful he was being considered, but in truth, why were they all so eager to be married?

"My brother knows better than to meddle into my personal affairs." He didn't mean to sound irritated, but he couldn't help it.

"I did not mean to offend you or intrude. But I wanted to broach the topic since I am aware my brother offered Elspeth to you on Islay. I do not know how much of the arrangement was settled or if you had even voiced your reply."

"If you recall, I believe you promptly interrupted that discussion."

"I had hoped that was what had occurred."

Magnus had to know. "Why do you ask of that now?"

"Because I have had an offer put to me for her that I am considering. But if an offer is already in place, I will honour it."

An offer? Magnus was ready to throttle the man for even suggesting it. No man would ever lay a finger on his woman not ever.

He opened his mouth to speak only to be met with Osgar's chuckling.

"You do not need to answer me now," he said. "From the look on your face at the moment, I believe I already know it."

"You do not need to wait," Magnus said. "I was offered Elspeth and was interrupted. I now accept. She will be my wife."

Magnus waited until Osgar nodded, a little of the colour having left his face in the process, then walked on ahead in the direction Elspeth had taken toward the keep. After a few strides he stopped and walked back to Osgar.

"Tell no one. Not even her."

"I'm afraid that will not be possible as the requestor is still present. He will no doubt put the pieces together once he sees you and your betrothed together. Truly, I do not know who you think you are fooling," Osgar said with a grin. "Anyone with eyes could see you have both already formed an attachment."

Magnus scrutinized the man's expression for jesting and found none. Truly, these Scots were a peculiar lot. Though he supposed Gunnar was not much different. Though he had not actively sought out these arrangements, he welcomed them when they landed on his doorstep.

"Come inside," Osgar said and clapped Magnus on the shoulder. "Let me welcome you to my home and share some ale."

Magnus followed Osgar inside the keep and looked around. He admired the way their structures were built with stone. After visiting MacDomnail Castle the first time, he considered using all stone to build on the piece of land Gunnar had laid out for him on Islay. It need not be anything as big as this place, but stone did have its merits.

The door to the entrance of the keep was as wide as two normal doors put together and was held together with long pieces of iron that were curved at the ends. He'd never seen anything like it in his life as most hammered metal he'd seen did not require such decoration.

Osgar pushed open the heavy door revealing a surprisingly bright entranceway, only then did Magnus realize there was a window high above the door allowing light to illuminate the entire entrance hall. It was a curious but brilliant addition and he found himself looking up at it from inside the keep.

"My grandfather fancied himself a bit of an architect. He recognized the need for protection, but he also enjoyed any opportunity to provide more light in the keep. Unfortunately, he didn't foresee the cold draft that usually comes from that window in the winter. We usually place a tapestry over it when it gets really cold."

They walked along the hallway and Magnus noted the tapestries dotting the walls. He understood they were meant to help stave off the cold, but some, as in this case told stories. He would ask Elspeth to explain them to him later.

Osgar turned right and entered a medium sized hall with a large hearth and many weapons on the walls. A large set of antlers rested on the wall behind an ornately carved wooden chair. All the others around the table were solid looking, but lacked the decoration of this one. The hall held a warmth he'd not felt at MacDomnail Castle, but reminded him of the tower.

There was something familiar about this place though he had never visited here before; somehow he had a sense of belonging for this room in particular. But how could that be, in a place he'd never entered before?

"Please make yourself comfortable," Osgar said and motioned toward large, cushioned chairs near the hearth.

Magnus sat in one and a moment later a servant appeared with a large pewter goblet. He looked inside and sipped. Liking the smoothness, he took a larger gulp of the ale and finished the offering. The servant promptly filled it again. Magnus looked up at her. She was young and sort of pretty in a childlike way. He couldn't understand why she waited.

"May I offer you aught else?" she asked with a smile.

"More ale," Osgar said as he took the seat across from Magnus. "And some meat pies."

She nodded and disappeared. Magnus looked around the hall again and wondered why he felt so at ease. That never happened to him. Normally he would not rest until he had completely scanned a place to ensure there was no one about intent on making trouble.

"You look like something is worrying you."

"Not at all," Magnus said. "I like this hall."

"Aye, my grandfather decorated it to be a place where the family could feel comfortable and gather to share meals and tales. He was quite the storyteller, my grandfather. Half of it I was sure was made up, that is until I followed my friend across the Firth of Clyde and landed in a Viking village and seeing your clan with my own eyes."

"Your grandfather told tales of our people?"

"Aye, he was fascinated with your gods and tried for years to learn as much as he could."

"And he educated his family?"

"He did. He told us all about Odin and Thor and Loki. Has Elspeth not told you this?"

"She has not. I suppose she has had other things on her mind."

"I imagine so," he said.

"So where is this other suitor?" Magnus asked, becoming increasingly aware of Elspeth's absence.

"She is speaking with him now," Osgar said.

"You have given him permission to do so?" Magnus asked.

He did not think this was the way these things worked for the Scots.

"I trust my sister," he said with a grin.

"And you do not believe she will accept this man?" Magnus' guts were ready to spill onto the stone floor.

"Nay, I do not. The man in question, is honourable as he is the king's cousin, is nearly twenty years her senior. I am not concerned in the least."

"But you would let him speak to her."

"Aye, he has been welcome here for many years. I would let him speak with her out of respect."

Magnus didn't understand. If Osgar knew Elspeth would not accept the man's proposals, why would he allow either of them to be put through it? Magnus would have just told the man outright, *my sister is not interested.* Magnus sat back in the chair and took another deep drink of his ale. The liquid soothed his parched throat and eased the tightness in his guts. He would not feel better until Elspeth joined them and the king's cousin was on his way.

~

Elspeth wasn't sure she'd heard him correctly. She'd known Malcolm since she was a wee lass and remembered him bringing her sweet honeycomb on his visits. It was the *now that you're grown* part that sort of stuck in her mind as the moment when she would never look at him the same. How could he possibly think she would be interested in marriage to him when he was always more like a much older brother to her? Her mind would not let her ruminate on the particular point he had considered her for marriage. Though it was not uncommon for betrothals to be decided upon when either party was younger, she'd never envisioned it happening to her.

"Malcolm, you honour me," she said.

"But…" he said and folded his arms across his chest.

"But you are one of my family's dearest friends. I could never think of you as a husband. Surely you must see that."

"I understand and in part I am relieved," he said and sat back on the bench with his hands on either side of him."

"I am confused. You asked me to marry you, but you are relieved I said no?"

"Aye."

Elspeth felt like she was losing her mind. She was not without intelligence, but this man made absolutely no sense whatsoever.

"Do you care to explain that?"

"I had heard of your brother's dealings with you and I came to ensure you were protected because it is the right thing to do and I need a mother for my children. I will never love another woman like I loved Marian and so by marrying you, I could have protected you and helped me as well."

"But in that scenario, I do not get to love anyone."

"Aye, that is true, and in part why I am relieved. I would protect you, Lady Elspeth, but I didn't say it was a perfect situation. At the very least your brother could not exploit you and you would have no chance to stow away in anyone's ship."

She could see his reasoning from his point of view and in his mind he was offering her a kindness. But there would absolutely be no life for her with him. She would be back to stitching pillows and boring conversation.

"I assume you had at least approached my brother?"

"I did and he laughed at me." He looked like he was about to vomit.

Elspeth tilted her head back and laughed. "Malcolm my friend, you are free and clear of saving me from harm."

"But what will you do?"

"Let us go inside and I will explain why I am in no danger anymore from my brother."

He nodded and offered his arm which she accepted. Bless him for offering to help her even though he obviously had his own trepidations around the match. Nay, he had not done anything that would result in her opinion of his honour being swayed in her mind. It was a comfort to know she had people around her who cared for her wellbeing and would sacrifice to keep her safe.

When they entered the hall she could feel the tension from Magnus. She'd only been out of his presence for an hour, but she could sense his unease. Had Osgar told him why Malcolm had come to visit? She smiled at him to try to ease the frown on his handsome face.

"Magnus, I would like to introduce you to an old family friend, Malcolm, this is Magnus of Islay. He is the reason I no longer need protection."

"You are wed then?" Malcolm asked as he moved toward Magnus and offered his hand.

Magnus looked at the man and his hand and at Elspeth. His raised eyebrows were almost comical. "We are not yet wed," she said.

Magnus locked gazes with her as he shook Malcolm's hand. He brushed past the man and stood in front of her.

"Can I speak with you for a moment?"

"Aye," she said.

They walked out to the gardens and chose a bench near the small stone birdbath.

"That man asked you to marry him."

"He did."

"And you said no."

"I did."

"Good. There will be no other men asking for you."

"There won't?"

"You will be mine and mine alone."

Elspeth couldn't help but grin at him. She loved how possessive he was at the moment and recalled a similar feeling when they'd first met. The feast on Islay seemed like an age ago though in reality it was only a few days.

"And you will be mine and mine alone," she said and placed her hands on her hips as if to enforce her point.

"Are we arguing and saying the same thing?" he asked, the tension slowly releasing from his body.

"I believe we are. I suppose if you are claiming me, we should go speak to my brother."

"There is no need as I have already done so."

"Before you even asked me?" Her voice was teasing and she loved it when he grabbed her around the waist and drew her in for a soul stirring kiss.

"You have already given yourself to me, many, many times. It is the rest of the world that will have to catch up to what we have already discovered. And I will hide my love for you no longer. Whatever you have to do to make arrangements, do them. I will sleep with my wife tonight."

He kissed her hard again then released her and walked back into the keep leaving her a little unsteady on her feet and more than a little breathless. That was the man who filled her soul so completely she was sure she would burst from it. Gone was the empty feeling she'd felt on the road. One look and one touch from him was enough to shift her whole world into focus.

Elspeth entered the hall to find her brother talking to Malcolm and Magnus. They all looked at her with different expressions; the first two with surprise, the latter with promise. She smiled at them all and joined them.

"I do not think I can arrange the priest so quickly," Osgar said to Magnus. "Surely you can wait one more day."

"We are anxious," Elspeth said. "Is there no one who can go fetch the Father?"

"I will see to it," Malcolm said. He shook his head and laughed. "When I arrived here, I thought I would be discussing my own wedding, not helping plan someone else's."

"Magnus," Osgar said, "while I appreciate your enthusiasm to marry my sister, she deserves a proper ceremony and feast and one that is carefully prepared. My cook will likely have an attack of apoplexy if he does not have the proper time to prepare a wedding feast. Please, give me a few days to do this right."

Elspeth was as driven as Magnus was to make their union a reality, but there was truth in what Osgar said. Once they did this there was no doing it again. So they may as well do it properly.

"What is your preference?" he asked her.

She saw everything in that question. Every memory they had made, every new one they would make, children, happiness, tears, and joy. He was her whole world and that had already begun. The beautiful part of this is that they already knew they were compatible, more than compatible. They were a perfect match. How many couples could claim that before they were officially married. And then there was the fact that they were already married in their minds and hearts. Aye, she could wait if it meant something to her family and likely his. His sisters would no doubt be eager to attend and she would love for them to be there.

Elspeth took his hand in both of hers and squeezed. "First of all, Magnus Haraldson of Islay, you have not asked me to marry you."

Without hesitation he cupped her face in his hands and whispered, "Will you be my wife again?"

She smiled when Osgar's head tilted in their direction as if to try to hear what he'd said.

"Aye, Magnus. I will be your wife."

"Was there a second of all?" he asked.

"Secondly," she said, "I would like my wedding to be as my brother suggests, with your family and mine present with a proper feast."

"Then, you will have it!" Osgar said and left the hall.

"Malcolm, you will stay and help us celebrate?" she asked. Considering the awkwardness from earlier, she hoped their relationship would return to how it had always been.

"Aye, I wouldn't miss this for the world."

She turned back to Magnus and smiled. She could see the eagerness in his eyes for them to resume their love, but he would have to wait. They would be wed in this time, and blessed by her God through their priest. And it would be forever.

# CHAPTER EIGHTEEN

The stag would be honoured at the wedding feast and Magnus was pleased for the invitation to hunt. It was a welcome distraction from the tension building in him having to wait days and days to officially claim Elspeth as his. When she'd said she wanted a proper wedding, he had not realized the effort that went into such an endeavour. In truth, he supposed, he didn't really pay much attention to such things in his village either. He hunted, he fished and someone else cooked it.

Now as he sat at the morning meal with his sisters and Freydis, a peacefulness washed over him. As if the madness of the past several weeks melted away. In a few short hours, Elspeth would be his and despite Osgar's offer to remain here for the winter, he longed to take her home, to what would be their home. They would stay with Gunnar for the cold months and come spring, he would take some men and start building their longhouse and other dwellings on the lands Gunnar had promised him. He'd seen so much now between Castle MacDomnail, this smaller keep, and even the structures in Iceland to know he wanted to build in stone. He planned to ask Osgar and Giric for advice on stonemasonry or to even help him find some men who knew the trade. He would pay them well and he would have his own Norse version of a castle and keep.

"You are lost in your thoughts, brother," Saga said.

"I am thinking of the future."

"You are thinking of your wedding night," she said in a teasing tone.

Magnus looked at Freydis then. Though they had not spoken of it, he sensed she knew more than she was letting on over the past couple of days since arriving. Her eyes narrowed on him as they'd done so many times of late. She could not read his thoughts, but she was perceptive, nonetheless.

"I am thinking that I am a lucky man."

"You are," Freydis said. "Do you realize just how lucky?"

"I do." It was obvious Freydis wanted to talk about their journey, but thankfully she kept her thoughts to herself. Today was not the day to delve into a philosophical discussion about gods and otherworldly beings influencing mankind for a higher purpose. Today was a day to celebrate a man and a woman declaring their devotion to one another before her god and their families.

"Do you plan to perform a blot sacrifice today?" Saga asked.

"I will wait until we return to Lagavulin," he said. "I wish my brother to be a part of that ceremony."

The blot was sacred to his people. It was a blood gift offered to the gods in exchange for good fortune and Magnus was not about to perform it without Gunnar's blessing as well.

"You're returning to Islay?" Freydis asked.

"We are," he said. "As soon as the celebrations are complete here. I want us to be settled before the snow flies."

"Have you spoken of this to Elspeth?" Vigdis asked.

"Ja, have you told her?" Saga asked.

"I have not had that chance, but I believe she will be in agreement. I can start preparing materials for our new home easier if I'm already on Islay."

Saga sat back while folding her arms across her chest and grinned.

"What?"

She shrugged. "You're making plans without consulting your future wife. That's very brave of you."

The turn of the conversation was something he'd not expected. There was no reason to believe Elspeth would disagree with his plan and it would afford her some distance from her brother Kenneth who had also returned in the last couple of days. The more time Magnus spent with him, the more he disliked him. He couldn't quite put his finger on it, but something was not quite right about the man.

"Would you like us to broach the topic with her when we help her prepare for the ceremony?" Vigdis asked.

"That will not be necessary," he said. "I will speak of it with her as soon as we are wed. I am sure she will agree."

"If you return to Islay, I wish to go with you," Freydis said.

Saga turned to her quickly. "You will not stay with me?"

"My purpose here is coming to an end and I am needed elsewhere," she said looking directly at Magnus.

Why did the woman have to be so cryptic? At least she appeared to be supportive of them leaving this place. Not that there was anything wrong with being here, and he supposed there would be time spent here in the future, but they would be better off on Islay at the moment.

"And who will keep me company when my husband is busy with his business and I am too fat with child to hunt or train?"

"I will," Vigdis said. "I wish to be closer to my betrothed as we too have a wedding to plan."

"There it is all settled," Magnus said and stood. Osgar had said he wanted to speak with him before the ceremony and he intended to seek him out, then prepare himself.

"Don't be late," Saga said.

Magnus rolled his eyes at her then left the hall. While he loved his sister, she could be irritating at times. Now was one of those times. He hadn't considered for a moment that Elspeth would oppose travelling to Islay as soon as the wedding responsibilities were satisfied. She wanted a lavish ceremony, and he was happy for her to have it. But there were more pressing things on his mind, including having to lie to everyone that they were not already man and wife. In his mind, they were just that.

"Magnus, wait for a moment."

He turned to see Freydis running to catch up to him. Something inside his guts twisted a little. He didn't like the look of concern crossing her face and the urgency in her stride.

"What is it, Freydis?" he asked. "I do not want to be late for my own wedding, and I have to make ready."

"I just wanted to let you know that all will be well."

"Freydis, I appreciate everything you are trying to do, but to be honest, it's all a bit too much."

"I know. I mean, I know everything. I spoke to Elspeth last evening, and well," she said with a smile, "I will let you find out on your own. I just want to wish you both many happy years together and you know I wouldn't say that if I had not seen that possibility."

"Thank you, Freydis. And if you wish to return with us, it will be so."

He leaned down and let her kiss him on the cheek and watched as she turned and climbed the stairs to the upper chambers. He shook his head and made his way to the kitchen. Osgar had spent much time in there over the past couple of days overseeing the preparations for the feast.

"Ah, there you are," he said to Magnus when he entered. "I want to make sure everything is perfect. I acquired this smoked salmon and want to make sure it is as close to what you are used to as possible."

Osgar offered Magnus some of the fish. The taste tantalized his taste buds and the aroma of smoke filled his head. He'd always preferred fish over meat and whoever the smoker was, clearly knew what he was doing. Magnus smiled to himself and appreciated that Osgar would take the time to consider his palate as well as Elspeth's favourite dishes.

"It is perfect," Magnus said. "Clearly the maker must have Viking blood flowing through his veins."

The cook stood a little taller and puffed out his chest. He nodded in Magnus' direction, then went about his business again.

"You truly like it?" Osgar asked.

"I do. I appreciate all your efforts on our behalf and I am sure everyone will compliment this as the greatest feast this region has ever seen."

Now it was Osgar's turn to puff up.

"Thank you. Now, there is one thing I want to mention to you, before the ceremony," he said. "I have assigned a large parcel of land to the North for you and my sister. You can stay here for the next few months and we can start a build for you in the spring."

Magnus's heart sank. It was a generous offer, but it was not what he wanted. He would have to speak to Elspeth as soon as possible about what she wanted. What if this was her greatest desire? Would he be willing to give up his plans if this was what would make her truly happy? For now he would have to put all of those thoughts aside and focus on today's ceremony.

~

*E*lspeth smoothed her skirt and lifted the fabric then let it fall. The heavy red velvet was glorious to the touch. The gown had been her mother's and had long since been put aside for her wedding day. Gold stitching framed the square neckline and an intricately stitched design of doves fronted the bodice panel. When Saga, Vigdis, and Freydis entered her chamber they all stopped and stared.

"Please speak," she said. "You're making me nervous."

Vigdis came forward first and lifted the fabric to examine it closer. "This is like nothing I've ever seen."

"'Twas my mother's and made for a time when she visited the king's court."

"This is why I must visit the markets in Edinburgh and York," Vigdis said. "I want to wear gowns like this."

"When you are the lady here, you may wear as many of these as you wish," Elspeth said.

Of all of them, Vigdis was bound to adjust to the differences in cultures the easiest. She was eager to learn everything there was to know about running a castle. In contrast, Elspeth, while excited to learn more about Magnus' life and village, she was worried the expectation would be more than she could satisfy. How would she fit in with the other Viking women? Those like Vigdis perhaps, but she had nothing in common with Saga. In fact, the only one of the three she could relate to was Freydis.

"Do you wear your hair up or down for your wedding ceremonies?" Vidgis asked.

"Down and veiled. Once I am married, I will keep it covered."

"Fascinating," Vigdis said and moved to the table on which rested Elspeth's hairbrushes and the rings and necklace she would wear on this day. They too had belonged to her mother. Four shiny round rubies were set to the sides of an oval one creating the central focus of the dark yellow gold necklace. Once clasped around her neck, the oval ruby would rest on her chest and a small droplet of gold would be positioned just above her cleavage. She'd always admired the piece and was excited to finally be permitted to wear it.

On her fingers were three gold rings that fit together, also with tiny rubies surrounding one large one in the centre. Once she was dressed, she sat so that her maid could remove the cloths from her hair allowing the tresses to flow down her back. She placed the necklace around her neck and her veil was pinned to her hair. Except that her belly was about to flutter apart, she was ready to begin her life with Magnus as her husband.

She'd spoken briefly with Freydis the day before and was now excited to share her wedding night with her husband. She had a surprise for him and she couldn't wait for him to discover it.

"You do not look as nervous as I would expect a bride on her wedding day," Saga said. "Though you do look lovely. I do not know how you can tolerate those heavy gowns. I wore them for a fortnight and was ready to burn them," she said and chuckled.

Elspeth could not picture the tall shield maiden wearing this sort of gown and smiled imagining it.

"You looked just as regal as you always do," Vigdis said. "Truly, I do not know why you fussed so much."

Elspeth watched the sisters banter as Freydis approached. She sat beside her and clasped her hand.

"All will be well, my lady." Freydis squeezed her hand and

Elspeth heard a soft voice in her mind say *the gods have confirmed it.*

"Aye," she said. "I know it to be true. I do not know how, but I believe you."

Freydis had shed some light on her theory of Elspeth's gift and she had to admit, the woman could be convincing, but Elspeth would make up her own mind in time. She'd also spoken to Father Fothad over the last few days and shared everything with him during confession. He had considered her to have had an episode of the mind and sent her off to prayer for the day absolving her of any wrongdoing and not believing her when she told him of her and Magnus' time together. Time, he'd said, does not work that way and only the glory of God can sanction a marriage. He'd claimed she was not married, and she'd not had a wedding night or any other night with Magnus and that had been that. It has all been a little bizarre, but she trusted that he knew best in terms of what would or would not offend God so she said her prayers and now here she was about to marry a Viking. Father Fothad had been surprisingly accepting of Magnus. A part of her wondered if that may have anything to do with the generous sum Osgar had to pay him for his services. She shook her head at the thought of it. Osgar had seemed fine with the arrangement as did the priest and so who was she to concern herself with it when she was getting what she wanted? The main thing was she truly felt safe for the first time since being in the tower with Magnus. Her mind boggled trying to make sense of time and so she focused her mind's eye on the man she would soon call husband.

She wondered if Osgar had told him of the land he had put aside for her. Magnus also had land set aside from Gunnar and so she was excited to talk to him about which they would accept. Elspeth cared not. She wanted to be wherever he was and if that was on Islay, Prestwick, or

Iceland, she would be happy. She couldn't wait to talk to him and plan with him.

A knock sounded at the door and then Osgar entered. He stopped when he saw Elspeth and grinned at her. "You look like our mother," he said. Elspeth had been very young when their mother had died and so did not have any visual memory of her.

"I thank you brother, as I believe she was a beautiful woman," Elspeth said, teasing him. She took his arm and together they walked down the stairs and outside of the keep and on toward the chapel.

"Did you tell Magnus about the land?" she asked him, focusing on the crunching sound of the stones under her feet to keep her thoughts away from her pounding heart.

"Aye. He seemed overwhelmed by the offer. I wonder if he realized that is the way of things for us. I will give him some time and I will explain how the title of the land will transfer to him. I have already petitioned the king."

"I am sure he understands," Elspeth said. "He is probably thinking of which parcel he will accept."

"What do you mean?"

"I mean his own brother has offered land to him as well. He may be thinking he has to make a choice."

"That explains a great deal," Osgar said. "I will be sure to make him understand that he can have both. And what about you? Do you have a preference for where you will live?"

"As long as 'tis with my husband, I care not."

"I couldn't agree more. I just want you to be happy. I have to say, Magnus is much changed from when I first met him. Back then I thought him to be pigheaded and a bully."

"Osgar!"

"Nay, 'tis true!"

"I certainly hope your opinion of him has now shifted."

"Aye, more than you can ever imagine. Today I will be

proud to call him brother and do not hesitate offering your hand to him."

Elspeth took a deep steadying breath. She was pleased to hear it. Disappointing her family would not be something that would ever sit well with her; however, if it was necessary to secure her own happiness she would do it.

They rounded the corner and the chapel came into view. She caught sight of Magnus standing on the steps and her breath caught in her throat. He wore his trews with a bright yellow tunic held in place by two wide, black leather straps crisscrossing over his chest. Thick, dark furs were draped over his shoulders highlighting his blonde hair. His face was smoothly shaven making her fingers itch to touch.

He locked gazes with her and everything else in the world fell away. This moment was for all time. This timeline or another timeline; this realm or another realm did not matter. All that did was this man and the commitment they were about to make to one another.

# CHAPTER NINETEEN

The moment Osgar placed Elspeth's hand in Magnus', a loud crash of thunder boomed around them. When she jumped, he squeezed her hand and smiled.

"You have no need to worry," he said. "It is Thor sending us his approval."

She looked up at the sky with wide eyes, then pointed upward. Magnus looked up to find several ravens circling overhead like they had done before.

He chuckled. "It appears Odin will not be outdone."

"Let us go inside before we become drenched," Osgar said, guiding them into the chapel and away from the sudden downpour.

Together they walked to the altar where the priest stood. He raised his arms in the air and brought them together, while raising his head skyward.

"Lord God, bless this union between our dearest Lady Elspeth and her pagan husband. Forgive him for his sins as he has not yet taken the sacraments."

He looked pointedly at Magnus. There had been no discussion with him about converting to her faith and there would be none. Elspeth tugged on his hand and when he looked down at her she was smiling and shaking her head.

The next several minutes passed by in a blur as he stayed focused on the woman before him. The priest said more of the same prayers for his soul and their marriage and for his God to guide Magnus to see the Christian light. Elspeth's hand squeezed his every time, he hoped in reassurance, or at least that was how he took it. How much longer did this ceremony have to go on? He wanted to hold and kiss his wife and this was fast becoming a new kind of torture.

"Do you accept this woman as your lawfully wedded wife, under the eyes of God and these witnesses; in the company of the greatly exalted Laird MacAlpin whose benevolence is unmatched; whose—"

"I do accept this woman as my wife," Magnus said. He couldn't take one more moment of this man's irritating speeches.

"Ahem," he said narrowing his eyes at Magnus before refocusing his attention on Elspeth. "And do you my dearest Lady Elspeth, take this pagan as your lawfully wedded husband, before the eyes of God and these witnesses; in the company of—"

"I do accept this man as my husband," she said.

"Indeed," the priest said. "Will there be an exchange of rings?" He practically smirked as he directed the question to Magnus.

"There will," Osgar said from behind them and produced two heavy gold bands encrusted with rubies.

Magnus had never heard of such a thing. He'd seen other people wearing such decorations, but it was nothing he'd ever even considered.

He tried to tune out the next instructions from the priest as he blessed the rings and instructed him and Elspeth to place the rings on the other's fingers.

After another prayer and another reference to Osgar's greatness, the priest said, "Go forth as husband and wife and may the Great and Almighty God bless your union."

And then it was over.

"You can kiss me now," Elspeth said.

Magnus needed no more encouragement. He slowly lifted her veil and everything and everyone else in the chapel melted away. Only they two remained as he gazed into her lovely eyes.

"You are mine now," he whispered, "For all time."

"And you are mine," she said.

Magnus leaned down and brushed his lips across hers. She smelled of lavender and cloves, scents he would always and forever associate with her for the rest of his living days.

"We should go to the feast now," she said with a chuckle.

"I don't care about the feast. I have missed you," he said and kissed her again ever so softly. "And I have missed this."

"Aye, I have as well, but remember no one else knows about our time in the tower."

"Freydis does," he said and leaned back to see her reaction.

"She does. And we have much to talk about, but for now, let us join the others at the feast. There will be plenty of time to reconcile all of that later. For now I want to sit beside you, hold your hand and thank all the gods responsible for bringing you to me."

That was good enough for him. But he couldn't let her go without lifting her up and swinging her around in an embrace to let her know just how happy he was they were now officially joined. Well, in her God's eyes anyway.

They held hands as they made their way outside and to the crowd that had still gathered waiting for them. The priest's eyes narrowed in on him again. Magnus wondered what would happen if he challenged the man. He suspected there would be cowering and grovelling considering Magnus was now a part of this *exalted* family and according to Osgar would be given title and lands. Perhaps some good could come from that arrangement after all.

Once they were back inside the keep and entered the hall, Magnus was impressed at how the place had been transformed to include many garlands of boughs and strings of dried flowers and herbs in arrangements placed on all the tables.

The main table was lavishly decorated with silver and gold goblets and pitchers; trenchers contained steaming meats, salmon, and breads; bowls contained a dark brown liquid and in the centre was a whole wild boar. The aroma in the hall was enough to make the juices flow in his mouth and he had to swallow hard to not embarrass himself.

"Here, you two," Osgar said. "You will take these seats."

Osgar directed them to two ornate wooden chairs at the centre of the table. Once they sat, a servant came by to fill their goblets with a dark red liquid Magnus had never seen before. He sniffed it then sipped. It was not unpleasant; not quite as sweet as mead, and not quite as bitter as ale.

"'Tis wine," Elspeth said. "I prefer it over mead so my brother gets it for me when he can."

"I shall make sure we are always stocked with it," he said.

Servants cut up samplings from all the food and placed a large platter in front of them so they could choose what they like. Magnus was not accustomed to such formality and so looked to Elspeth for help.

"Take what you like for yourself and for me," she said. "I promise we won't eat like this always, but there is a certain expectation with so many present."

"I choose your food?"

"Aye, it is technically yours to give."

"But your brother is laird here."

He didn't understand, but as he waited for her reply he used the two tined fork to lift out the best pieces of meat he could find and placed them on her trencher. He chose a piece of smoked salmon like that which he had tasted earlier. He also chose pieces of bread and lifted the small bowl of the brown substance toward him so he could smell it.

"That's gravy," she said. "We pour it over our bread, or you can dip into it."

"Which do you prefer?" he asked.

"I like to pour it over everything," she said. "Well, maybe not the salmon."

He nodded and drizzled the gravy carefully over all her food leaving the salmon off to the side. He sat back and waited for her to eat.

She laughed. "Now you must fill your own trencher and we will eat the first bites together."

This was far more complicated than he preferred. Magnus took mostly the same as he had given her and when his plate was full, he drew the gravy bowl near, but did not pour any out.

"I will not ruin my food if I do not like this gravy of yours."

"A good plan," she said. "Now take a piece of meat."

Once he had it in his hand she encircled her arm around his and motioned to put her food in her mouth. He did the same and they ate the first bites together. He'd taken a piece of the wild boar which was the most tender and juicy meat he was sure he'd ever eaten.

"Take a piece of your bread and dip it into the gravy. The juices they use to make it would likely come from the rabbit, which is my favourite."

"Then we will always be well stocked in rabbit as well," he said.

He'd need to make a list.

*E*lspeth loved watching him explore all the different food laid out before them. She had enjoyed the feast on Islay, and their cooking was delicious, but different and the presentation somewhat less formal.

Magnus filled his goblet with wine a second time and offered to fill hers again but she put her hand out to stop him.

"I prefer to sip mine. It has a tendency to sneak up on me."

"The taste is growing on me."

The next couple of hours were filled with guests offering their gifts and congratulations. Magnus was quizzical every time someone came by with their tokens which aligned with that particular person's trade. Though the item may appear small, the intent was grand. Osgar had always taken great care to ensure those who worked for the success of the castle and their lands were always cared for. He never abused his people and the outpouring of well wishes this day was a testament to it. Elspeth smiled at the sight of the smiles on everyone's faces. Only Father Fothad seemed offended by Magnus' beliefs. Not one other person had expressed concerns over his faith or his heritage.

"You seem lost in thought," he said to her.

"I am wondering how I became so fortunate to have so many blessings."

"I hope I am counted among them."

She turned to him and met his gaze. Uncertainty rested in his expression. "You are my grandest blessing. Truly, I do not care whose god sent you to me."

"Your brother offered me lands and title," he said.

She hadn't wanted to get into any of the details of that aspect of their marriage yet, but it appeared he did.

"You are sure you want to talk about this now?"

"I am," he said. "What we do once this feast is over is too important to leave it until the time comes and I want to be sure we understand each other."

She wasn't sure she liked the sound of that or where the conversation could be heading.

"Magnus, I know your brother has also offered you lands."

"He has. On the southern portion of the island. There is stone to cultivate for building, and lush farmlands not yet tilled."

"And you want to build our home there."

His brow furrowed. He looked so forlorn that she placed her hand on his cheek. "Magnus, my home is wherever you are. Don't you know that already?"

He released a deep breath as if he'd been holding it for an age. Placing his hand on the back of her neck, he drew her forward so their foreheads touched.

"I was worried you would insist on staying here and I would have stayed with you, but of the two offers, I promise you with my heart and soul you will be happy on Islay. I will build us our very own tower and you can help decide where all the chambers will be situated."

She leaned back and gazed into his eyes. "You want me to help you build a tower? Like *our* tower?" Not that the tower they stayed in was theirs, but in her mind it was theirs for a time.

"I do. If we travel to Islay once the wedding feast is complete, I can start to work gathering materials. By the time the spring comes, I should have enough of everything to start building. I am certain Gunnar will provide me with enough men to help clear the land and with the build."

He had it all planned out and she loved the sound of every

detail he shared. "Magnus, I love it and cannot wait to start planning."

Magnus cupped her face with his hands and kissed her deeply. The second his lips touched hers she could see his vision in full form. An image of a tower house, smaller dwellings, gated sheep, and young children running through tall grass filled her mind. Her heart was near to bursting with the essence of the life he envisioned for them.

When he leaned back, the look of contentment now resting on his face was infectious. Her heart, nay, her very soul was full of such happiness and joy that she could scarce contain it.

"You are sure you accept this path for us?" he asked.

"I have never been more certain of anything in my life," she said and grasped his hand. "I have seen the path as you do and I cannot imagine a happier existence."

"How long must we remain here?"

"This day? Or do you mean how long will the feast continue?"

"Both."

"Today we must remain here for a while yet. There will be dancing and much music and Osgar will likely want to formally announce his betrothal to Vigdis. But be patient," she said, feeling just as eager as him to be alone. "After today, we only need to partake for our meals and if we need a break…"

He smiled broadly at her. She already knew what a skilled lover he was and also knew that their appetite for one another was not easily satiated.

"Then I will be patient," he said. "For I already know the reward is worth a thousand feasts."

Magnus leaned forward and filled his trencher and hers again. When she made to stop him he shook his head. "You will need your energy, my darling wife. For you are in store for an evening where you will get no sleep and I plan to make up for each of the last seven days since we have been together."

Heat pooled between her thighs and more rose to her cheeks. She grabbed a big piece of rabbit and bit into its succulence. Seven nights to make up was a great deal and he was right, she'd need the energy.

After they ate their meals, they sat back and watched as the musicians played their various instruments. Magnus asked about each and every one of them. His curiosity appeared to have no limits and she loved sharing all that she knew with him. And she was more than aware that once they went to Islay, she would have just as many questions. She wanted to take the time over the winter to learn as much about their ways so she could find a way to blend them both. After all, they need not be bound to one or the other way of doing things, rather take the best of both cultures and form something new. Her whole outlook on their future changed the moment she saw his vision.

She had no sooner felt that realization when an image of Kenneth floated into her mind. *Danger*. He was in danger. She looked first at Magnus, then at Osgar who had been nearby the entire evening.

"What is it?" Osgar asked.

"Kenneth," she said and felt a powerful pressure on her head. A second later it was gone. She glanced around the table to see Freydis focusing intently on her.

"You and your wife should retire for the evening, now," Freydis said.

"What is going on?" Magnus asked.

"You do not need to worry," Freydis said. "She is safe."

Elspeth could feel Freydis' protection from across the table. The strain on the woman's face told Elspeth she may not be able to hold out much longer and luckily no one else had noticed what was going on.

She stood and took Magnus' hand. They made their thanks and left the hall. Out of the corner of her eye, Elspeth caught sight of a cloaked figure leaving the keep and before she could say anything, Osgar and some of his men were laying chase.

"Come upstairs," Magnus said. "I trust Freydis' advice."

"As do I," she said and took his hand and led him upstairs. Something strange was happening and though she was worried about Kenneth she had to question if she should have put aside her fear of him. Whether he was in danger or not she was not about to risk hers or Magnus' safety to find out.

They walked down the hall to her chamber to find a spray of lavender, rosemary, and cloves pinned to the door. Once she opened it, she noticed a white crystal substance spread just inside around the perimeter of the chamber. She bent down to touch it then lifted a pinch to her tongue. Salt. It appeared Freydis had been doing some of her own preparation for their wedding night. On a table sat a pitcher and pewter goblets, no doubt a touch added from her brother.

Magnus closed the door and bolted it. He turned to her and stepped inside the circle with her. For some reason she expected…what? Some sort of change or something. Whatever Freydis was doing with the salt didn't appear to have an impact on her. It was no matter. The door was bolted and she was finally alone with Magnus. The rest of the world could wait. She had a husband who needed pleasing.

# CHAPTER TWENTY

The strings used to tie Elspeth's bodice to her skirt were proving temperamental. Magnus had long since removed his furs, tunic and boots. He stood before her in nothing more than his trews and loved the way her hands stroked his chest then tugged at his hips.

"You're not very good at undressing your wife," she said.

"I want to know who made a gown meant to send a man into madness. Why can I not cut these strings?"

"This gown belonged to my mother and you will take care with it," she said and reached around to cup his behind.

"That's not fair," he said. "I can't even get you out of any of this contraption and you have almost full access to me."

"Very well," she said. "Here, tug on the strings like this." Using her fingernails, she loosened the knots and released the parts of her gown.

Magnus didn't waste another moment. He pulled the bodice over her head and tugged at her skirts until they fell to the floor.

"Step this way," he said as he held her hands to keep her steady. Now she only wore her ornate necklace and her rings. He carefully removed all but the ring he'd placed on her hand during the ceremony. His felt foreign but at the same time comforting. As if it would always serve as a reminder of their commitment to one another. He supposed that was the point.

The fabric of her shift was sheer revealing her pink nipples. He reached out to stroke them with the backs of his fingers and smiled when she sucked in her breath. He picked her up and walked with her to the bed. He placed her there then lay beside her.

"Now you're wearing too much," she said as she stroked his leg with her bare foot.

Magnus shimmied out of his trews and threw them on top of her gown then reached for her. He pulled her atop him and lifted her so that she hovered over his hard erection. He'd been dying to drive himself inside her all day but in the back of his mind he still questioned whether any of it had been real. He didn't want to hurt her in case her maidenhead was still intact so he would take it slowly, tease and taunt her for a little to see how high he could bring her desire.

He rubbed the tip of his cock across her slick opening and drew in a deep breath when she pushed her body down to take his tip inside.

"Not yet, wife," he said and flipped her over onto her back.

"You plan to torture me then?" she asked a little breathless.

His answer was in the form of pulling her body toward him and positioning her legs above his shoulders. He buried his face between her legs and sucked hard on her bud. She bucked off the bed when he drove two fingers inside her. She was hot and tight and soaked. Her flesh clenched hard around him as her body pulsed through her climax. Thor's breath, she was as desperate for release as he was. And if he didn't get himself under control, his plans to take things slow with her would fail.

As her body settled, Magnus lifted her shift until it was over her head then wedged his body between her legs. He peered into her eyes and leaned down to kiss her sweet lips. When she opened her mouth he slipped his tongue inside to dance with hers. She tasted of the sweet wine they had shared and he marvelled at how perfectly her body melded to his as if they had been made from one of Yggdrasil's branches.

"I need to feel you inside me," she whispered as she gazed up at him.

His need was greater now than any other time in his life including his other times with her. This time, this connection was so much more than physical. This was a branding upon each other's souls that time and place could not touch. He felt so raw, so exposed in the moment he pressed into her welcoming body. At her entrance, he waited. If she were a maiden still, she would need to adjust and he would not barrel forward like one who has not yet earned his manhood.

"Magnus, please," she said as she tried to push him forward using her on his buttocks.

He looked deep into her eyes as he pushed into her. The moment was at hand and when he felt no barrier his soul overspilled with joy.

It had been real.

All of it.

How or why he didn't care.

Now he could love her they way he wanted; the way she wanted.

He shifted his arms underneath her shoulders and thrust hard. She gasped. He pulled back and thrust harder this time and loved the way she threw her head back and lifted her hips to meet his. Her body tightened around him as he thrust harder and faster, their bodies slapping against the other in mad rhythm to a song only they could sing.

Tingling started at the base of his spine signalling his nearing climax, but he didn't want this feeling to ever end. He pulled out of her body and flipped her over onto her belly. He lifted her hips and drove into her from behind.

Elspeth grabbed hold of the pillows and pushed her body back in time with his thrusting. Higher and higher he climbed, but he would not release until he was sure she had been completely satisfied as many times as she could. Her body tensed and her climax pulsed around him then she would build again. He lost count of the number of times this occurred for her before her body finally relaxed. Only then did he unleash his own tension and let the tingling spread up his spine allowing his own orgasm to spread through his body.

Tensing, he became lightheaded as his seed shot out of his body and into hers. Magnus had never felt so coiled. And never so unleashed.

Moments or eons passed as he lay beside her stroking her hair and waiting for his heartbeat to return to normal.

"How do you feel?" he asked her.

"Like all the bones have been removed from my body."

Her voice was soft and sleepy. But he'd made her a promise to get no sleep this night. Magnus stroked her back and her round bottom. He brushed the back of her thighs with his fingers and slipped them between her legs. She sucked in a breath when he stroked her hardening bud.

"I am very pleased," he said.

"For which part?"

"That it was all real." He looked into her eyes and watched a solitary tear escape the corner of her eye.

"I knew it but wanted to wait for you to discover for yourself."

"And I am glad you did. I cannot imagine a more beautiful way to discover all that we had shared was not some imagining on either of our parts."

She smiled at him as he brushed the tear away. "There's more that I am pleased with," he said.

"Oh? And what is that?"

He turned her onto her back and leaned onto his elbow so he could better examine her body. "This one is tasty, but I think this one might be my favourite," he said as he sucked gently on one nipple, then the other. Back to the first and the nipped it with his teeth. "Ja, this one is my favourite."

"Oh!" She flung her arm over her eyes as he played with her nipples. "What else do you like?"

While still flicking her nipple with his tongue, he reached down to stroke her again. Her hips shifted as if to encourage his movements. He shifted his body again until he was again between her legs and driving his tongue within her. He pressed hard and drew circles with his thumb on her clit while he tasted her. As soon as he felt her shake he drove himself within her and thrust hard and fast to capture each and every wave of her orgasm which drew his to a dizzying height. Magnus tensed as heat washed over him and he spilled into her again.

This time when the waves subsided, he collapsed beside her. Perhaps a little rest was warranted if he was to fulfill his promise to her.

Elspeth rose from the bed and brought back a goblet. She spilled a small amount of the wine on the sheets then placed the goblet back on the table. Was she losing her wits?

"Father Fothad will insist on proof I was a maiden."

Magnus shook his head. Would he ever understand these customs?

*E*lspeth cuddled into Magnus' side and inhaled his masculine scent. He was all leather and wine and that intoxicating scent after they'd shared their bodies. She would never get enough of it or him. Not ever.

His gentle snoring made her grin. True to his promise, he had not let her sleep the entire night. When they were not ravishing each other, they were replenishing their energy with the food and drink that had been placed outside their door at some point in the night. Magnus had dressed and was on his way to get something for them when he discovered the offering outside. He'd stripped again in record time and they sat by the fire eating and sipping some wine until they were both roused again.

She loved making plans for the tower with him. Never in her wildest dreams had she considered being part of planning the build with him. Even when she considered he may want to live on her lands, she didn't see herself in the planning of it.

And she couldn't be happier.

Streams of sunlight cast through the window and highlighted the mound of their clothes upon the floor. She slipped out of the bed and put more wood on the fire to break the chill that had started to settle through the chamber. Elspeth grabbed her shift and tugged it over her head and slipped back into bed to snuggle next to Magnus. Her eyes finally grew heavy as she absorbed more of his warmth.

She had no idea what time it was when she was awakened by a knocking on the chamber door. She arose to grab a covering gown and answer the door leaving her still snoring husband sound asleep in the bed.

Her two maidservants, Sheona and Isobel, came into the chamber with fresh bed linens and were followed by two men carrying her large wooden tub.

"The water will follow shortly, my lady," Neville, one of Osgar's manservants said. He'd never served her so she assumed he was there to assist Magnus.

She looked back toward the bed to see him now sitting up and barely covered by the quilts. The two maids looked at her and cast their gaze downward.

"My lord, if you come with me, I will see to your comfort. You too may have a bath if you wish."

He flicked back the covers and stood. The two maids yelped and left the chamber. Neville quickly scanned the floor then grabbed the discarded tunic and handed it to Magnus.

"My lord, I do believe you may wish to have a care around the maids as they are not accustomed to seeing a man about without his clothing."

"Then the maids should not enter a man's chamber while he is still abed and especially on the morning after his wedding."

Magnus came over to her and kissed her on the head then on the lips. He motioned to the red stain on the bed sheets and winked at her.

"Enjoy your bath, wife," he said. "I believe I may take you up on the offer of a bath," he said to Neville. "My wife did not let me sleep much last night." He quickly stepped out of reach of Elspeth as he made the last comment. The look on Neville's face was almost comical and she had to lower her gaze in mock embarrassment, though she absolutely felt none.

Once they were gone, the maids came in again and stripped the bed. One giggled and quickly stifled herself when Elspeth caught her. They would surely know the stain was not her virgin's blood, but the priest would not. They bundled all the clothes up and remade it with the fresh linens.

"We will be sure to alert Father Fothad that the marriage has been properly consummated," Sheona said.

They returned a while later once the water arrived and proceeded to scrub every inch of her and wash her hair. Elspeth had to admit, the heat from the water was soothing the ache in her joints and between her legs from the vigorous night she'd spent with Magnus.

Her maids, normally chatty little birds, were thankfully quiet this morning. The quiet gave her time to think about the occurrence at the feast the night before. Magnus had done a superb job of eliminating all thoughts from her head except those that directly related to their physical enjoyment of one another, and their future life together.

The maids left with the promise to return in a little while to brush dry her hair. Elspeth took advantage of the quiet and rested her neck on the edge of the tub. Steam arose in tufts and between the lavender and rose scented water and the crackling fire, her eyelids drooped slowly until they remained closed.

When she awoke, the maids had returned with a small platter of food and a fresh pitcher and goblets.

"'Tis a good thing we came back when we did," Sheona said. "You fell asleep and your head was almost in the water."

Elspeth sat up and rubbed her eyes. She was a little disoriented for the moment and had to look around a little to remember where she was. She blinked a few times and asked, "How long was I asleep?"

"Almost an hour," Sheona said.

An odd, unsettling feeling washed over her. For as long as she could remember even the smallest of naps resulted in a vivid dream that could be about nothing, but more than likely was something that she later related to something real. Now she thought about it, she hadn't dreamed when she'd slept with Magnus earlier that morning either. Did the salt on the floor have anything to do with it? Had Freydis somehow blocked her mind from dreaming or receiving whatever messages entered her mind when she slept?

"Is the Viking seer belowstairs yet?"

"Aye, she has been up since dawn broke."

Elspeth stood and reached for the cloths to dry her skin. "I must speak to her," she said to Isobel. "Go and ask her to join me here while Sheona brushes my hair."

"Aye, my lady," she said and left the chamber.

"Are you unwell?" Sheona asked her.

"Nay, I am well, Sheona. You need not worry about me."

"I cannot help it," she said. "I have known you for so long and I find that you are different since you went away with your brother."

Elspeth was more than sure she had left the lass she once was somewhere along the road of her adventures. She would scarce recognize that lass any longer and though her adventure was far more outlandish than she could have ever imagined, she would not change one second of it because it had put her on a path leading directly to Magnus.

"I have seen much since leaving here all those weeks ago," she said. "And I am happier for it."

"Your husband is an imposing man," she said.

"You do not have to worry about him," Elspeth said. "His ways may be different from ours, but he is honourable and would not harm one hair on anyone he considers unable to defend themselves. Did you know his sister has trained the maids at Castle MacDomnail?"

"My cousin works there," Sheona said. "I love my work here, but I would love to know how to keep groping hands at bay."

"Then we will have to be sure we can make that happen. I am certain when Vigdis becomes lady here, she will ensure everyone is properly able to defend themselves."

Elspeth was glad the topic of conversation had steered away from her specific adventures. She trusted her servant, but was not prepared to share the incredible happenings that offered little to no viable explanation. Nay, she would keep the details of her journey closely guarded. She was even hesitant to ask about Kenneth, lest Sheona be inclined to gossip. She would have to wait for Freydis' explanation and Magnus' observances.

Elspeth sat by the fire waiting for Freydis as Sheona brushed her hair until almost dry. The door opened quietly and for a moment, Elspeth couldn't make out who it was. That is until Freydis stepped over the salt threshold and her head was filled with dozens of images from the evening before and right up to her climbing the stairs and standing outside the chamber door.

"Sheona, would you please leave us now." It wasn't mean to be a question, rather as much of a direct order as she'd ever been comfortable giving.

"Aye, my lady. You will let me know if you need help dressing today. Remember, now that you're married, you must cover your hair before you come below."

"I will remember and I will be able to manage on my own."

Sheona left and Elspeth stared hard at Freydis. The woman had some explaining to do.

# CHAPTER TWENTY-ONE

The tension in the hall was thick enough to cut with a knife. Kenneth gripped the man who had proposed to Elspeth by the throat and Osgar was trying to hold him back.

Magnus approached and slammed his arm down across Kenneth's forcing him to break his hold on Malcolm; the man crumpled to the floor.

"What is going on here?" Magnus asked.

Malcolm coughed and sputtered as Kenneth turned on Magnus.

"I'll tell you what's going on. I'm the only person in this family who has the sense and decency to keep your kind out, that's what."

Magnus stepped toe-to-toe and looked down at him. He would be easily bested in a fight, but something told Magnus that it wouldn't be enough. That simply beating this man to a pulp would not change one part of his behaviour and his clear dislike of him.

"That's a far cry from a few weeks ago when you tried to pawn your sister off on my brother. What has brought about this sudden change? Or are you running out of options to line your pockets?"

Magnus was starting to figure the man out and the extent he was willing to go to gain control over Elspeth or anyone else who could possibly help him gain power and wealth. The end result was easy to identify, but the question that remained, was why. What could turn a man so vile as to put his own family's safety at risk?

"Magnus, you had better sit down," Osgar said. "There's much you do not know."

Malcolm got to his feet and made for the door. "The king will hear of this," he said as he left.

Giric made to go after him, but Osgar stopped him. "Let him go," he said. "He has a right to his grievance as he has been ill used."

Magnus had no idea what was going on and looked from one man to the other hoping someone would soon fill him in on the drama he'd obviously missed.

"Come and sit with me," Osgar said.

"I would rather stand," he said and crossed his arms over his chest.

"Very well," Osgar said. "It appears my brother secured a contract sanctioned by the king for Elspeth to marry Malcolm."

"But he had said he was offering marriage only to protect her."

"That was part of the deal. He was not to tell her about the contract."

"And he bailed on his oath and he will pay for it," Kenneth said.

"That's enough, Kenneth," Osgar said. "You have cost this family thousands in what I will have to pay out for a dowry that was promised and a wife who is now legitimately married to another."

"That is by your wrongdoing, not mine."

"I said that's enough!" Osgar looked down upon his younger brother and held his stance.

Magnus shook his head at all of them. So obsessed with money and position and power that they would be willing to trade off their family to secure it. Giric had been no different when he'd first sailed to Islay to secure arrangements with Gunnar. And Kenneth was no different now. The more he thought about it, the more it enraged him.

The fact that Kenneth had tried to work against a match between Magnus and Elspeth after trying to secure it merely proved that the man was the worst sort of opportunist. That was a well-established fact in Magnus's mind now.

So where did that leave them? Magnus didn't want to spend one more night anywhere close to Kenneth and he was sick to his back teeth of Freydis' obsession with Elspeth's gifts. He was sick of all of it.

"So what now?" Giric asked.

"Now, Kenneth will tell us about his conversation with the king and Malcolm concerning Elspeth and any other dealings he has had resulting in lining his pockets of late."

"I will tell you nothing," Kenneth said.

"You will tell us of your links to Athelstan," Giric said. "We know you have been meeting in York."

"How do you know that?" Kenneth asked.

"Because we had you followed," Giric said.

"You didn't think to tell me that?" Magnus asked. "I thought the alliance you struck with my brother extended to me."

Magnus grew more irritated by the minute. They were supposed to be aligned to push Athelstan back if and when he attacked, but it appeared the Scots were not willing to share information that could determine the ultimate outcome.

"You were preoccupied with protecting Elspeth at the time and we didn't think you needed to know."

Magnus nodded. He saw everything clearly now. The Scots only wanted the Viking strength of arms, not their insight into strategy in battle. They did not view this as an equal partnership.

"What's done is done," Giric said. "We must work together now more than ever. Kenneth you must tell us everything."

"I do not need to tell you anything," he said. "And there's nothing you can do to me to make that happen." Kenneth grabbed a goblet and a pitcher, sat in a large chair by the hearth and poured himself a drink.

Magnus had had enough of all of them. He strode over to Kenneth, knocked the goblet out of his hands and raised him to his feet by his tunic.

"You will tell me everything that has to do with Elspeth and any arrangement you presumed to arrange for my wife."

"My sister first!" Kenneth tried to pry Magnus' hands loose but he lacked the strength. The man was weak in more ways than one.

Magnus shook him hard enough his teeth rattled.

"All right I will tell you," he said. "I promised the king that if he arranged for Elspeth to marry Malcolm, I would spy for him, but it would cost extra because of the dangerous roads in and around York."

"How much did he pay you?"

"Five thousand marks," Kenneth said.

"And where is the money now?"

"Mostly gone."

"Gone?" Osgar asked. "Christ's teeth how could you spend so much money so fast?"

"Because he was paying it to someone he owed," Magnus said. He understood desperation when he saw it and there was only one thing that could make a man so desperate as to make such stupid decisions as this man.

"How can you owe anyone money?" Osgar asked.

"It is a long story," Kenneth said.

Magnus didn't want to hear it, but released the man as he told his tale of trying to always live up to his family name and his perfect older brother. Magnus could somewhat relate, but he would never resort to jeopardizing his sister's safety. His judgement might have lapsed on one or two occasions when he'd taken more than was agreed upon when raiding, but that was different. And he would fully expect to have to pay back anything that was deemed excessive by his brother the chieftain.

This was different.

Kenneth didn't care who he hurt in the process as long as his personal gain was satisfied in the process. In any case, he'd heard enough. As he turned to go, Giric caught up to him.

"You and I will talk later of our plans for Athelstan."

"No we will not. I go to speak with my wife and we will leave here at first rise on the morrow. When I share what I have learned with Gunnar, I suspect you will have some explaining to do to him. Remember, Giric, you approached us for an alliance. If you wanted mercenaries, you could have gone anywhere else. Rather, you entrenched yourself into our family and now you presume to pick and choose our involvement."

"That's not how it is. Your family is as much mine as possible. For God sake, your sister is my wife."

"And that was an effective way to gain Gunnar's alliance. And look at me, I am now as entrenched as my sister."

"What do you mean by that?" Elspeth asked from the staircase.

Magnus looked up to see her shocked look. Before he

could explain what he meant she turned and ran back up the stairs. He turned back to Giric and pointed his finger in his face.

"This is why we are leaving. You are all mad in the head and obsessed with a king who is hundreds of miles away and little threat to us. I said this from the beginning."

"You could not be more wrong, Magnus. But if you need to go tomorrow, will you do me one thing?"

"And what is that?"

"Will you bring a missive to Gunnar explaining everything that is going on?"

"I can, but he cannot read it."

"Elspeth can read it," Giric said. "I will go over it with her to be sure."

Magnus was too irritated to answer and merely walked away from him and toward the stairs. He knew how his statement sounded and prayed his wife was in a mood to listen. He could not battle her as well as everyone else.

~

She was going to vomit. Of that she was certain. From her discussion with Freydis to the words she could not believe she'd heard fall from Magnus' lips and the possible implications of it. Could it be possible he felt trapped? Her heart felt like it was being ripped from her body. She wrapped her arms around herself and stared out the window at the ravens who again circled overhead. The dream of their tower and their happy life together was real wasn't it? He couldn't possibly regret loving her as much as she did him. But they'd never said it. Mayhap it was all in her head, and the result of an incredible set of circumstances.

The door opened and quietly closed again. She didn't have to turn around. His footfalls grew until large, strong arms encircled her. His scent, his strength, his very essence was home to her now and by God, if he didn't feel what she needed him to she didn't know what she'd do.

"What you heard was out of context," he said quietly. "I feel that Giric and your brother are acting outside of the alliance they forged with my brother that includes our union. The argument was not about you and I and what we have come to mean to each other. The argument is that they want our alliance, but not our council. Do you understand?"

"Somewhat," she said quietly. It was difficult to shut off the hurt even if his words did make sense. She had seen what he described with her own eyes during their time on Islay. Osgar had acted like he was Magnus and Gunnar's better and they had been too gracious to point it out. So that part made sense. Perhaps all she needed was some reassurance.

She turned in his arms and rested her head on his chest focusing on his heartbeat. Its strong *thud, thud* calmed the torrent of emotions washing through her. It was as though she was the storm and he was the only calm that could settle it.

"You are my heart, Elspeth. You are the only thing that matters to me. I want us to leave here tomorrow instead of in a few days' time. All of this drama with your brother and deceit from Giric is too much. I want us to go to where there is less possibility of you being harmed. To where your dreams, or gift, or whatever you want to call it can be dealt with peacefully and without the constant threat of someone or something interfering."

"I want that too," she said. Truly she wanted nothing more. Freydis had cast her runes again and found a different meaning this time. She supposed she should share that with Magnus, but first she needed his love to fill the cracks that had found a way into her soul.

She reached up and pulled him down for a kiss. He

squeezed her tight and he kissed her like there was never to be another day for either of them. When he leaned back, she was breathless.

"Do you feel a little better?" he asked.

"A little," she said and smiled shyly at him. How could she tell him she wanted to hear the words?

"What can I do to prove to you that I love you more than my own life? That I would do anything to make you happy even if it meant tolerating either of your brothers and MacDomnail for another few days."

Elspeth drew a deep breath and smiled. That was all she needed to hear. He was as committed to her as she to him. Sometimes the words mattered.

"We will leave here on the morrow together and make our way to Islay."

He raised his eyebrows.

"You see, Husband, I love you more than *my* own life and would not see you miserable in the company of any man. If you want to go, then go we shall."

"You are certain you do not mind leaving early?"

"I am certain," she said. "I want the dream you shared with me. I know it will take a long time, but I believe in it."

"And how do you feel about your dreams? I will have to let Freydis know we will be leaving early."

"She's already gone."

"She is? Where? How?"

"You might want to sit for this, Magnus."

They sat opposite one another near the hearth. Elspeth didn't know where to begin really. She supposed at the beginning was as good a spot as any.

"Freydis believes she is on a spiritual journey and that I was a part of that. She was confusing the powers she believes she has with my gifts."

"How is that possible? You and I shared visions, the tower, all of that couldn't be just Freydis."

"You're right. That wasn't Freydis. The truth is I don't know where my gift originates. Based on my discussions with Father Fothad, I do not believe they're from God. Perhaps the Celtic Goddess, Brigid has seen me worthy to be blessed with such a thing. I may never know."

Magnus pinched the bridge of his nose and shook his head. Elspeth understood where he was coming from perfectly. She'd really believed Freydis was the answer to her journey. Now to hear the woman say she was mistaken didn't make a whole lot of sense.

"So what now?"

"Now we do what we said we would do. We travel to Islay and begin our life together," she said.

A knock sounded at the door and Magnus answered it. Sheona and Isobel entered with the contents of their evening meal and as she and Magnus ate, the maids began folding and packing Elspeth's clothes into large chests.

"Your brother said you will be gone for the winter so we will make sure you have everything you need."

They ate in silence as the maids continued to pack her belongings. It was strange to think it may be months or years before she returned to her chamber. One more night here and the rest of her life's journey would begin. How many nights had she lain awake in bed dreaming of a handsome stranger whisking her away on a large white horse? Those silly thoughts didn't seem so silly anymore now that she was about to move away from everything she ever knew to live in a Viking village with a man even her wild imagination could have never conjured.

"I should go speak to my brother," she said. "I would like to reassure him this is my decision too."

"Then I will go with you," he said and held out his hand.

"Always my protector."

"I will never falter in that regard," he said. "I may make many mistakes as a husband, but I will always love you and I will always protect you."

She didn't doubt it for a second now and she never would again. Together they left her chamber and made their way to the hall. The second she crossed the salt threshold, her mind's vision cleared. It was as though she'd been trying to see through a veil and that veil was now lifted.

Osgar sat alone in the hall bathed in firelight and candlelight. He appeared lost in thought as they entered.

"Have I failed you?" he asked without looking up as she drew near. His voice was solemn.

"Nay, brother, you have not failed me," she said and sat near him. "The time has come for us to leave. My mind cannot find peace. These last few weeks have taken a toll on me and I do not want to add any further stress on myself or my husband. You must deal with Kenneth as you see fit and I fear I could no longer be objective where he is concerned. I am caught in the middle."

"And what about these talks with the Viking healer?" he asked. "Do you have any resolution there? Was the Father any help? I feel like I have not been protecting you or helping."

"You don't need to protect me any longer, brother," she said. "My husband will stave off the wolves at the door."

"I am sorry for my part in keeping anything from you, Magnus," he said. "I assure it was not done intentionally and Giric is writing his letter to your brother as we speak. He values the alliance more than you can imagine."

"Maybe, or perhaps he is just afraid of my sister," Magnus said. She appreciated him trying to lighten the mood in the room. This hall was supposed to be a comfort but at the moment it was filled with gloom. She couldn't abide it any longer.

"We will retire now," she said.

"I will see you off in the morning. Your belongings will be packed and ready to go."

The sadness in his voice was difficult for her to accept, but she had no choice. Leaving here was a necessary part of her wellbeing now and her only concern going forward was Magnus.

# CHAPTER TWENTY-TWO

The sight of the longhouse lifted his spirits. He never thought he would ever be so glad to see his home. He wrapped his arm a little tighter around Elspeth's shoulders. The crossing had been calm thankfully, but it was cold and he was eager to get his wife inside where the fire would be warm and the company warmer. He'd had enough adventure and he was looking forward to some quiet days and planning the tower house. Contentment settled over him as the galley docked. All his life he has longed to leave this place and see the world. Now all he wanted was constancy with Elspeth.

"Welcome home, wife."

He looked down at her. Her cheeks were red from the biting wind, but she looked relaxed. She smiled at him and hugged him tight.

"The last time I was here, our tour was stopped short," she said. "I am looking forward to learning everything about the way of things here."

"Then I look forward to showing you."

Together they walked to the longhouse, but the door

KATE ROBBINS

opened before they reached the end of the wharf. Gunnar walked quickly toward them and looked behind them. He frowned for a moment, but he appeared to mask his expression again.

"I am pleased to see you brother," Magnus said. "Elspeth and I have been married and have come here to make plans for our future."

"Welcome to our family," Gunnar said to Elspeth and kissed her on both cheeks. "I am afraid though that planning may have to wait."

"What's happened?"

"Come inside," he said. "Magnus. I need you on your best behaviour."

"Gunnar, what's going on?" he asked not liking the sheen of sweat on Gunnar's brow or how pale he looked.

"Einar is here. And Short-Beard. They are trying to claim the lands I put aside for you."

"Do not bring her inside." Magnus left Elspeth with Gunnar and marched to the hall. Once inside he quickly located the two snakes and stood over them with his arms crossed.

"Will you two never cease to stir trouble?"

"Magnus, before you blow that hot head of yours—" Earl Einar said.

"I will blow more than my hot head if what Gunnar tells me is true." To Short-Beard he said, "You know you have no claim on any lands outside of those you currently occupy. We have returned all that was taken from you in this summer's raid and you have no reason to be here."

"My family is expanding," he said. "We have just as much right to this land as you do."

"That's not true," Magnus said. "All of Islay was granted to my grandfather except the portion set aside for you. And you own a quarter of the island. That is enough for you."

"I disagree," Einar said. "As Earl of this region—"

Magnus leaned down close enough to the man that he was forced to stop talking. "Hear my words, and hear them now. You have been stirring trouble for an age. You have no power here and you have no authority to reassign land that was legitimately granted."

"I am an Earl!"

"You are pathetic." To Short-Beard, he said. "What did he tell you to persuade you to travel all this way? Did he say he can speak for the king?"

"He said he has documentation that proves he has authority over Islay."

"Does he now? Well this is documentation I would like to see."

"I obviously do not have it with me." Einar said. "I have it in a safe place."

"And you think to come here to convince me that you have imaginary authority."

"The last I checked, your brother was chieftain," Einar.

A month ago, even a week ago, Magnus would have grabbed Einar by the scruff of his neck and thrown him out of the hall. Now he felt only pity, rather than rage.

"Short-Beard, you are welcome to stay and partake of the wedding feast we will host in my honour and perhaps we can discuss why you need to press your land boundaries.

"Einar, you are not welcome here. As you have not been welcome here for a long time. You have insulted every member of this family and you have proved time and again that you are not deserving of the Earl's title. Your desperation for land ownership is doing nothing to benefit Short-Beard or us. Leave here now."

His voice was calm and clear. Perhaps it was that calmness that seemed to draw a reaction from Einar. He paled and looked quickly between the two men.

"You are married?"

"I am."

"To whom?"

"Lady Elspeth MacAlpin," she said from behind Magnus. "And I believe you have been instructed to leave this hall." She stood beside Magnus with Gunnar on her other side.

Einar stood. "Are you going to let them treat me like this?" he asked Short-Beard.

"I am," he said. "You have manipulated me, Einar. I thought it before, but I know it now. These are my neighbours and our relationship was good until you interfered."

"You will all regret this," Einar said. "I will return and when I do, you will see I have the authority over all of you and your lands."

"And I look forward to seeing this imaginary document of yours," Magnus said. Why was Gunnar being so quiet? He would usually have tossed Einar out on his ear by now, rather he seemed at a loss for words.

The hall fell awkwardly silent after Einar left. "Should we ask Bjorn to follow him to make sure he leaves?" Magnus asked Gunnar.

A moment later the man was on his arse on the floor. "Come help me get him up," Elspeth said to Magnus and Short-Beard.

They lifted his dead weight onto a chair. "Thor's breath, what's going on, Gunnar?" His brother had always been the strongest man he'd ever met. This was not something he could have ever imagined. Wasn't he part god himself?

"Your brother is sick," Elspeth said.

"I need Freydis to help me," Gunnar whispered.

"She did not cross with us," Elspeth said. "She said there was a place she must visit and would not tell me where that was."

"I will not live if she does not heal me," Gunnar said.

"Yrsa's father would not let her continue to learn the healing arts and we only have a young woman who has been helping the sick."

"Perhaps I should leave," Short-Beard said.

Something was not right. His brother never fell ill. "When did you arrive here?" Magnus asked.

"Yesterday," he said. "Gunnar let us stay here in the hall overnight."

"And how was he when you first saw him yesterday?"

"He was not well then, but I just thought he'd been into too much ale."

Gunnar heaved his guts onto the floor; the foul stench filling the air around them. Magnus' stomach was strong, but even this was a bit much for him to handle. He and Short-Beard helped him into his chamber whilst Elspeth summoned some servants to scour the floors.

They got Gunnar into his bed and covered him with furs. There were all sorts of illnesses Magnus could think of that could affect a man so. But he would feel a whole lot better if Freydis was present. In the meantime, he prayed to Odin, Elspeth could help.

"How is he?" she asked when Magnus and Short-Beard returned to the hall.

"He needs a healer," Magnus said.

"I have sent the servant to find a woman in the village who can help," she said. "We must find out if anyone else is sick or if it is just Gunnar."

As she said the words she examined all the food around the fire-pit in the centre of the hall. She lifted pieces of meat and fish and brought some to her nose to sniff.

"Do you think the food is bad?"

"Did you eat here last night?" Elspeth asked Short-Beard.

"I did and this morning."

"And you are well?"

"I feel no illness," Short-Beard said. "But I meant what I said earlier. I do not wish to overstay my welcome. I will take my men and leave here now. We do not need to talk about boundaries and lands at the moment."

"At the moment?" Magnus asked. "So you do have a dispute over your border then?"

"I do. But now does not appear to be a good time to discuss the issue."

"You mean, you now realize you have nothing to use to make an argument besides greed, and so you will skulk away until you find another way to lay claim to that which is not yours."

Short-Beard shook his head. "You mistake me, Magnus. You always have. Though you are a married man now, you are still too quick tempered. I would not negotiate with you if you were the last man standing."

"Then our business here is done," Magnus said.

Short-Beard left then. Elspeth went with the servants to collect the new healer and for the moment Magnus was alone in the hall. Short-Beard's words weighed on him. He wanted peace, but it appeared peace did not want him.

~

*E*lspeth spoke very little Norse, and the young healer spoke no Scots. Magnus was trying to help translate, but it was frustrating. She wasn't a healer. Of course she knew some basics, Nana Besse had taught her, but she wasn't prepared to be responsible for someone's wellbeing. She wished now she'd persuaded Freydis to come with them. Though she respected the woman's need to find her own path, the truth was the woman had gifts Elspeth could not define.

And what of her own gifts? She was no closer to determining their extent or origin. Freydis had been somewhat helpful in suggesting the origin was not relevant, but insistent on Elspeth determining the extent.

To what end, though? What good could she do if she could see into people's thoughts? How could that help her in say this situation? She watched the young healer, Ulfhild, whose name she could not grasp until Magnus said it slowly. The woman touched Gunnar's forehead, cheeks and grasped one of his hands in hers.

"What is she doing?" Elspeth asked Magnus.

"Healing?"

After an hour of these motions, Elspeth was losing patience. It appeared to her, the woman had no idea what was wrong with Gunnar and even worse, how to help him. A prayer, a concoction, something, anything would be better than watching her falter in her duty to help him.

"This is ridiculous," she said to Magnus. "Please have her returned to her home. I will find a way to help Gunnar myself. It is clear to me, she does not possess the skills to help him."

"You are certain of this?" Magnus asked.

"Aye. I'm sure. She has done nothing but touch him for an hour. Get her out of here." To the servant waiting outside the door she said, "Bring me hot water and cloths and warm up some mead."

The servant left to do as she was bid. Magnus spoke quietly to Ulfhild. The girl looked upset and would not make eye contact with Elspeth as she passed by and out of the chamber. Elspeth had more on her mind than the feelings of a young woman who misrepresented herself as a healer.

"She thinks you are too harsh in your judgement of her," Magnus said.

"And she is entitled to feel that way, but she was doing nothing to help your brother."

"She told me she was praying to Odin to send someone to help Gunnar for she knew she lacked the skills. She says that since you have decided to be that someone, she will now pray for you."

Drawing a deep breath, Elspeth thought about what the woman meant and pushed it aside. The greater issue here now was Gunnar and he did not look well at all. He'd fallen asleep a while ago and Elspeth would make sure he was tended properly. Prayers were appreciated, but this man needed help in this realm.

She stretched her neck after several hours of mopping the sweat from his brow. His skin was clammy and he still slept. She was getting more and more worried. She wanted to get some mead into him, but he'd need to be awake for that. And shy of shaking the man she had no idea—

But she did have an idea. She did know how to reach him, didn't she? She could draw him out and let him know they were there to help him.

Nay, she had vowed she would never do that again without permission. It was different with Magnus now. He'd given her nearly free reign to explore his mind during their intimate times and which elevated their lovemaking in ways she could not describe. Nay, this was different and felt too invasive. Suddenly Freydis' voice was in her head. *You can help him, Elspeth. Please do it. Please help him.*

Was this part of what Freydis was trying to tell her from before? That she could find ways to use her gift for good purposes?

"You look troubled," Magnus said. "What is it?"

She'd never known anyone who was as in tune with her as he was now. Every time she was worried, excited, or angry, it was like he felt it right along with her.

"Gunnar needs to wake so I can get him to drink this mead." She'd gone to the stores earlier and found some of the things Nana Besse always sowed into her memory as treatment for someone who was sick. She crushed mint and cloves and rosemary and mixed it through the liquid. While she knew mead had its own special healing properties, adding the other ingredients made this especially helpful to stave off whatever affliction held him.

Magnus reached for Gunnar's shoulders and Elspeth almost laughed when she realized his intent.

"Nay," she said. "I will rouse him."

Magnus sat back. His brow furrowed for a minute then his eyes grew wide. "You cannot," he said. "Gunnar has not granted you permission. I will not allow you to do this."

"Magnus I must find a way to rouse him so we can get him to drink. I promise I will not engage any longer than I have to."

"And I will not see you collapse when it becomes too difficult for you and I have to tend to you both and watch Ulfhild pray for not one, but two of you."

"Magnus, this is the best, easiest way."

"No, Elspeth. Find another way," he said. "He is my brother and you are my wife. Freydis is not here to help you this time. And I cannot help you with this. Do not do it."

"Magnus, I must. I am worried about your brother and if we do not find a way to help him now, I do not know what will happen."

Gunnar coughed from the bed and they both looked over to him. She hoped he'd wake again, but after calling his name several times, there was still no response.

"Magnus, you must trust me. You must let me try to reach him."

"I do trust, you," he said. "It is this gift of yours I do not trust."

Her heart was punctured. "How can you say that after everything you and I have shared? Freydis was not present when we shared my gift in the tower and she was not needed then. I understand this now. And I know how I can be useful."

Magnus shook his head. "I do not like it. And you were safe in the tower because I kept you safe."

"You had less control over what happened there than you care to admit."

"What does that mean?"

"It means there are other forces at play here that are much bigger than you and I and any idea that we are fully in control is a fantasy."

"You are bent on doing this, aren't you?"

"I am. I believe I can help your brother."

Magnus scrubbed his hand down over his face. He looked tired and worn. While she understood his concern, she knew with every fibre of her being this was the right thing to do and she believed in her ability to do so without Freydis' or anyone else's help.

She didn't wait for his approval. Lifting his big, meaty hand into hers she focused on his face and closed her eyes. She focused on the place where their hands connected and envisioned energy passing from her to him and back again. Slowly, she willed that connection to travel up his arm and could feel him responding with little jerks from his hand and arm.

When she reached his neck, she paused. No more time for doubt, no time for anything but to fulfill her purpose. *Odin help me.*

Elspeth turned around and opened her eyes. She was in a large grassy field with cattle being called home by a beautiful young woman. Gunnar gazed upon her with such love and light in his eyes. She watched the couple as they laughed when the cattle came running to the woman. Elspeth had heard of this, it was a kulning song, specific to one group of cattle. Only the group who'd been taught it from infancy responded and were drawn to it.

The young woman's song ended and then she turned. She smiled at Elspeth and reached up to Gunnar and kissed him on the cheek. She walked away to the other side of the field. Gunnar watched her go then walked toward Elspeth and frowned.

"I want to stay here," he said, his voice filled with anguish.

"You cannot," Elspeth said. "We need you."

"And I need her."

Elspeth had no words of comfort for him. She nearly doubled over with the ache consuming his heart.

"Please Gunnar, you must wake. I am here to help."

A single tear slid down his cheek then he reached out his hand to her.

# CHAPTER TWENTY-THREE

With a great gasp of air, Gunnar awoke. Magnus had watched tears fall from his brother's eyes and Elspeth's too. He would never understand how this worked, but he was grateful for the moment that it was over. Gunnar sat up in bed a little and reached for the cup Elspeth held out then downed it and passed it back to her. She refilled it and gave it to him again.

"How do you feel?" Magnus asked him.

He looked over and blanked as if he just realized Magnus was there. "I feel like horse shit."

Magnus smiled. He was awake and coherent. That was a good sign. "You gave us a bit of a fright."

Gunnar looked at Elspeth again then down at the cup in his hand. He emptied it and passed it back to her again. "I will be well."

Elspeth placed the pitcher of mead and cup on a small table beside Gunnar, collected the used cloths and pan of water, and left the chamber.

"What happened with Einar and Short-Beard?"

"I sent Einar away and Short-Beard went of his own

accord not long after realizing he had nothing to bargain with. He'll be back, but he will need more than a falsified document from Einar before he can push his borders east."

Gunnar tilted his head, a little of the usual glint entering his expression. "You handled all of that without me? And you didn't toss them out on their arse?"

He chuckled. Elspeth may have been given a gift of sight straight from Odin, but he'd been given a gift too. One of patience. Perhaps the gods were smiling down on him and showing him his path too.

"I did not. And I don't think you'll hear from either any time soon though."

Gunnar flicked back the furs and swung his long legs over the side of the bed. His boots hit the floor with a loud *thunk.*

"Where do you think you're going?" Magnus asked.

"I have work to do, Magnus. My little brother has just gotten married and proved himself a right and proper leader in this clan," he said. "I have a feast to prepare."

Magnus helped Gunnar out to the main hall which was thankfully empty except for two men stoking the fire-pit. Once seated, Gunnar asked Magnus to fetch Elspeth.

"You wanted to see me?" she asked when Magnus returned with her a short time later.

"Thank-you," he said. "I know how much that must have cost you and I hope you are not harmed."

"She is not harmed," Magnus said. "And I was there the entire time. You know I would not let anything happen to her."

"I do know that," he said. "And I appreciate you both being here and am grateful for the company. I am getting sick of listening to Bjorn lament over having no one to love." He rolled his eyes and started to laugh then went into a fit of coughing.

"Seriously, Gunnar how long have you been unwell?"

"Not long," he said. "Now that I have some of my family back, I will take better care of myself, I promise."

"I am glad to hear it," Elspeth said.

"And now we must plan a feast in your honour," he said. "My lady, what is your favourite meal? And we must talk about the blot sacrifice. I will marry you both this day to honour our gods and be sure your marriage is also recognized by them."

Magnus listened as Gunnar told Elspeth all about the purpose of the sacrifice and how he was pleased to be able to perform the ceremony himself.

"Is it your wish to engage in this ceremony today?" he asked her a time later when Gunnar was off talking to the cooks. New life appeared to have been breathed into him now he had a function to plan.

"I am looking forward to it and learning all about each and every one of your gods. I believe I know one fairly well already."

He chuckled. "I have not yet told you how grateful I am."

"For what?"

"What you did for my brother," he said and kissed the top of her head.

"I am happy you think so. I know you were worried."

"I was worried about his wellbeing as well as yours. I don't know what I would do without you now."

"The gods have offered you good fortune and I do not think you will ever have to worry about being without me."

"What is it like? I mean, when you and I connect, we share all of the feelings we have for one another. How is it with someone else?"

"It's difficult to explain," she said. "But I can somehow feel what the other person is feeling."

"And what is Gunnar feeling?"

He didn't know why it was important to him to know what was going on with Gunnar, but his brother seemed different.

"I do not think it would be appropriate for me to share his most private feelings with you, Magnus. And nor would I share yours or Freydis'."

"I can accept that. But will you do me a favour?"

"Anything."

"If you detect anything that you think needs to be addressed, you will come to me. You will not try to deal with anything like this on your own."

"Aye, Magnus, I will make that promise to you."

"Good, now go get yourself dressed and meet me back here for our ceremony. I had the men bring the chests to our chamber while you were sitting with Gunnar."

Elspeth kissed him on the cheek and went off into the back chamber with two young servant girls following.

He sat quietly for a time while he waited for Gunnar to return. When he did, he was followed by six other men all carrying armloads of provisions. He gave instructions and sat by Magnus who passed him a horn of ale.

"You enjoy this don't you?" Magnus asked him.

"I am never happier than when this hall is full and bustling with people." His voice trailed off and his gazed was fixed on the door.

"Gunnar she will be back."

He shook his head. "You don't know that."

"You're right, I don't. But you cannot fill your days pining for her either. We are here with you now and will be here until the spring. I need your help planning the build for my home. I think it will be a good distraction for you."

Magnus described his vision to Gunnar and the moment he mentioned stone and tower in the same sentence, Gunnar perked up.

"It will take some time and I will need some men," Magnus said.

"You will have all that you need. Your lands are fertile and firm. I believe the structure you plan will be perfectly situated there."

"There's also the matter of our alliance with MacDomnail and MacAlpin."

"What of it?" Gunnar asked. "I have heard no news for weeks."

"Elspeth has a letter for you from Giric detailing everything that's happened. She read it to me during our travels. I was not happy that he was making decisions and plans without involving you or me so he has sent you information that should shed some light as to everyone's involvement."

"I am glad to hear it. I was feeling quite abandoned for a time," he said. "What does the letter say?"

"Our alliance with Olaf is sound, but there are rumours Athelstan plans to push his campaign forward in the spring."

"That means we will need to assemble our numbers and be ready. That is a long way to travel to go into battle. But we have time to plan. I am glad you are here, Magnus."

"As am I, and you will have your feast and all the company you can muster for the next few months. Vigdis will stay with Saga for the winter until she and Osgar make their nuptials and perhaps they will also visit next summer depending on what comes of Athelstan's plot."

Gunnar seemed to perk up with each passing moment and Magnus was glad for it. The man possessed the strength of ten men normally and to see him deflated was disconcerting.

"Shall we see if your bride is ready for the blot?" Gunnar asked.

"Ja. She seems fascinated by all our ways and I think we

might be able to persuade her to teach some Scots tongue to any villagers who want the lesson."

Gunnar nodded then sat back again staring at the door. Magnus didn't like being out of the company of the woman he loved for even a few moments, so he couldn't imagine how difficult Freydis' absence was for Gunnar. The problem was, Gunnar had only realized the extent of his feelings apparently, after she left. The lesson was to be acknowledged that no moment was more appropriate to tell someone you love them than the present.

~

Their marriage was now blessed by her god and his gods. Elspeth sat beside her husband and viewed the crowd gathered to celebrate with them. Her own wedding feast had been cut short at her home so she was bent on enjoying this one. When Gunnar had asked her what she preferred in meat she had said rabbit, thinking perhaps he would have a little as part of the feast. Instead there were several different ways the meat was prepared and she thoroughly loved trying each and every one of them.

Mostly, she loved the glances she stole at her husband who seemed more relaxed and happier than she'd seen him since their time in the tower. For all of the strife and challenge they'd endured, the respite right now was enough to make her intoxicated though she'd not consumed any mead or ale.

The change in Gunnar was incredible. The man was now jovial and enjoying the antics of the men and women gathered who appeared to thoroughly enjoy the opportunity to celebrate. And how they'd all embraced her. Never in her wildest dreams could she have imagined herself in such a place in such a circumstance.

"You seem lost in thought," Magnus said.

"Aye, I am lost in pleasant thoughts."

"Am I in them?"

She chuckled. "Always."

Magnus reached under the table and stroked her thigh. "You know there's no expectation for us to stay here all evening."

"You mean we can go whenever we like?"

"We can," he said as his gaze flicked to the square neckline of her gown. She'd chosen the red one she'd worn when she married him the first time. She recalled how he'd gotten her out of it and now longed for him to remove it again.

"Your guests will not think less of me for being a wanton woman who is driven to distraction with thoughts of the pleasure she shares with her husband?"

Magnus stood and held out his hand for hers. She looked around as the hall fell silent; all eyes then directed toward them.

"I thank you, Gunnar, for preparing a feast fit for a king. I am honoured by your hospitality," Elspeth said.

Gunnar stood. "The honour is mine. I am proud to welcome you into this family and I speak for the entire clan when I say we are pleased you have chosen to turn my brother into an honourable married man."

She was well aware of the jest, but Magnus seemed a little put off by the remark. She decided to turn it around. "It is he who honours me."

Magnus picked her up and flung her over his shoulder then walked to the back of the hall and to the chamber. At her home, she would be mortified by such behaviour, however here she could only laugh in delight as the crowd cheered and yelled *SKOL!*

Once inside the chamber, Magnus closed the door. There was no need to bolt it. No one would bother them for the rest of the night. It had only been a few hours since she'd left for the blot, but somehow the servants had organized all her gowns and pushed her trunks back to the edge of the chamber out of the way.

The fire burned brightly and several candles were lit around the chamber. Several furs were stacked upon the bed and a table near the hearth was topped with a pitcher, goblets, and a tray of meats and bread.

Strong arms encircled her as Magnus pressed his hands onto her belly and pulled her back to him. She'd kept her hair down for this ceremony and the servants had added some braids to keep it away from her face. Magnus pulled the hair away from her neck and kissed her softly.

"I could hold you like this forever."

"And I could let you."

He pulled on the ties that held her bodice to her skirts, this time being far more deft than the first time. Sliding his hands under the bodice, he lifted it over her head and placed it on one of the trunks. She shimmied out of her skirt and turned around to face him. He was working his way out of his tunic and she was happy that this time, he wasn't wearing his trews.

Standing naked before her, his gaze trailed down the length of her.

"Take it off," he said.

She watched the heat in his eyes as she drew the garment up over her legs and higher up, then let it fall, only to draw it up a little farther each time.

The air hissed through his teeth when she pulled it all the way up over her head and dropped it to the floor.

He took the steps to reach her then lifted her up so her legs could wrap around his waist. He kissed her then. A deep, penetrating kiss that was seared onto her soul. Nothing that was happening outside the chamber mattered any longer. Only the two of them and the unbreakable bond they'd built.

Magnus walked forward until they reached the bed then dropped her on it and jumped on top of her. She laughed and tried to scooch away, but he was having none of it.

"You are mine, wife and I want to please you until you cannot be pleased any longer."

His words and his hard body shot thrills through her as he wedged himself between her legs and drove himself hard inside her. She gasped and threw her head back as he thrust harder and faster until her climax burst upon her and liquid pleasure flooded her veins. He tensed and thrust hard a few more times which brought about a second and even more intense climax than the last.

Throughout the night they loved and laughed and slept and started all over again. How many hours they shared themselves in the chamber she did not know. And she didn't care. All she cared about now was the man who snored lightly beside her as she stared into the dying embers of the fire.

Everything that had happened that led them to this moment was a blessing. She could see that now. Even the turmoil she'd endured kept her on the path that had eventually crossed with his.

Stroking his hair she adored it when he snuggled closer to her in his sleep. She wanted to get up to get some more food, but she didn't want to lose the feeling of him holding her so tight.

"You're awake?" he whispered.

"Aye, my love. Sleep now."

"Thank the gods," he said. "I thought you were ready to go again. I am a strong man, but even strong men have their limits."

Elspeth tilted her head back and laughed. "I believe I am the luckiest woman in the world," she said.

"Then I am the most fortunate man."

He leaned back and sat up for a moment.

"Is aught all right?" she asked him.

"It is. I feel safer here," he said. "And I want to make sure again that you do not feel pressured in living in a place that is so different for you."

"You do not have to worry about me, my love. As I told you before. I am happiest wherever you are."

He reached over and kissed her softly then gazed into her eyes. "I do not know which god is responsible for bringing you to me, but I will get down on my knees and thank each and every one of them right now. I love you, my beautiful wife. I love your heart, and your mind, and all your gifts," he said, his voice going hoarse.

"And I love you, my hot-headed, Viking husband."

"Hot-headed, hey?" he asked with a grin. "I'll show you who is hot-headed."

Magnus flipped her onto her back and raised her arms over her head then began a maddeningly torturous onslaught with his tongue starting from her neck then trailing down her body until he had tasted every inch of her and she was breathless once again.

Her rumbling stomach after her last climax was the only thing that stopped him from continuing.

"Come, my wife," he said, pulling her up. "Let's get you fed."

"I admit, I have worked up quite an appetite." Then she thought of something. "How long are we permitted to stay here until we have to acknowledge your guests again?"

"My mother and father stayed in their wedding chamber for four days."

"Four days?"

She loved the sound of it, but she realized she'd need some serious sustenance if they were to break that record. Elspeth hopped out of the bed and began loading up a trencher with bread and meat and filled a large goblet full of ale.

Magnus' laughter was a delight to her very soul. Aye, whichever god was responsible, she owed them all her blessings.

# EPILOGUE

Her belly heaved as the bairn she carried kicked hard. Elspeth held little Astrid's hand as Magnus covered her eyes. Four summers of hard work and labour had come to this moment. They'd cleared the land, they'd set their gardens, and he had built her tower house. Well, most of it. Right now it was only one level, but he'd said he would keep building until he reached the sky if she wanted. The world outside their little haven had gone mad, yet they managed to create a world that was safe for their family. Sometimes she envisioned them under the dome of an enchantment. It was a beautiful thought.

"Are you ready, love?" Magnus asked.

"Aye! I want to see!"

"Me too, Fader!" Astrid said.

She could barely speak, but she was picking up new words every day. Elspeth was so proud of the family they were building and of the place they were about to call home. The roof had been secure for a week, but Magnus would not let her enter because he said it had to be perfect for her first time in her new home. The dwelling they'd been living in would eventually be offered to someone else. Magnus had been grappling over who he would gift the place, and she'd agreed to leave the decision up to him. They'd had a great deal of assistance over the years and there were a few who deserved the place. But for now the moment was at hand for her to enter her new home.

Magnus lifted his hands from her eyes. She looked at the door and a flood of memories returned of a place she'd only seen again in her dreams. He'd fashioned iron bands across the oak panels making up the door. She lifted the latch and let Astrid push the door wide open. What met her view made her breath catch and tears pool in her eyes.

A fire roared in the hearth and a long table exactly like the one in their tower rested nearby. To the left she viewed the kitchen area which wasn't as large, but was arranged in exactly the same way, and stocked in the same manner. On the other side of the main hall, were the bed chambers. They were small, but they would do, until the second story was complete.

Elspeth stepped into the first chamber to find it decorated exactly like the tower she and Magnus had shared all those years ago. Tears slid down her cheeks as she turned to him. He was dusty and dirty and looked exhausted, but he'd never looked more wonderful to her.

"How did you do this?" she whispered.

"I have it all up here," he said, tapping his temple. "I remember every second of our time there and every detail in this chamber. I had Vigdis scour Scotland for the right materials and have these bed clothes made for you."

Elspeth could not hold back her tears as she stroked the beautiful coverlet as the memories consumed her.

"Magnus, it's more than I could have ever imagined."

"You are more than I could have ever imagined," he said and cupped her face in his hands. He brushed his lips across hers and lifted Astrid to show her all the different details in the chamber.

"Mama, it's exactly like your tower," Astrid said, when he set her on the floor again.

"What did you say?" she asked her. The bairn inside her kicked again as her daughter climbed upon the bed.

"This is just like your tower." She drew circles on the coverlet and tilted her head back and forth whilst humming a little tune.

"Did you hear your father say that?" she asked, unwilling to accept the alternative.

"I told her nothing. This has been a well-kept secret," Magnus said. "There's no way she could have known."

"Then how did you know?" Elspeth asked Astrid as she sat beside her on the bed.

"I saw it when I was sleeping," she said.

Elspeth locked gazes with Magnus. She had not considered that Astrid could inherit the same gift she possessed.

"Ulf says you're hungry," she said then. "Fader, Mama should eat now."

"Darling, who is Ulf?" he asked her.

She patted Elspeth's belly and hopped off the bed skipping out toward the hall. Elspeth didn't know what to make of it. She'd never explored the idea that her children could possess her gifts and was a little frightened and a little excited by the prospect at the same time.

"You said your Nana Besse guided you when you were very small, Elspeth," Magnus said.

"Did you know about her?"

"I have suspected for some time. She has brought me different tools before I have even asked for them, or even knew I needed them to be honest."

Elspeth needed a moment to absorb the extent of what this meant for her daughter. She would do everything in her power to guide and protect her and ensure she never had to go through self-doubt and confusion Elspeth had.

Magnus wrapped his arms around her. "It will be all right," he said. "You will guide her, and I will protect you all."

Elspeth didn't doubt it. "But she named the bairn. Do you suppose 'tis a lad as she said?"

"I do not know, but I will love lad or lass, and if we have a dozen more, I will love them all just as much."

Right on cue, Elspeth's belly rumbled loudly. Magnus chuckled. "Someone *is* hungry. Come, let us share our evening meal in our new home."

Elspeth sat back and watched Magnus and Astrid a while later once her belly was satisfied. Magnus was playing a game with her where he made a stone disappear from his hand and appear behind her ear. She squealed in delight each and every time. It appeared her blessings did not end with her and Magnus and the home they had built together. Here she was safe, and her children would be safe. The best she could offer them was the same guidance she'd been given and more love than they could imagine. That would be the best protection of all.

## THE END

Pre-Order The Wildcat, Spirits of the Norse, Book 3

# PRE-ORDER THE WILDCAT, SPIRITS OF THE NORSE, BOOK THREE

Only survivors can speak of the storm. Gunnar Haraldson is chieftain of his clan and proud of his lands on Islay. Sustaining a peaceful existence on an island off the coast of mainland Alba is not easy considering his ancestry is Norse. Like his fathers before him, he will do everything in his power to preserve the Viking way. Those are his thoughts every morning—and then reality finds a way to intervene. Most notably in the name of the village healer, Freydis.

Freydis has understood her place between the worlds of the gods and men her whole life. She can see into their hearts and the future, but she cannot see why Odin placed her on the same path as the most infuriating man ever spawned from Loki. So why does she not take up permanent residence on the mainland where she could live out a happy life free from the man her heart won't release?

Gunnar and Freydis will have to look past more than their stubborn nature to combat the uncertain times ahead. What must they sacrifice to secure their future?

# ACKNOWLEDGMENTS

So I almost messed up. And it might just be true what they say that the road to hell is paved with good intentions. I set up pre-orders for this series to make me more accountable and finish the books in this series within a certain timeframe. But what I didn't account for was life getting in the way. And so I started this book on January 4, 2022 and finished on February 27, 2022. Just shy of eight weeks of creative frenzy while working a stressful day job and also a part-time job. How did I do it? Spite. Nothing more, nothing less than purely driven spite that I would not let myself fail. So I have myself to pat on the back in these acknowledgements which is something I've never done.

"Good job, Debbie."

"Thanks, Kate."

To my sons who watch me slip into alternate human form to create the stories I adore so much—you are the reason I want to succeed. I love you both so much for your endless support.

To Michelle O. Always, always, always for offering your editorial services to a stubborn writer. You make me readable. Your insight helps me link everything together when I don't know how. Thank you.

To Roy. For listening when you need to, for challenging when you need to, thank you for everything, always.

To Melanie and Vicki. Thank you for cheering from the bleachers as always!

To Suzan. For all the crazy questions, for all the snarky

rants, for your shoulders, and your ears, and your heart, thank you!

To Victoria Z. We still got this, lady!!! #rockstars

To my beta readers, Maria, Stefanie, and Cynthia. Thank you for your feedback on the advanced read. I love getting your emails with your comments about the characters and what you hope will happen. :) I love you all!

To my readers. Thank you for taking a chance on a little maid from the Cove all those years ago and for putting up with me delving into a new series before finishing the last one. I will get to it, I promise. You have reached out to me many times over the years with helpful critique and kind words and your support has been unwavering. I sincerely hope you enjoy The Raven and I will continue to work hard to provide you with good quality entertainment. Please keep reaching out over all my platforms.

Much love to you all!!!

Kate/Debbie

## ALSO BY KATE ROBBINS

Bound to the Highlander: Highland Chiefs Book 1

Aileana Chattan suffers a devastating loss, then discovers she is to wed neighboring chief and baron, James MacIntosh -- a man she despises and whose loyalty deprived her of the father she loved. Despite him and his traitorous clan, Aileana will do her duty, but she doesn't have to like it or him. But when the MacIntosh awakens something inside her so absolute and consuming, she is forced to question everything.

James MacIntosh is a nobleman torn between tradition and progress. He must make a sacrifice if he is to help Scotland move forward as a unified country. Forced to sign a marriage contract years earlier binding Lady Aileana to him, James must find a way to break it, or risk losing all—including his heart.

From the wild and rugged Highlands near Inverness to the dungeons of Edinburgh Castle, James and Aileana's preconceptions of honor, duty and love are challenged at every adventurous turn.

~

Promised to the Highlander: Highland Chiefs Book 2

Nessia Stephenson's world was safe until a threat from a neighbouring clan forces her to accept a betrothal to a man whose family can offer her the protection she needs. The real threat lies in her intense attraction to the man who arranged the match—the clan's chief and her intended's brother, Fergus MacKay.

When powerful warlord Fergus MacKay arranges a marriage for his younger brother, William, he has no idea the price will be his own heart. Fergus is captivated by the wildly beautiful Nessia, a woman he can never have.

When the feud between the MacKay and Sutherland clans escalates,

Nessia, William, and Fergus all must make sacrifices for their future. Longing and loss, honour and duty. How can love triumph under such desperate circumstances?

∽

### Enemy of the Highlander: Highland Chiefs Book 3

Two years ago Freya MacKay walked away from the only man she would ever love, her family's bitter enemy, knowing her clan would never accept their love. A fragile alliance has been forged and now he has returned to warn of a terrible threat. Freya MacKay is torn between the familiar surge of passion he evokes and her promise to wed another man.

Ronan Sutherland has lost everything to a cruel uncle who will lay the entire north Highlands to waste if he is not stopped. There is only one who can help—but seeking alliance with his former enemy, Fergus MacKay, means encountering the woman who left him two years ago, breaking his heart.

A bitter feud keeps their clans at one another's throats and it seems nothing will stop one from destroying the other. Will Ronan ever forgive Freya for leaving him? Can he trust her again? Or will the decades of hatred and deceit between their families prevail?

∽

### Prisoner of the Highlander: Highland Chiefs Book 4

Annabella Beaufort, cousin to the Queen Consort of Scotland, visits court in Edinburgh upon the queen's urging. She has little interest in this wild and rugged land and is pleasantly surprised to find Linlithgow Palace and King James' court quite refined. An attack on Edinburgh Castle by a savage Highlander results in her capture. This flaxen haired giant is like nothing she's encountered before, but her fear of him quickly turns to lust and she prays he will not also claim her heart.

Son of the great Alexander MacDonald, beloved Lord of the Isles, Angus MacDonald refuses to bend to King James' tyrannical rule.

After his father is imprisoned, he becomes acting chief. Unlike his father and his schemes, Angus will attack and bring this king to his knees. His attempt to release his father is thwarted and instead he abducts the Queen's cousin. His desire for her is intense and immediate, despite her flawed Sassenach ways. But he must keep her at arm's length regardless of the raging passion she evokes in him. She is his pawn—his prisoner—and he must always remember that.

Though they fight on opposite sides of the battle for power over Scotland, Angus and Annabella discover a fire that will not be ignored or denied. Will their loyalties to their families tear them apart? If he sets her free, will she return to him? Or will she in turn imprison his heart for all eternity?

∼

### Heart of the Highlander: Highland Chiefs Book 5

Devastated to learn the betrothal to her beloved Rorie has been broken, Muren Grey vows to take control of her life once and for all. But independence is not an easy path in a world dominated by men. Can she love a man who wants to control her? Muren must gather her strength and find the essence of who she truly is—even if it means losing the only man she will ever love.

Rorie Mackenzie has inherited a clan he will do anything to protect. Drawn into the king's schemes involving Muren, diplomacy will only take him so far before he must make a stand, for her and for the Highlands.

Facing impossible odds from their world and beyond, Muren and Rorie seek the one power that can obliterate any barrier.

∼

### Highlander Bewitched: A Highland Chiefs Novella

Stripped of her title and wealth at a young age, Gwendolyn MacGregor was put into service for the chief of the Chattan Clan. Determined to embrace her new life, she shed her noble expectations and even her religion. As a pagan wise woman, she developed a gift for channelling nature's energy and became a contented free spirit in every way—until she meets Calum MacIntosh.

Brother of the great MacIntosh chief, Calum MacIntosh believes virtue is the most important gift a husband and wife can bring to a marriage. He is prepared to join his name with another noble lady when the time is right, until his path crosses with the enchanting lady's maid, Gwendolyn. Despite his efforts to forget her, he is drawn to her as though an invisible tether connects them.

Caught between longing and duty, Gwen and Calum discover a powerful bond that will not be defined by social expectations or status—and will not be denied.

### One Knight in Stirling

Sir William MacPherson is honoured by the queen mother's invitation to protect her from her enemies. The only catch: he must reside at Stirling Castle where he will encounter Coira MacLaren; the one woman who can bring him to his knees and keep him there. Her refusal of his marriage proposal a year ago hit him hard and he has not seen her since. Can he harden himself against her, or will their insatiable lust for one another burn them to cinders this time?

### Christmas Crackers: A Short and Spicy Smalltown Romance

Travelling home to spend Christmas with her parents, Caroline finds herself the victim of a nasty patch of black ice and an ill-placed snowbank. Her saviour is none other than the all-grown-up version of her many teenage fantasies, Kirk Drodge. Meeting him again stirs old feelings she thought were in the distant past. Not so much, apparently. This Christmas, maybe she's not the only one with a surprise in store.

The Serpent: Spirits of the Norse, Book One

Oceans of blood have stained Scotland's shores for a century. Forging peace between the Vikings and Scots seems an impossible task, but Giric MacDomnail is resolute. Giric meets with Gunnar, chieftain of Clan Haraldson on Islay, with a proposal to end the carnage. But there's more at stake than peace when he meets Gunnar's sister.

Saga is a shield-maiden who fights her clan's enemies with abandon—backing down from no one. This Scot, come to play them with his pretty words, deserves an axe in his chest. Instead, his reason and his words penetrate her defences.

Giric and Saga must mend the hatred and prejudice between two fiercely proud cultures. Can love be the binding ingredient for a peaceful future?

## COMING SOON!

My Eternal: A Kate Robbins Short Story
The Lady's Portrait: An Isle of Skye Novella
The Wildcat: Spirits of the Norse, Book Three

# ABOUT THE AUTHOR

Amazon internationally bestselling author of the award-winning Highland Chiefs series, Kate Robbins writes historical romance out of pure escapism and a love for all things Scottish. She thoroughly enjoys the research process and delving into secondary sources in order to blend authentic historical fact into her stories.

Ranging a thousand years, Kate's novels are filled with passion, adventure, and political intrigue.

Kate is the pen name of Debbie Robbins who lives in St. John's, Newfoundland and Labrador, Canada.

Stay up to date with new release information by joining my Facebook Group, Into the Highland Mist with Kate Robbins.

Manufactured by Amazon.ca
Bolton, ON